Second Chance Christmas

by

Alison Packard

This is a work of fiction. Names, characters, places, and incidents are either the product of the author's imagination or are used fictitiously, and any resemblance to actual persons living or dead, business establishments, events, or locales, is entirely coincidental.

Second Chance Christmas

Cover Art by *The Wild Rose Press, Inc.*

The Wild Rose Press, Inc.
PO Box 708
Adams Basin, NY 14410-0708
Visit us at www.thewildrosepress.com

Publishing History
First Edition, 2022
Trade Paperback ISBN 978-1-5092-4601-4
Digital ISBN 978-1-5092-4602-1

Published in the United States of America

Still holding hands, they walked the rest of the way in companionable silence. Maddie tilted her face to the sky, marveling at the stars above. In Los Angeles, the stars weren't nearly as bright. She'd forgotten how brilliant and beautiful they could be.

As they approached her car, he let go of her hand, and immediately, she missed the warmth of his touch. "Thanks for walking me to my car." She pulled her keys from her coat pocket, and before she could hit the button to unlock the car door, he took a step forward to brush away a few errant strands of hair from her face. His gaze roamed over her, and the sensuality in his eyes seemed to suck the air out of her lungs.

"So tell me the truth. Did you want to make out during the movie?" The low husky tone of his voice sent a vibration of tingles throughout her body.

"Yes. Did you?"

He leaned in close. So close the warmth of his breath brushed against her cheeks; so close his clean male scent invaded her senses. Her pulse raced as his gaze lowered to linger on her lips, then lifted.

"It's all I thought about." He raised his fingertips to caress her cheek.

Her heart skipped a beat, and pleasurable goose bumps prickled her skin in response to the gentle touch. "Ben," she whispered.

"What?" His eyes burned into hers.

She shivered in anticipation. "Kiss me."

Dedication

For Suzanne. An amazing friend and an even better
human.

Acknowledgments

Although writing can be a solitary endeavor, no book is created entirely alone. I was blessed to have the assistance of Angie Shiroff, JoJo Christophor, Dawn Alexander, Kat Sheridan, and my Wild Rose Press editor, Josette Arthur. Thank you all for your contributions to *Second Chance Christmas*. You're the best!

Chapter One

"Hey, aren't you the gal in those constipation commercials?"

Glancing over her shoulder, Maddie Hart flashed a weak smile at the attractive guy standing behind her, then turned back to the mini-mart cashier who'd recognized her and was now eagerly awaiting confirmation.

"Yes, that's me," she said quickly, hoping the cashier wouldn't launch into her own experience with the product. She was amazed how many people didn't seem to mind sharing the most private details of their lives.

The woman, whose oval metallic name tag identified her as Anita, chuckled. "I knew it. I'm sure people must tell you this all the time, but you have such an expressive face. You'd win hands down if they gave awards for acting in commercials. You really look like you're constipated."

"Thank you." While acting in those particular commercials wasn't what Maddie had envisioned for herself, she was pleased by the compliment.

"I love the one where when the stuff kicks in, you do the shimmy to the bathroom." Anita slapped the counter and cackled. "It's a hoot."

A stifled laugh sounded behind her, and Maddie's cheeks grew warm. Why did this always seem to happen when she had an audience? The series of semi-comedic commercials she'd done for a popular constipation

1

remedy didn't air as often as they had in the past. Still, almost everywhere she went, someone invariably recognized her.

"I'm glad you enjoyed it." She set the bag of cheese puffs she'd been craving for the past hour on the counter. "How much do I owe you?" She pulled her wallet from her purse.

Once inside her warm car, she ripped open the bag and shoved several cheese puffs into her mouth. Groaning in pleasure as the fake cheese melted on her tongue, she chewed and stared at the cars whizzing by on the highway leading to Summerwood, the town she'd grown up in and left four years ago. She hadn't been back to Oregon since, and her stomach churned at the thought of returning as a failure.

Maybe failure wasn't the right word. She'd managed to eke out a living in LA. The constipation commercial was a little embarrassing, but it had paid the bills for a while. That had to count for something, right? And she still had a couple of irons in the fire. Her career might be sputtering, but it wasn't over yet.

Last week she'd had two auditions. One of them had been a callback for a lead role in a new Netflix series, meaning she'd made it one step further. The other had been for the pilot episode for an over-the-top family drama. But instead of pacing her apartment while she waited to hear from her agent, she'd decided to return home to spend Thanksgiving with her family. She hadn't seen her parents since last year when they flew to Los Angeles for a weekend visit. It had been even longer since she saw her sisters.

As much as she looked forward to seeing her family, she might not be able to avoid one particular person, and she dreaded coming face-to-face with him. Even now, she could still conjure the image of his handsome face in her mind. Sparkling blue eyes, hair the color of rich dark caramel, and a smile that could go from disarming to flat-out sexy in less than two seconds. The last time she'd seen Ben Ashford, a smile would have cracked his hard-as-granite expression, and those beautiful eyes had definitely not been twinkling. Instead, they'd been filled with pain. Pain *she'd* caused. She hadn't seen or spoken to him since she left him standing on his front porch on a rainy October evening, but not one day had passed in four years that she hadn't thought of him.

Forcing the painful memories from her mind, she set the cheese puffs on the passenger seat before she was tempted to scarf down the whole bag in one sitting. After buckling the seat belt, she started the engine and pulled out of the parking lot. But even as she tried to channel her thoughts elsewhere, they kept circling back to Ben. What was his life like now? Was he still working for the police department? Was he married? Did he hate her? She couldn't help but hope the answer to the last question was no. The thought of Ben hating her was something she didn't think she could bear, even if she deserved it. And she *did* deserve it.

Maddie exited off the highway, and within two miles, she passed a cheery welcome sign. About an hour south of Portland, Summerwood was a small town located in the Willamette Valley. She'd lived in smoggy and congested Los Angeles for so long that the gently rolling hills dotted with trees and punctuated with long rows of grapevines were a soothing balm to her soul.

At the outskirts of downtown, she eased the car to a stop at an intersection; simultaneously, a silver sedan pulled up to the white line on the street to her right. Remembering the courtesy rule her father had drilled into her when she was a student driver, she waited for the other car to pass through the intersection, but the vehicle didn't move. She made eye contact with the driver and motioned with her hand for him to proceed. After a few seconds, she shrugged when he still didn't move. "Fine. I'll go."

She hit the gas, and her car moved forward; the silver sedan accelerated into the intersection. Maddie gasped and stomped on the brake pedal, but the front end of the silver sedan collided with her car's right front side panel.

Heart pounding, she released her iron grip on the steering wheel and took a deep breath. She sat there, stunned but not in physical pain, for several seconds. As she debated her next move, a car door slammed, startling her. She glanced to her right as a bald man of about fifty strode past the passenger side of her car. Where was he going? Spurred into action, she unbuckled her seat belt and jumped out of the car.

"What are you doing?" she asked, wrapping her arms around her coat to ward off the chilly afternoon air.

"Making sure I get your license plate number." He pinned his accusing gaze on her, then took a picture of her license plate with his phone. "It was your fault."

"Excuse me?" Forgetting the cold, she put her hands on her hips and glared at him. "I gave you a hand signal to go, but you just sat there. So *I* went. If anyone was at fault, it was you."

"We'll see about that." He hit his phone screen with his fingers before putting it to his ear. "Yes, you can help me. I'm calling to report an accident at the intersection of Brookstone and Deerfield. Some lady hit me, and she's got road-rage issues."

"Road rage?" Maddie exclaimed. "What the... I don't have road rage. I was trying to be courteous. And *you* hit *me*!"

"She's yelling at me."

"I'm not yelling." She released a frustrated breath and took a step back. The guy wanted her to lose her cool; she wouldn't give him the satisfaction.

"Can you send someone right away? Who knows what she's capable of?"

Disgusted, Maddie threw up her hands and moved to stand by her car's driver's side door.

A large SUV approached from the opposite side of the intersection, then slowed to a halt next to her. The window slid down. "Are you okay?" the woman inside the vehicle asked, her expression concerned.

"Yes. I'm fine. Thanks for checking. You didn't happen to see the accident, did you?"

"No. Sorry." With a wary gaze, the woman glanced toward the man. "Do you need me to stick around?"

"Thanks for the offer, but I'm fine."

"Are you sure?"

Maddie nodded. She'd forgotten how friendly people were in Summerwood. "He's on the phone with the police. I'll wait for an officer to arrive and explain the situation."

After the woman drove away, Maddie opened the car door and grabbed her phone. The odious man wasn't the only one who could take pictures. And judging by where his car hit hers, anyone could tell she'd been farther into the intersection than him. Surely, whoever showed up from the police department would see that and ticket the man accordingly. Justice would prevail, and it would be in her favor.

****

Ben Ashford walked into his office at midday and couldn't miss the large box of chocolate-covered macadamia nuts sitting on top of his desk. Irritation bubbled up inside of him. After his last conversation with Traci, he'd hoped she'd stop leaving goodies from her various vacation getaways and weekend trips on his desk, but she appeared not to have gotten the message. So now he would have to do what he should have done initially and tell her he wasn't interested in dating her.

When Traci started working in the Emergency Communications Center a few years ago, he'd thought the treats were her way of making friends with her co-workers. But then he noticed she never brought anything for the other sergeants, or even the officers, for that matter. Also, she never made a point of lingering in any other office when she stopped by during a break or lunch hour. Then she'd started dropping suggestions about hanging out after her shift. That was when he finally admitted to himself that she wanted more than friendship *and* that he would have to find a way to discourage her without hurting her feelings.

Easier said than done.

He sat in his chair and moved the box aside with a resigned sigh. Later he'd take it into the break room. When the officers came in for shift change, they could sample the contents. Before he pulled up the patrol report he'd been working on, an exchange between dispatch and one of his patrol officers played over the radio attached to the epaulet on his shoulder. He listened intently, then pressed the talk button. "208, do you

6

copy?"

"This is 208. Go ahead." The officer's voice crackled over the line.

"I'll take the code nine at Brookstone and Deerfield. Take your meal break. Over."

"Copy that, Sarge."

Ben pushed his chair back, then got to his feet and grabbed the keys to his cruiser. Usually, he wouldn't jump in on a routine traffic incident, but after sitting at his desk since 0600, he could use a break from his computer. The one downside to his promotion was less time in the field and more time sitting at a desk. Slipping on his sunglasses, he left his office, informed Cora Jean, the front desk receptionist, where he was headed, and walked out of the building.

Hopefully, when he arrived on the scene, the two parties involved in the accident wouldn't be hurling insults or, worse, engaging in a physical altercation. Even the most minor of accidents could bring out the worst in people. No one ever wanted to admit they were at fault. Even when they obviously were.

Instead of driving through downtown Summerwood, Ben took a quicker route. As he rolled up on the intersection of Deerfield and Brookstone, the first thing he observed were two citizens, a man, and a woman, standing approximately six to ten feet from each other near their vehicles. They weren't arguing, which was a relief, so he pulled his cruiser into the bike lane, killed the engine, grabbed his citation booklet, and got out of the car. Luckily, Brookstone, an ancillary road, wasn't as heavily traversed as Highway 99 or Central, and the accident wasn't causing a traffic jam at the intersection.

Summerwood in late November was anything but summer-like, but the Kevlar vest he wore under his long-sleeved shirt kept him warm enough. The wind had picked up and whipped the woman's hair around her head, obscuring her face. The man turned as Ben crossed the street and moved toward him, obviously determined to tell his side of the story first. In his experience, that meant this guy was probably the cause of the accident.

"Officer, that woman has a bad case of road rage." The man, who looked in his mid to late fifties, used his phone to point toward the woman in question.

Ben didn't bother telling the man he was a sergeant. Most civilians didn't know about the insignia on his shirt sleeves or paid enough attention to his badge to read the title inscribed on it. He glanced at the woman. She didn't appear to be in a rage—road or otherwise.

She lifted a hand to brush the hair away from her face, and their gazes collided. As her eyes widened in stunned surprise, Ben's stomach bottomed out, and he sucked in a shocked breath.

Son of a bitch. Maddie Hart was back in town.

The man was rambling on about the stop sign and right of way, but Ben could barely hear him over the thundering inside of his chest. He hadn't seen Maddie in four years, and yet as she moved toward him, it seemed like it was yesterday. Her hair was now reddish blonde rather than golden blonde, but her eyes were the same, as clear and blue as a warm summer day.

He'd thought about this moment many times. But when he imagined seeing Maddie again, he hadn't expected to feel like he'd been punched in the gut. And he hadn't expected her to look as beautiful as she did the last time he saw her. The night she'd left him standing

8

on his porch with an engagement ring burning a hole in his pocket.

Maddie approached him and the older man cautiously, her mouth pressed into a tight grim line as she halted in front of them. She searched his face, and he was grateful for the cover of his sunglasses. If she could see his eyes, she might be able to tell how much her presence affected him, and he couldn't have that, not after everything that had gone down between them.

Propping his hands on his utility belt, Ben cocked his head, looking from Maddie to the older man. "If your cars are drivable, I need you to move them out of the intersection in a few minutes. You're blocking traffic," he said gruffly.

The man, whose head was as bald as a bowling ball, scowled. "I tried, but she stole my keys. Took 'em right out of my car."

"Is that true, ma'am?" He kept his tone professional.

Maddie lifted her chin. "I was trying to preserve the scene of the crime, Sergeant," she said after a cursory glance at his insignia.

Ben's stomach tightened. *Damn it*. Even her voice sounded the same. Slightly husky and incredibly sexy.

"Yeah. The crime *you* committed," the man grumbled. "She ran the damn stop sign."

"I most certainly did not," Maddie said hotly. "We got to the intersection at the same time. The rule is the driver on the right has the right of way, so I waited for you to go." She glared at the man, her eyes flashing. "I even waved at you to go, for Pete's sake. But you didn't move, so I went, and that's when you stepped on the gas and hit me."

"That's a damn lie!"

"Calm down." Ben held up a hand. "Both of you." His gaze bounced between them. "Please give…" He looked at the man. "What's your name, sir?"

"Leland Spevins."

"Please give Mr. Spevins his keys, ma'am," Ben said to Maddie, his tone brooking no argument. "I'm going to take a quick look at the scene, and then I'll need you both to move your cars to the side of the road."

Maddie narrowed her gaze but handed over the keys. Spevins snatched them out of her hand and stalked toward the two cars.

"You know I know the intersection rule," she said before whirling around and marching after Spevins.

She was right. Ben *did* know. She'd always been a good driver, and before she left Summerwood for Hollywood, she'd worked at a driving school in town. Releasing a long breath, Ben waved a car slowing to a stop next to his cruiser through the intersection. After the vehicle maneuvered around the two cars, Ben strode toward Maddie and Spevins. They were staring at each other like two prizefighters facing off in the ring before a title match.

As he surveyed the two cars, he was more aware of Maddie than he cared to admit. Aware of her watching him intently, aware of the fullness of her lips, and aware of the way her coat clung to her soft curves. She looked even better than she did in those ridiculous constipation commercials. Not that he watched them. Much.

With no witnesses, two similar accounts, no injuries, and minimal damage to both vehicles, no way he was going to side with either Maddie or Spevins. Especially since he knew Maddie. He'd write up a report, including their statements, and they could each contact their insurance companies.

After taking a final look at the vehicles, Ben pulled a pen out of his breast pocket, flipped open his citation booklet, and made notes on the notepad opposite the citation tablet.

"I hope you're writing her a ticket."

"I'm making notes for my report," Ben said, not looking up. "You can pick up a copy at the police station tomorrow."

"You're not giving him a ticket?" Maddie asked incredulously.

"Neither of you are getting a ticket." He jotted down her license plate number. "After you pick up the report, you can file a claim with your insurance companies, and they can determine who's at fault."

She set her hands on her hips, her light-blue eyes flashing with annoyance. "I thought you were a trained professional. Do you need me to draw a diagram for you?" She pointed to a small dent on her front fender. "See where he hit me? That proves I entered the intersection first. If he'd gone first, his car would be damaged on the side, near the driver's side door."

His jaw tightened at her imperious tone. "It looks to me like your vehicles entered the intersection simultaneously. If you'd like, I can write each of you a ticket, and you can talk to the judge and let her decide." He stepped back and made a note of Spevins' license plate number. "Either option works for me. Now I'd like you to move your cars out of the intersection and show me your license and registration for my report. After that, you can exchange insurance information and be on your way."

After recording Spevins' information and

instructing him to wait until he was done with Maddie before exchanging their insurance info, Ben walked toward Maddie, who'd gotten inside her compact SUV to wait for him. As he approached, she glared at him in the side mirror.

"License and registration," he said, then noticed the bag of cheese puffs on the passenger seat. Its sight brought back memories of them sharing junk food while binge-watching their favorite television shows. Gritting his teeth, he forced himself not to think about the past. "I'm surprised to see you back in town."

"Why?" She opened her wallet to pull out her license. "It's my home."

"I thought Hollywood was your home now." He was unable to keep the bitterness out of his voice.

She handed him her license along with her vehicle registration. "If you must know, I'm home for Thanksgiving."

"Only Thanksgiving?"

"Yes," she said sternly, turning her head and staring straight ahead.

Ben copied her information, not quite sure how he felt about that. Maddie Hart was the only woman he'd ever been in love with, and he'd honestly believed she'd loved him in return. But then, out of the blue, she'd decided to move to Hollywood to pursue an acting career.

Performing with the local theater company hadn't been enough for her. That's what she'd said. But what she *hadn't* said hurt the most. Now she would be in town for a week, which meant he'd probably run into her again. In a town the size of Summerwood, it was inevitable. After all this time, it shouldn't matter. But it did. He'd been in her presence for less than an hour, and he could barely think straight.

Leave it to Maddie Hart to show up and turn his life upside down.

Chapter Two

Seeing Ben after four years had been a major shock to Maddie's system. Her trembling body as she'd driven away from the intersection was evidence of that. That she'd managed to keep her emotions in check as he strode toward her and Leland Spevins was quite possibly an early Christmas miracle. Or it could be his cool and unruffled demeanor helped her disguise how affected she was by his presence.

She drove into Summerwood on autopilot with more than a few regrets weighing heavily on her shoulders. Leaving town to pursue her acting career was one of those regrets. Another was one she hadn't yet forgiven herself for. And neither would Ben if he found out.

But if you hadn't left, where would you be now?

Still working a going-nowhere job?

Still a disappointment to her father?

Check. And double-check.

But maybe you and Ben would still be together.

She shook her head to chase the thought away. She'd made her choice, and now she had to live with it.

In a stroke of luck, Maddie snagged a parking spot directly in front of Sweet Temptations. After getting out of her car, she admired the quaint downtown corner storefront. A cream-colored façade was topped with a pale-gray and white striped awning above the entrance, and the cotton-candy pink door offered a cheery welcome. She grinned. Mallory always did love a pop of color.

After crossing the sidewalk, she pushed open the door, and the comforting aroma of sugar and cinnamon invaded her nostrils, triggering a sudden desire for something sweet. Her gaze was drawn to a colorful display of cupcakes placed under a domed glass tray on a nearby table, and her mouth watered. At the counter, Mallory was assisting a customer.

Older than Maddie by fifteen months, Mallory was the middle sister and arguably the nicest person in the world. Mallory was also the peacemaker. Lauren, the eldest of the three, had always been the bossy sister.

Mallory's light-brown hair was pulled up in a messy bun, and the faint white streaks of flour on her apron indicated she'd spent the morning in the store's kitchen.

She glanced over the shoulder of her customer and gasped. "Oh my God." A delighted smile tilted the corners of her mouth. "You're home." She handed the woman a bright-pink bakery box. "Enjoy the pie, Mrs. Beasley," she said, then rounded the end of the gleaming white counter, flew across the shop, and wrapped Maddie in a tight hug.

Maddie absorbed the warmth of her sister's embrace and blinked back the tears suddenly swimming in her eyes. She'd spoken to Mallory dozens of times over the past few years, but it wasn't the same as seeing her in person.

"It's so freakin' good to see you." Mallory pulled back, her eyes suspiciously moist. "Mom and Dad are thrilled you decided to visit for Thanksgiving. Have you been to the house yet?"

"No. I figured they'd be working, so I came by here

first." She slanted a covetous glance toward the cupcakes. "Those cupcakes are calling my name."

Mallory's amber eyes twinkled with amusement. "Still haven't lost that sweet tooth, I see."

"That's one battle I'll never win. But I did manage to keep it under control. The camera does add ten pounds."

Mallory lowered her arms, stepped back, and gave her a quick once-over. "I don't think one cupcake will do much damage."

"Who says I'm going to eat just one?" Maddie winked.

After Mallory's assistant returned from lunch to take over the front counter, Maddie sat on a tall wooden stool at the large stainless-steel island in the small but serviceable kitchen where Mallory sat across from her rolling out sugar cookie dough. Taking a bite of the decadent chocolate fudge mini cupcake she'd selected, she let out a low moan. "Your buttercream frosting is to die for. I've been dreaming about it for months."

Mallory let out a soft chuckle. "Remember when we were kids, and you would eat the frosting and leave the rest?"

"The frosting is the best part." Maddie licked a dollop of chocolate buttercream from the tip of her finger. She surveyed the kitchen, her gaze resting on a tiered rack filled with assorted pies. "Do you need help boxing up those pies?"

Mallory sent her a grateful look. "I'll take any help I can get. I'm not complaining, but I've gotten way more orders than I anticipated this year, and my best part-time employee has been sick for two days."

Maddie wasn't surprised her sister's small business

had taken off. Mallory had known since the eighth grade that she wanted to open her own bakery and worked her butt off to achieve it. Including winning one of those kids' baking shows when she was twelve.

Both of her sisters were successful in their chosen fields, and while she was proud of them, their accomplishments only seemed to underscore Maddie's many failures. She *had* to land one of the roles she auditioned for. High-profile projects like those could jumpstart her acting career and lead to even more significant roles.

"I watched you on one of those true crime shows last week."

"Which one? I've done a couple." She pulled her phone out of her purse and quickly checked her messages, hoping to see one from her agent. She hadn't gotten a single call or email all morning. Disappointed, she set her phone on the countertop.

"I don't remember the show's name, but it's the episode where you were the conniving mistress who killed her lover's wife."

Maddie suppressed a shudder. "It's called *LA Crime*. Honestly, I was happy to get the job, but knowing it was a true story was disturbing." The low-budget show was filmed in Los Angeles, and she'd been hired for a few episodes as reenactment talent. It wasn't her dream job, but she had to pay the rent, and the residual compensation she received from the commercials was decreasing now that they weren't getting as much air time; being picky about paying gigs wasn't an option.

"Yeah, I guess it would be." Mallory selected a turkey-shaped cookie cutter from an assortment on the counter next to her. "Do you have any jobs coming up?"

"I'm hoping to hear from my agent soon. I had two auditions last week. One of them is for the lead in a Netflix series."

"That's great." Mallory's smile brightened her face. "How did the auditions go? Were you super prepared, as usual?"

Maddie chuckled. "You know me too well. By the time I auditioned, I had created an extensive backstory for each character. It helped me find the motivation for the characters in the scenes."

"I'm sure you nailed it. I hope you get offered both parts." Mallory pressed the cookie cutter into the dough. "So what about your love life? Anything new there?"

She shifted uncomfortably on the stool. The question was to be expected. Mallory was a hopeless romantic and had watched almost every rom-com ever made. Still, despite the many men Maddie had met in Los Angeles, she'd only gone on a handful of dates. As much as she tried, she couldn't stop comparing every guy she met to Ben. And none of them ever measured up. "I had coffee with a guy from my Pilates class last week. But all he talked about was himself. I could feel my eyes glaze over with boredom."

Mallory's brows lifted. "So no second date?"

Maddie snorted. "Hardly."

"That seems to be a pattern."

"What are you getting at?" Her tone was defensive even though Mallory's slightly sardonic comment wasn't far from the truth.

"You haven't dated anyone seriously since Ben."

"I've been busy trying to establish my career. I don't have time."

She rested her forearms on the counter as Mallory

pressed the cookie cutter into the dough, making several turkeys. Turkeys she would artfully decorate after they were baked.

"Speaking of Ben, I ran into him today."

Mallory looked up quickly. "Where?"

"At an intersection outside of town. I was involved in an accident, and Ben showed up to take the report." At Mallory's anxious expression, she continued, "Don't worry, it was a minor fender-bender. I'm fine, and so is the other driver."

"Oh, wow. I'm glad you're okay. So what happened?" Mallory set aside the turkey and picked up a giant acorn cookie cutter.

"Well, it was the other guy's fault, but he accused *me* of having road rage. Can you believe that?" She let out a soft snort. "Jerk."

Mallory's lips quirked with amusement. "I was talking about Ben. How was it seeing him?"

"It was a little tense," she said, remembering Ben's cold demeanor. Not that she had expected him to greet her any other way, but it still stung.

"I'm sure you were the last person he expected to see. The next time you run into him, it should be easier."

"I doubt there'll be a next time. I'm only here for a week."

"Oh, you'll see him," Mallory said with a knowing grin. "Dad will expect you to come to the annual football game on Thanksgiving morning. Ben will be there, as will his adoring fans, I'm sure."

"Adoring fans?" Maddie echoed. She was well aware of the yearly football game between the police and fire departments, but she didn't remember a large crowd.

"Yeah, I know of four women in town that would

love to get a piece of him." Mallory waggled her eyebrows. "If you know what I mean."

She had no problem believing Ben had women panting after him. Four years hadn't diminished Ben's appeal. He was still six feet of pure hotness, and judging by the fit of his uniform, he was still in excellent physical shape. The thought of anyone else getting a "piece" of him shouldn't bother her, but it did.

Maddie eyed the remaining cupcake on her plate, then casually asked, "So he doesn't have a girlfriend?"

"Not that I'm aware of. Would you care if he did?"

"No," she said quickly. "Of course not. Ben and I are ancient history."

"History has a habit of repeating itself."

After the way she'd treated him? "Not this time."

"Hey, I'm just saying that neither of you has been in a meaningful relationship since you split up. Maybe you needed time apart."

"Ben needs someone who lives in Summerwood, not Los Angeles. And that isn't me. I need to make it as an actress, Mal, and I can't do that here."

Mallory looked up from her task, her gaze shrewd and assessing. "I noticed you said need, not want. Tell me the truth. Are you happy living in LA?"

Happy? Not even close. But admitting that, even to Mallory, would prove that moving to Los Angeles based on a flimsy offer from a casting director she'd met only once was one of the most idiotic things she'd ever done.

"What I'm happy about is this second cupcake." Maddie picked up the lemon cupcake topped with raspberry buttercream and bit into it.

****

Ben's mood hadn't improved by the time he

returned to the station, and when he pushed the door open and spotted Traci Kemp at the front counter talking with Cora Jean, he wanted to turn around and walk right back out.

Before he could act on the inclination, Traci caught sight of him and left Cora Jean in her dust as she hurried toward him. "Hey, Hawaii was fabulous. Did you see the surprise I left on your desk?"

"I did. Thank you. I'll share it with the officers," he said politely. "It'll probably be history by the end of the week."

Her smile faltered slightly. "Do you have a minute?"

He glanced at his watch. Now could be his opportunity to have the conversation he needed to have with Traci, but at the moment, he didn't have the time. "That's about all I can spare. I have a meeting with the chief in five minutes."

"It won't take long. After shift tonight, a few of us are heading over to JD's Pub for drinks and darts. Why don't you join us?" She gave him a cajoling smile. "C'mon. Sam will be there. I ran into him at the diner this morning and invited him."

As much as he'd like to see his brother, Ben hesitated. He didn't much like the idea of going home and stewing about Maddie, but he also didn't want to lead Traci on. She was a nice person and an excellent 911 emergency operator, but he wasn't attracted to her.

"Come for one beer. And maybe a game of darts." She put her hand on his arm and squeezed. "I bet I can beat you."

"You think so?" He deliberately stepped back to dislodge her grip on his forearm.

"Yes. I'm very good." Her bright smile returned in

full force. "What do you say? You work all the time. You deserve to have some fun."

"I second that," Cora Jean interjected. "All work and no play makes—"

"Fine," Ben said sharply, sending Cora Jean a stern look. "I'll be there. What time?"

Traci's smile held a hint of triumph. "Eight." She turned and waved at Cora Jean as she left the building.

"That girl's set her sights on you, Benjy."

He sighed. He'd known Cora Jean Beck since his family moved to Summerwood, and when she applied for the front desk position and was hired, he'd thought she'd be a great fit. But since then, he'd realized that Cora Jean was more interested in gossiping than actually doing her job. A few times a day, she would call him up to the front to answer a question from a citizen she could have easily answered herself.

"Cora Jean, I'm not a kid anymore. Please don't call me Benjy."

"Can't help it. I looked after Sierra and cooked for you boys when you first moved to town. You'll always be Benjy to me." Behind the wire-framed glasses perched on her nose, her dark eyes were filled with amusement. "Look on the bright side. Maybe you'll get laid tonight."

His jaw dropped. "What the—"

"Ashford."

The chief's commanding voice startled Ben. He spun around to find Eli Hart standing at the doorway leading to the back of the station where the squad room and individual offices were housed.

"Are you done socializing?" His tone was as sharp as the stern glint in his hazel eyes.

"Yes, sir." He scowled at Cora Jean and followed the chief to his office.

"Sit down." The chief rounded his desk and settled his tall frame into his well-worn leather chair.

Ben sat ramrod straight across from the chief's uncluttered desk. The chief was a stickler about wearing the uniform with pride. That meant no missing buttons, no stains, and no slouching. Eli Hart was a tough taskmaster, but he was fair and walked his talk. He believed in the chain of command but was approachable and genuinely cared about each officer who worked under him.

That said, Eli Hart didn't have a problem letting his officers know when they fucked up. His only soft spot, at work anyway, was Cora Jean. Everyone in the station had complained about her poor work performance at one time or another. But other than a minor reprimand, the chief didn't seem to have the heart to fire the older woman. Maybe he hoped she'd retire soon or pack up and move to Seattle where her daughter and grandchildren lived. But until one of those two things happened, they were stuck with her.

"Captain Daniels tells me he selected you to be a part of the team putting together our strategic plan for next year."

"That's correct, sir. The team is meeting next week to finalize our immediate and future goals as well as our strategic objectives," he said, proud to have been appointed to the team and taking it as a good sign for his prospects within the department. Usually, newly promoted sergeants were assigned less critical tasks.

"What, in your opinion, is our most important immediate goal?"

Surprised the chief was asking him instead of Captain Daniels, Ben leaned forward, eager to share his input on one of the key goals and one he championed. "Considering the rise in domestic violence calls, I believe it's imperative we continue to enhance our response to those types of calls and provide in-depth training for our sworn officers."

Chief Hart steepled his fingers under his chin and studied him thoughtfully. "I'm inclined to agree with you. Since last year, DV calls have increased, and while our officers received the standard training in the academy, specialized training is warranted. I expect you to provide a cost analysis summary for the training and a list of accredited instructors when I meet with the team next month."

Pleased he'd anticipated the chief's needs, Ben nodded. "That's my plan."

"Good." Hart nodded. "You can go."

"Yes, sir." Ben stood and turned to leave.

"Oh, one more thing."

Shit. Had he spilled hot sauce on his uniform at lunch? He resisted the urge to check as he turned to face the chief.

"Are you ready to kick the SFD's ass on Thursday morning?"

Relieved, he grinned. "More than ready. Those smoke eaters won't know what hit 'em."

Eli Hart's jovial mood turned somber. "Look, I've debated telling you this, but all things considered, I think you should know. Maddie's coming home for Thanksgiving."

Surprised, Ben kept his expression neutral. In the past four years, the chief had mentioned Lauren and

Mallory's accomplishments but rarely mentioned his youngest daughter. At least not when Ben was around. Eli probably figured it was a sore subject, which wasn't far from the truth. Ben had been happy not to discuss Maddie, especially with her father or other family members.

"I know. I ran into Maddie earlier," he said, resting his hands on his utility belt.

Eli's bushy eyebrows lifted. "You did? Did she stop by the station while I was at lunch?"

"No." He was surprised Maddie hadn't already talked to her father. "She was involved in a minor traffic accident, and I took the report."

"Is she okay?" The concern on the chief's face was evident.

"She's fine. It was a minor collision at an intersection. I didn't ticket Maddie or the other party. Neither of them was happy about it. Each of them thought the other one was at fault."

"Well, Maddie was always a good driver, but she's lived in Los Angeles for four years. Who knows what bad driving habits she's picked up from those fools in California." A shadow of emotion Ben couldn't place crossed Eli's face. "I wish…" he began, then shook his head and waved a dismissive hand. "You've got work to do. I'll see you at 0900 sharp on Thanksgiving Day."

"Yes, sir," he said, then left the chief's office.

Back in his office, Ben worked for two solid hours on the report he'd started on earlier in the day, then, as he usually did, he checked in with each of his patrol officers as they filed in at the end of their shift. After preparing for his briefing for the following day, he let Cora Jean know he was done for the day and was heading home. To his surprise, he was looking forward to going to JD's Pub to catch up with Sam. His brother had been working long hours on a building remodel downtown, and they hadn't seen each other in a while. A beer and catching up with Sam was what the doctor ordered to take his mind off Maddie.

Make that two beers.

Chapter Three

After helping Mallory box the pies, Maddie left Sweet Temptations with a promise to meet her sister after dinner at JD's Pub for a drink. Mallory was bringing along the guy she'd been dating for a few months, and Maddie was eager to meet him. For reasons Maddie could only guess, Mallory hadn't been forthcoming about him. The two things she knew about him was that his name was Tanner, and Mallory had met him through an online dating app. Hopefully, this time she had found a nice guy. One who would treat her the way she deserved to be treated. Too often, she chose men who were controlling. One had even been verbally abusive, and her sister had waited way too long to end the relationship.

As she drove along Main Street en route to her parents' home, Maddie passed Callie's Diner where she and her friends from the community theater used to hang out after their performances, drinking pots of coffee and talking for hours about acting. Down a half block was Summerwood's original movie theater where she'd had her first official date with Ben. Now refurbished, it resembled a retro Hollywood theater. The large marquee advertised a recently released action movie and a reminder that, beginning on the Friday after Thanksgiving, their annual Friday Holiday Movie Night would start and continue each Friday until the Friday after Christmas. Their first movie selection, *Christmas Vacation*. Maddie was thrilled they'd continued the tradition, and she couldn't wait to see what other movies they'd selected.

Once she left the downtown corridor, she drove along the familiar route to her parents' neighborhood on the outskirts of Summerwood. When she arrived at the house, she pulled up to the detached garage, turned off the engine, and climbed out of the car. Closing her eyes, she breathed in the fragrant scent of the pine and chestnut trees dotting the property and sighed with contentment. Nothing in Los Angeles smelled this good. Nothing. And then there was the quiet. The blessed quiet. How she had missed it.

Opening her eyes, she moved from the driveway to the brick path that curved toward the front of the house. Built in 1930, the two-story Cape Cod with its light-gray siding and bright-white trim looked like one of those fabulous houses in the movies that no one had ever seen in real life. The house hadn't always been this amazing. Her parents had purchased it as a fixer-upper before she was born, and over the years they had renovated it. Their care into each renovation phase had transformed the once neglected house into a warm and inviting home.

Before she could make it to the steps, the front door opened, and her mother stepped onto the porch, her smile wide and welcoming. "Oh, honey, I'm so happy to see you."

"Hi, Mom." Maddie hurried up the stairs and hugged her mother. "I've missed you." She inhaled the faint antiseptic scent that clung to her mother's clothes after a long day at her dental practice. As odd as it might seem, every time she went to the dentist in LA, she'd come down with an acute bout of homesickness.

"I've missed you too." Her mom pulled back and searched Maddie's face, her eyes filled with emotion. "You have no idea how much."

She followed her mother into the house and closed the door behind her. "Is Lauren here yet?" she asked as they moved across the formal living room and into the cheery blue-and-white kitchen.

"No." She brushed back hair that had more silver-gray than blonde strands in it since Maddie had seen her last. "There was a last-minute change to her schedule. Lauren won't make it for Thanksgiving, but she promised she'd be here for Christmas."

"Oh, no. I won't get to see her." Maddie tried to infuse some regret in her tone, but in truth, she was somewhat relieved. She loved her eldest sister, but Lauren Hart was a hard act to live up to. Lauren had always been the smartest, the most popular, and the prettiest, but now as an ICU nurse at a major hospital in Philadelphia, she was the one that saved lives. In short, she had achieved sainthood status in their parents' eyes.

"Are you sure you can't stay through Christmas?" Her mother's voice penetrated her thoughts. "It's not like you're all that busy, right?"

"I went on two auditions last week." This wasn't the first time one or both of her parents assumed she sat around with nothing to do in between jobs. Preparing for an audition was time-consuming. Learning her lines and figuring out her character's motivation might sound easy to someone who hadn't done it before, but it wasn't. It was a process, and it took time.

"But even if you get either of those parts, wouldn't you start working after the holidays?"

"Yes, but I have to be available to audition at any time," she said and wasn't stretching the truth. Thousands of talented women in their mid to late twenties were competing for the same number of limited parts; she couldn't afford to miss a single audition. Slackers didn't get anywhere in Hollywood; she'd learned that fact very quickly.

"Well, I guess that makes sense. It's just that I haven't had all of you home at the same time in four years," her mom said as her phone rang. "Sorry, honey, I need to get this. I worked today, but even though I'm off the clock until next week, I'm on call for emergencies." She picked up the phone from the granite countertop and gave Maddie an apologetic smile.

"It's okay." Maddie returned her smile, somewhat relieved the call had interrupted talk of her career. "I'll go get my stuff out of the car."

Outside, she popped the cargo-hold door, then turned around at the sound of a car pulling up behind her and smiled at the familiar face behind the steering wheel. "Hi, Dad!" She waved as her father got out of his unmarked police vehicle. Leaving her suitcase in the trunk, she hurried toward him and threw her arms around him.

"How's my girl?" He wrapped her in a hug.

"Happy to see you. It seems like ages." She pulled back and looked up at him. Like her mom, her father's hair was a bit grayer than the last time she'd seen him. "Did you catch any bad guys today?" As a kid, that had been her standard question every time he came home from work.

He laughed, his accompanying smile crinkling the corners of his eyes. "Not today, but I did hear about your little traffic incident."

Damn Ben. Of course, he had to go and tattle.

She stepped back, raising her hand like she was taking an oath to tell the truth, the whole truth, and nothing but the truth. "Dad, I swear it wasn't my fault. This guy and I got to the intersection at the same time. He was on my right, so I motioned for him to go. But he just sat there, so I went, and that's when he decided to hit the gas."

Her father chuckled. "I believe you. Now let me help you with your suitcase." They moved toward her car. "So how long are you staying?"

"A week. Then I have to get back to LA." She halted beside her father as he reached into the trunk and pulled out her suitcase. "Auditions and all." She shrugged. "I never know when something will come up."

A frown deepened the creases on his forehead. "Seems like acting is more about waiting for the phone to ring than anything else."

"It's a lot more than that." She pasted on a smile. "C'mon. You get the suitcase, and I'll get the pies Mallory made for Thanksgiving. Then I want to hear all about what's going on at the station."

After dinner with her parents and a quick shower, Maddie changed into a pair of black jeans and a cream chenille sweater. She applied her favorite red lipstick and checked her appearance in the mirror. Satisfied she wasn't overdressed for the pub, she slipped the lipstick tube into her purse and moved from the dresser to the closet to retrieve her coat. She had just shrugged into it when her phone rang. She made a quick dash to the bed, and when she picked it up, her heart tripped at the sight of the large initial M on the screen. M was the first initial of her agent's name. "Hey, Margo. What's up?"

"I heard from each of the casting offices on those auditions you went on last week." Margo Loughlin's tone didn't indicate whether the news was good or bad.

"What did they say?" She crossed her fingers. Finally. This could be it, her big break.

"I'm sorry, Maddie, but both of them passed."

Tears pricked her eyes as she sagged onto the bed. "Both of them?"

"Yes, but I heard from my sources that *A New Dawn* is looking to replace one of their current actresses, and you'd be perfect for the role. I'll keep you posted."

"Okay. Thanks." Disappointment churned her stomach into a tight knot. *A New Dawn* was one of the few remaining soap operas on network television. It wasn't the direction she'd wanted for her career, but she hoped they would at least ask her to audition. After all, a job was a job.

"Don't get discouraged." Margo's tone was sympathetic. "You made it to the final round of auditions in the Netflix project. That's significant progress."

"Yeah. Right." Even though Margo was right, she couldn't muster any enthusiasm. "I appreciate you letting me know. Have a nice Thanksgiving."

"You too. I'll talk with you soon."

After Margo hung up, Maddie sat on the bed, staring blankly at the wall. When the bedroom was hers, she'd painted it her favorite color. Pale yellow. But now it was a guest room, and her mother had repainted it a soft cream color. Too bad it wasn't black—to suit her current mood.

The last thing she wanted to do now was go out among people or face her family. But she'd promised

Mallory, and if she didn't go, all she would do was sit and wallow in self-pity. She could do the same thing at the pub *and* have a few drinks to go along with her pity party. Getting drunk sounded pretty good right about now.

She trudged down the stairs, pulled on her gloves, and headed toward the family room that adjoined the kitchen. As she approached the kitchen, she heard her name and paused at the entrance.

"Maddie's an adult, Eli." Her mother's voice was low but still audible. "We can't tell her what to do or how to live her life."

"I know that, Rena. But I'm afraid, like always, she bit off more than she can chew." Her father's deep voice shot across the room like an arrow and pierced Maddie's heart. "She's been in Hollywood for four years, and her major claim to fame is a constipation commercial."

"Maddie's a good actress."

"I'm not saying she isn't a good actress, but maybe she's just Summerwood good."

Maddie stifled a gasp. *Summerwood good?* That was a bit harsh.

"It's a tough business, and you have to give her credit. The four years she's spent in Hollywood is the longest she's ever committed to anything."

"I wish she was more like her sisters. Especially when it comes to life decisions."

Maddie didn't stick around to hear her mother's response. She turned and rushed out of the house. As usual, she'd been compared to her sisters and come up lacking. What else was new?

****

Ben wasn't sure if trivia night was the reason, but

JD's Pub was remarkably busy for a Tuesday evening. Summerwood was growing, but at its heart, it was a small town, and because he'd been on the police force for nine years, he knew pretty much everyone. As soon as he walked in, he'd been flagged down by at least five people wanting to shoot the breeze with him. When he finally made his way to the gleaming oak bar, Traci was annoyed, and his brother amused.

Fortunately, Traci was easily appeased, and when she reluctantly left him and Sam at the bar to play a round of darts with her friends, he'd been relieved. However, the way she'd been hanging all over him made him suspect that agreeing to her invitation had given her the mistaken impression he was interested in more than a round of darts. He had to set her straight and soon. Putting off the uncomfortable conversation would only give Traci hope for something that could never be. The longer he waited, the more he could hurt her, and he didn't want to do that.

But now wasn't the time or the place. He shifted on the leather stool and looked at his brother. "How's the remodel going?"

"Can you say renovation hell?" Sam's usually cheerful expression darkened. "Dealing with the new owners is a pain in the ass."

Ben had heard the new owners were from California. Like many Oregonians, Sam believed transplanted Californians were the main cause for the population growth in the Willamette Valley and the increase in housing prices.

"Keep changing their minds, do they?"

"Every damn day. But it's their money, and they have a lot of it, so I'm going with the flow." Sam took a draw on his beer, slanting a glance toward Ben. "What time will you be at the house on Thanksgiving?"

"I'll be over around noon. I've got the football game in the morning, remember?"

"Oh, yeah. I forgot. Are you QB again?"

Ben lifted his bottle. "Yep, and I think we have a shot this year." He took a long pull of the ice-cold brew.

"I'll come by and check it out." Sam glanced toward the section of the pub where it looked like Traci and her friends were talking and drinking more than they were shooting darts. "What's the deal with you and Traci? Are you hooking up with her?"

Shit. Even his brother thought he might have something going on with her. "No. And I'm not going to."

"Why?" Sam looked at him like he'd lost his marbles. "She's hot."

He scowled. "Why don't you hook up with her if you think she's so hot?"

"Dude, she's not interested in me. It's you she's trying to get horizontal with. I thought she was going to mount you right here at the bar."

"Can we not talk about Traci?" Ben wished Sam would drop the subject of Traci altogether.

"You're wound a little tight there, bro." Sam grinned. "What's got your shorts in a wad?"

"It's not what. It's who." He blew out an exasperated breath. "Maddie's back in town."

Sam's eyes widened. "Seriously? I talked to Mallory the other day, and she didn't mention it."

"She probably didn't know. Maddie likes surprises."

"So you saw her?"

"Yep." He'd seen her and, much to his annoyance,

hadn't been the same since.

"And how'd that go?"

"We barely spoke. She was involved in a minor car accident, and I took the report."

"Is she home for good?"

"No. For Thanksgiving." And why did that bother him? Even if she was home to stay, it didn't change the past. She'd be gone at the end of the week, and he'd be set for another four years.

"That's probably for the best." Sam finished his beer and slid off his stool. "I gotta go to the john. Order me another beer."

As much as he hated it when Sam was right, in this case, his brother had pretty much hit the nail on the head. It *was* for the best. He'd made a fool of himself over Maddie Hart once; he didn't need to go down that road again. He swung his gaze in the direction of Traci and her friends. She looked toward him and gave him a luminous smile. He acknowledged her with a nod and pushed his empty bottle aside. She was dressed to kill. Wearing a sparkly red halter top and tight jeans that more than accentuated her smoking-hot body. Any other man would take advantage of what she'd been offering him for months. What the hell was wrong with him?

The answer to that question wasn't something he wanted to dwell on. He motioned to the bartender, ordered two more beers, and stared at the television screen mounted over the bar. He watched the hockey game until his brother returned and elbowed him in the side.

"Ex-girlfriend in the house." Sam settled himself on his stool and slid his newly opened beer in front of him. "Yours, not mine."

"Where?" Ben turned and discreetly searched the pub but didn't see Maddie at any of the nearby tables.

"Sitting alone at a table near the hallway that leads to the restrooms. She didn't see me. I thought about asking her to join us, but I wasn't sure how that would sit with you. Or your date."

"Traci isn't my date," he snapped, taking the teasing bait Sam had served up on a silver platter.

"Try telling her that." Sam grinned.

Ben shook his head as he slid off his stool. He needed a break from his brother. "I'll be right back." He grabbed his beer and threaded his way around the room until he reached Maddie's table.

Staring at the glass in front of her, she appeared to be oblivious to his arrival.

He let his gaze wander over her beautiful face and tamped down memories that were still potent even after four years. "Mind if I join you?"

With a jerk of her head, she looked up at him, a mix of emotions flashing in her eyes before they became flat and unreadable. "Sure, why not? It's not like my night can get any worse."

"Rough night?" He sat across from her and set his beer on the table. "Is that why you're drinking alone?"

"I won't be alone for long. Mallory's meeting me here." She picked up her glass and narrowed her gaze on him. "Oh, by the way. Thanks for telling my dad about the accident. I bet you couldn't wait to get back to the station and drop that little tidbit," she said in a tone laced with sarcasm before she sipped her drink.

"I hadn't planned on mentioning it at all. It came up when he told me you were coming home for Thanksgiving. I told him it wasn't a big deal. As

37

Alison Packard

accidents go, it was minor."

"To you, maybe."

"What do you mean? Was he angry?"

"No. But let's just say that little fender-bender is one more reason for my father to assume I'm incapable of managing my own life. And now that I didn't get—" She didn't finish her sentence and this time took more than a sip of her drink. Probably a Tom Collins—she'd never liked the taste of beer.

"Didn't get what?"

"Never mind. It doesn't matter." She set her glass on the table and gave him an apologetic smile. "I'm sorry I snapped at you. How's your family?"

Something other than the accident was bothering her; he'd bet his life on it. But her deliberate change of subject was a sure sign she didn't want to talk about it.

"Doing well. My dad still has the construction company. Sam is working with him now. He's doing a remodel on Main Street. Some folks from California bought the Rosebud property."

Her eyes widened. "Rosebud's went out of business?"

He nodded. "They couldn't compete with the online booksellers. Rose and Bud sold everything and moved to Florida."

"Wow. Lauren's going to be upset when she finds out. She practically lived in Rosebud's. I think she was born knowing how to read." Maddie flashed a grin and leaned forward. "Speaking of brainiacs, how's Sierra?"

"The same. Driving Dad crazy with her causes. Last summer, she organized a protest at the library. About half the town showed up."

Her eyes widened. "What were they protesting?"

"The library district's decision to ban a controversial book. In the end, they changed their minds and allowed the book to remain on the shelves."

"I'm not surprised." Admiration shone in her eyes. "Your sister was always a force of nature."

"Yeah," he said proudly. "I'm going to miss her when she goes to college next year. I'm sure she'd love to see you while you're in town."

"Really?" she said, her expression one of surprise. "She doesn't hate me after I—"

"Hey, Maddie. Long time, no see."

He started at the sound of Traci's voice. She halted next to him, and while her expression was pleasant, her eyes held a hint of irritation. Maddie and Traci had known each other since grade school, but they'd never run with the same crowd, according to Maddie. When he and Maddie were together, they had encountered Traci a few times around town, and he'd always sensed some tension between them, but Maddie had never elaborated. As for Traci, she'd never spoken ill of Maddie unless he counted the time she'd made fun of Maddie's commercials. But to be fair, half the town joked about them too.

"Hi, Traci." Maddie's tone was cool but polite. "It *has* been a while. How are you?"

"Fabulous." Traci gave Ben a suggestive smile before redirecting her attention toward Maddie. "Are you back in town for good? Or just visiting?"

Maddie reclined in her chair. Her sweater clung to her breasts, and Ben quickly averted his gaze. Admiring her physical attributes wouldn't get him anywhere except frustrated.

"Visiting."

"Oh, well, it's great to see you." Traci rested a proprietary hand on Ben's shoulder. "You promised me a round of darts."

He gave her a tight smile. "I'll be over in a bit. I'm catching up with Maddie."

"Okay, but don't take too long." She squeezed his shoulder before turning and heading back to the bar.

"I hope she brought a coat. It's cold outside," Maddie said with a wry smile once Traci was out of earshot. "Are you seeing her?"

"Would you care?" He wondered what Maddie would say if he led her to believe he was dating Traci.

"No."

Her swift, emphatic denial stung. And was another reminder of how easy it had been for her to leave him. "Then why'd you ask?"

"Just curious." She shrugged.

Her indifference sent a surge of anger through him. If he ever believed Maddie had regretted her decision four years ago, she'd just proved him wrong. "What about you? Is there anyone in LA you're serious about? Oh, wait." He pointed at her. "I forgot. You don't do serious."

She shot up straight in her chair, her eyes flaring with indignation. "What does that mean?"

"You know exactly what it means." He pushed his chair back and got to his feet. "Have a nice night," he said harshly and walked away, leaving her sitting at the table.

Chapter Four

Eli Hart's motto had always been *if you're on time, you're late*. That motto was why Maddie and her parents arrived thirty minutes early on Thanksgiving morning at the Summerwood Sports Complex.

For the past ten years, the town's police and fire departments had engaged in a flag football game on Thanksgiving morning. It had started as a worthy endeavor to raise money for a local charity, but not long after had turned into a rivalry of epic proportions. Both chiefs had started wagering on the outcome, with the losing department having to provide a service or complete menial tasks for the winners.

Maddie sat in the car with her mother, keeping warm while watching her father and the fire chief confer with the donation station volunteers near the bleachers. Under a cloudless blue sky, the early arrivals were stretching or warming up with wind sprints on the freshly chalked football field.

As soon as they pulled into the parking lot, she'd searched for Ben, but he wasn't on the field. Ever since he walked away from her at JD's, she'd been unable to forget his parting shot. Maybe because he'd struck a nerve. A nerve already exposed and raw after overhearing her parents' conversation.

"It's cold. Did you bring gloves?" her mom asked. "I hope this thing doesn't go all morning. The turkey's

41

ready to go, but I need to get it in the oven no later than noon."

"Yes, on the gloves," Maddie said. "And if it looks like the game won't be over by noon, I'll drive you home and come back to pick up Dad."

"Thank you, honey." Her mom glanced over her shoulder. "Have you heard from your agent?"

Maddie's body froze, including her brain. "Ah…" She cleared her throat. "Um, yeah. She called to wish me a Happy Thanksgiving."

"Oh, that was sweet." Her mother didn't seem to notice Maddie tripping over her tongue. "I hope she has good news for you soon."

"Me too." Maddie's cheeks grew hot like they always did when she lied. But technically, she hadn't lied to her mother, right? Margo *had* wished her a Happy Thanksgiving. All she'd done was omit the part of the conversation where Margo had informed her that she'd tanked her auditions. Okay, fine. She was exaggerating, but the last thing she needed was to provide further evidence of her failures. She could turn this around. All she had to do was get through her visit, go back to LA, and keep auditioning. And who knew, maybe she'd end up on *A New Dawn*. Her mom would be thrilled. It was her favorite soap opera, even though she was still angry they'd killed off her favorite character in a freak ice storm.

Ten minutes before game time, she sat on a mid-level bleacher bench, unable to keep her eyes off Ben, who had arrived as she and her mother were getting out of the car and heading for the bleachers. Dressed in a pair of black sweats that emphasized his muscular thighs and a long-sleeved gray Summerwood Police Department shirt, he looked every bit the athlete he'd been in high school. She hadn't known him then. He'd graduated the year before she was a freshman, but she'd known *of* him from all the Friday night football games she'd attended with her family to support Lauren, who'd been in the marching band all through high school.

"Hi, Maddie, welcome home!"

She turned and smiled at Clarice Worley, an insurance agent and one of her former employers, sitting next to her mother, who had moved to talk to a friend a couple of rows up.

"How's that constipation? I hope you're not too backed up." Clarice let out a hearty belly laugh as if she'd said the funniest thing on earth.

"I'm good, Clarice, thanks." She smiled despite herself at Clarice's attempt at humor. Clarice was a wonderful woman and had always been good to her. Turning her attention to the field, Maddie spotted Mallory and her boyfriend, Tanner, moving along the walkway in front of the bleachers. "Mallory!" She waved a gloved hand. "Over here."

By halftime, she wished she'd worn thicker socks. Her feet were freezing, and she'd had to turn down the cuff on her knit cap to cover her ears. Although she'd never been a huge football fan, the game so far had been exciting. Both teams were playing hard, and the score was tied. She opened the travel thermos her mother had given her, sipped the warm cocoa, and discreetly scanned the bleacher seats nearer to the sideline benches where Ben and the rest of his team were in a huddle, probably discussing their second-half strategy.

As Mallory predicted, a few women had spent the first half cheering wildly for Ben. She wasn't surprised one of them was Traci Kemp. She and Traci had gone to school together. Maddie hadn't much cared for how Traci treated some of their classmates. Unlike Maddie and her drama-geek crowd, Traci had never gone through that awkward teen stage. Smart and popular, the stunning brunette and her striking green eyes had sailed through high school without a single zit or a day in detention.

At the pub on Tuesday night, Traci had made it a point to stake her claim on Ben, and by the time Mallory finally arrived with Tanner in tow, Maddie had had her fill of watching Traci fawn over Ben as they played darts. In LA, she was surrounded by beautiful people, and if she was honest, Traci could hold her own against any of them.

A tap on her knee roused her from her thoughts. She turned toward Tanner, who'd scooted over to sit next to her after Mallory left them to buy two cups of coffee at the refreshment stand.

"Who's the guy talking to Mallory?" Tanner said, adjusting the dark knit cap partially covering his dirty blond hair.

Following his line of sight, Maddie searched the crowd and zeroed in on Mallory standing at the far end of the bleachers, holding two cups of coffee, and chatting with Ben's brother.

"Oh, that's Sam Ashford. He and Mallory have been friends since junior high." She turned to look at Tanner, whose brooding gaze had stayed fixed on Mallory and Sam.

"Did they date?"

"No," she said and sipped her cocoa. Last night, Tanner had been polite but distant. He hadn't spoken much and kept a proprietary arm around Mallory's shoulders until they left the pub. Now, the way Tanner was watching Mallory and Sam troubled her. She hoped he wasn't like Mallory's last boyfriend. "So you said you're a web designer, right?"

"I'm a web *developer*. There's a difference." He looked at her with exasperation and, of course, proceeded to tell her the difference.

After what seemed like an hour but in reality had been about five minutes, she breathed a sigh of relief as Mallory rejoined them.

"Hey, babe. You've been gone a while." Tanner's tone was sulky. "I hope the coffee's still warm."

"It is." Annoyance pinched Mallory's face as she handed him his cup. "Sam said to say hi," she said to Maddie as Tanner moved over so Mallory could reclaim her seat between them. "And guess what? He offered to help me renovate the storage room in the back of the bakery. I've been using it for both an office and a pantry. When he's done, I'll finally have a separate office."

"That's nice of him." Maddie glanced surreptitiously at Tanner, who was displeased judging by his dour expression.

"Isn't it?" Mallory nodded and sipped her coffee.

"Shouldn't you hire a professional for a job like that?" Tanner asked.

"He *is* a professional," Mallory said, her tone defensive. "He's a licensed general contractor. He's working on a remodel a few blocks away from the bakery."

Tanner's eyebrows drew together in a scowl. "How can he do that and help you at the same time?"

"In his spare time, I guess." Mallory shrugged. "It's

not like I'm in a hurry. After he looks at the space and we discuss what I want, he'll draw up some specs and give me a quote for the materials. He's not charging me for labor."

"Big of him," Tanner muttered as he swung his gaze to the field where the second half was getting underway.

Maddie grinned as Mallory turned to her and grimaced. Tanner wouldn't last through Christmas if Mallory had learned her lesson about dating possessive men.

****

After shaking hands with the fire department's players, Ben walked off the field with his teammates in a much better mood than last year. Losing again would have sucked big time, but a late-game field goal had won the game for the SPD, saving them from performing whatever tedious task the fire chief had dreamed up for them if they'd lost.

Moving to the bench that flanked the sideline, he reached for his jacket and pulled it on. It was almost noon, but the weather hadn't gotten any warmer, and now that he was cooling off, a chill was invading his body.

As Officer Dodd's eight-year-old son ran up to him, he zipped the jacket.

"That was a great game!" Cole's eyes were lit with excitement. "That touchdown pass you threw to my dad was *ah-mazing*!"

"I'm lucky I caught it," Dave Dodd said from a few feet away where he was taking off his cleats. "My hands felt like ice blocks for most of the game."

"You did good, Dad." Cole beamed proudly at his father.

"Yes, he did." Shelly Dodd ambled up, carrying a large tote bag stuffed with blankets. "Hi, Ben." She smiled and looped her free arm around Cole's slim shoulders. "Hon, we've gotta get moving. Your parents are expecting us at three. We need to get on the road in an hour."

Dodd slipped into his sneakers and started tying the laces. "Hang on. Almost done." He stood and gave Ben a nod. "Good game, Sarge." He hurriedly shoved his cleats into his gym bag and grabbed the handles. "See you next shift."

"Copy that." Ben watched as the Dodd family strolled off the field toward the parking lot.

Cole, a miniature version of his father, turned and waved at the edge of the grass. "Bye, Sarge! Happy Thanksgiving."

"Same to you, champ." Oblivious to his teammates milling around him, Ben gazed at the trio with more than a bit of envy. At thirty-one, he'd expected to have what Dave Dodd had. A family of his own. That he didn't was solely on him. After his relationship with Maddie hadn't worked out, he'd focused on his career instead of his personal life. He'd told himself he'd get back out there once he made sergeant, start dating, and find someone to settle down with. But a year after his promotion, he was still single, dating sporadically, and no closer to finding someone to share his life with.

"Benjy!" The only other person who called him Benjy, his sister, Sierra, hurried toward him, her cheeks rosy from the cold. She was out of breath when she reached him. "Why didn't you tell me Maddie was back in town? I saw her after halftime, so I went and sat with her."

"Because I haven't seen you since she got back." He shoved his hands into his pockets, forcing himself not to scan the small crowd vacating the bleachers. Not long after stepping onto the field to stretch before the game, he'd located where Maddie was sitting. After that, the bright-pink hat she wore acted as a beacon, drawing his attention each time they'd changed downs, and he headed for the sideline. And worse, knowing she was there watching him had scrambled his damn brain. He'd played like shit. His team would have lost if it hadn't been for the last-minute field goal.

"She's going to run lines with me." Sierra rubbed her hands together to warm them. As usual, she'd forgotten her gloves.

Puzzled, he cocked his head. "Run what with you?"

"I'm in the Christmas play at school, remember? Maddie offered to run lines with me. You know. Lines of dialogue. This is *so* awesome," she gushed, practically vibrating with excitement.

Seeing her so happy made him glad he hadn't gone into detail about his and Maddie's breakup. Just because he'd been disillusioned didn't mean Sierra had to be as well.

"What's awesome, Skittles?" Sam appeared behind Sierra and gently tugged a few strands of her long hair, which she'd recently dyed light purple.

"Maddie's going to run lines with me." Sierra pulled her phone from her coat pocket, surprising Ben by not giving Sam a hard time about the nickname. "I've gotta text Faith. She is *so* gonna freak out. See you guys later." With her head bent over her phone, she turned and headed toward her car.

"I haven't seen her this excited since we took her to

that boy band concert when she was eleven," Sam commented as Ben sat on the bench and pulled his sneakers out of his gym bag.

"Don't remind me," Ben grumbled. "That was two hours of my life I'll never get back."

Sam burst out laughing and sat on the bench, stretching his long legs out in front of him. "You lucked out, bro. Traci left before the game ended. But before she left, she told me she can't wait to get you in the sack."

Ben snorted as he unlaced his cleats. "You're full of shit. There's no way in hell she said that." When Sam remained silent, he turned to look at his brother. "Did she?"

"No. I just like messing with you." Sam chuckled and got to his feet. "She asked me to wish you a Happy Thanksgiving. And on that note, I'll see you at Dad's. I've gotta stop by my place and pick up the pies I ordered from Mallory's bakery."

Ben quickly slipped on his sneakers. "I hope at least one of them isn't pumpkin." He stowed his cleats and water bottle in the gym bag.

"Don't worry. Your aversion to pumpkin pie was duly noted a long time ago. I had Mallory make you a lemon—oh, hey, Maddie."

His senses suddenly on high alert, Ben jerked around as Maddie approached. Like Sierra, her cheeks were pink from the cold air, almost matching the color of her knit cap.

"Hi, Sam. I saw you at the pub the other night but didn't get a chance to say hello. It's good to see you." The genuineness of her greeting and the luminous smile she directed toward his brother felt like a knife in Ben's gut—sharp and painful. He used to be on the receiving end of her smiles, and now he wasn't. He shouldn't care, but he did.

"It's good to see you too, Maddie," Sam replied warmly.

"I'm sorry to interrupt, but…" She looked at Ben, her smile fading. "Can I talk to you for a minute?"

Ben's pulse accelerated. After their interaction at the pub, he didn't think they'd talk again before she left town. "Sure."

Sam's curious gaze bounced between the two of them. "Well, I'm out of here. Happy Thanksgiving, Maddie." He pointed at Ben. "I'll see you at Dad's. Don't forget the beer."

"Happy Thanksgiving to you too," Maddie said, and as Sam strode off the field, she swung her gaze back to Ben.

The light breeze ruffled the length of her hair not covered by her cap, and he tamped down the urge to reach out and touch it like he used to.

"I won't keep you long. I did something earlier and afterward realized I probably should have checked with you first."

"If you're talking about running lines with Sierra, she told me about it." He tried to ignore how her jeans clung to her curves. Her hair wasn't the only thing he missed touching.

"She's coming over to my parents' house on Sunday afternoon. I hope that's okay."

"Of course." He waved a hand. "This is the first big role she's gotten since she started taking drama classes, and she wants to make her teacher proud. Running lines with a professional actress will give her a lot of confidence."

Her brows kicked up in a question. "You think I'm a professional?"

"Yes."

"Even though I haven't…" She raised her arms and made air quotes with her gloved fingers. "Made it yet? I mean, I'm hardly famous."

"What does being famous have to do with it?" He frowned. "You've been a working actress for four years. That makes you a professional, or it does to me." The surprise in her eyes baffled him. Why would she have gone to Hollywood if she didn't believe she was a professional actress? "I've never doubted your talent, Maddie." How could he when he'd been mesmerized the first time he saw her on the stage?

"Thank you," she said softly as her entire face, not just her cheeks, flushed pink.

"You're welcome." He shoved his hands into his jacket pockets, and after several silent seconds, he continued, "About the other night at the pub. I was out of line."

"No," she said with a vehement shake of her head. "You have every right to hate me. The way things…no…" Lifting her chin, she met his gaze levelly. "The way *I* ended our relationship, I—I'm not proud of it. You deserved better."

"You're right. I did." Ben tried to keep his bitterness in check. "So why did you do it?"

She bit her lower lip and sighed. "It's complicated."

"Complicated is a word people use when they aren't willing to tell the truth."

Pressing her lips together, she averted her gaze. Annoyed, Ben stooped to pick up his gym bag. He'd gone as far as he wanted to go with this conversation.

And did they need to? The bottom line was she'd wanted a career in Hollywood more than she'd wanted him.

"Forget about it. It's in the past. Thanks for running lines with Sierra. It means a lot to her and me. See you around," he said and headed for the parking lot.

"Happy Thanksgiving," she called after him, just as she had to Sam.

He raised a hand in acknowledgment but didn't look back. Looking back still hurt too damn much.

****

The morning after Thanksgiving, Maddie slept late and didn't feel guilty about it. In LA, her early morning routine always started with some sort of exercise. Unfortunately, she didn't enjoy working out and got bored quickly, so she usually switched it up to keep herself interested.

She'd managed to stay in shape between Pilates, a barre class, and swimming laps at the local community center. Today, she planned on taking a long walk, hopefully, while not thinking of Ben and their conversation after the game. It was official; he hadn't forgiven her. And never would.

Not that she was surprised. Blurting out she was leaving for Hollywood right after he'd confessed he'd never loved anyone as much as he loved her was the most insensitive thing she'd ever done. It didn't matter that she was young, trying to find her place in the world, or intent on proving herself any way she could; it was wrong. *So wrong*. And she had no clue how to make it right. She doubted she would see him again before she left on Tuesday, which was best. For both of them.

The enticing aroma of bacon drifted upstairs, and her stomach rumbled in response. She flung the sheet and blanket aside and got out of bed. Forcing Ben from her mind, she used the bathroom before splashing some warm water on her face and brushing her teeth. Then, slipping on her robe, she trudged downstairs to the kitchen where her father was sitting at the table in the cozy breakfast nook, reading the newspaper. No online news from a phone or tablet for him—he liked the feel of a real newspaper in his hands.

"There's scrambled eggs and bacon warming in the oven." He glanced at her over the top of the paper.

"Where's Mom?" She padded to the counter and retrieved a mug from the cupboard.

"Christmas shopping. Mallory came by to pick her up at the crack of dawn."

"Oh, that's right. I forgot." Maddie smothered a yawn as she poured herself a cup of coffee. She hated shopping on a good day, let alone on Black Friday. Online shopping was more her speed. "Do you have to work today?" She opened the fridge and grabbed the creamer.

"I'm going in for a couple of hours. I've got some paperwork to catch up on." He folded the newspaper and set it on the table next to his plate, then picked up his fork and set about finishing his breakfast.

Maddie poured a splash or two of the creamer into her coffee and mixed it with a spoon. "Do you miss being out in the field?"

"Sometimes. I love the job, but it's all politics when you get to my level. It's frustrating as hell," he said as his phone rang. He picked it up and frowned. "Oh Lord, help me," he muttered, shaking his head as he answered the call. "Hello, Cora Jean. What can I do for you... *What?*" His eyes widened. "Three weeks!" His bushy

53

eyebrows bunched together in a frown. "No. No, I understand. Family comes first… No, don't worry about it. We'll muddle through until you get back. I'm sorry to hear about your daughter's situation—yes—fine. Thanks for letting me know."

From her father's side of the conversation, it sounded like something was wrong with Cora Jean's daughter. Concerned, she leaned forward. "What's going on?"

"Cora Jean has to take some time off." He stared at her blankly.

"Why?" She set her mug on the table.

"She went up to Seattle to spend Thanksgiving with her daughter and grandkids." He placed his phone on top of the newspaper next to him. "Turns out her daughter's husband decided right at the dinner table to announce that he's in love with someone else and wants a divorce."

"Holy crap," she exclaimed. "In front of his kids? What an ass."

"She asked for three weeks off to help her daughter adjust to this new reality." Her father grabbed the napkin from his lap, balled it up, and flung it on his plate. "This is the last thing I need right now."

"Can you fill the position temporarily?"

"If it were any longer than three weeks, I'd hire a temp until she gets back. But with all the hoops human resources makes us jump through, it'll take at least that long to hire someone. I can't spare a day-shift officer or sergeant to sit up at the front desk right now, but it looks like I have no other choice."

His hopeless expression tugged at her heart. He was in a tough situation. One she was more than capable of helping him handle if she wasn't planning on returning to LA in a few days. Her gaze lingered on his face, and she made up her mind right then. It was only three weeks, and it wasn't like she had any auditions lined up yet.

"I'll do it. I worked in Clarice's insurance office, and in LA, I've worked temp jobs to make extra money. I can do customer service and admin work in my sleep. Plus, I'm familiar with the police department, remember?"

"That's true." The tautness eased from his expression. "Can you really do this?"

She nodded. "I'm positive."

His brow furrowed. "But I thought you had to get back to LA."

"I can rearrange my schedule," she assured him. "It's not a problem."

Her father sagged in his chair, the tension leaving his body like a deflating balloon. "I can't thank you enough, Maddie. You saved your old man from a boatload of aggravation."

"You're welcome." She smiled, sipped her coffee, and basked in her father's gratitude. It didn't happen often; she would enjoy it while it lasted.

Later it occurred to her that one person at the station might not be happy she was helping out—the man who'd never forgiven her for breaking his heart and leaving town, all on the same night.

It was going to be a long three weeks.

Chapter Five

Ben stared at the statistical data in front of him. Destruction of SPD property was frowned upon, but he really wanted to punch the computer screen. November was drawing to a close, which meant his monthly report had to be compiled and turned in to his captain the first week in December. Since making sergeant, he'd met his deadline every month, but not without a lot of blood, sweat, and cursing. The damn thing was his Achilles heel, mainly because he'd yet to figure out a way to pull the data more quickly. But he wasn't giving up. There had to be a solution; he just hadn't figured it out yet.

The distinctive double knock on his door brought welcome relief. "Come on in," he said and swiveled his chair around.

Carolyn Knight opened the door but didn't venture over the threshold. Instead, she leaned her tall, lanky frame against the doorway as her dark eyes took stock of the stacks of papers and folders strewn haphazardly across the top of his desk. "I don't know how you find anything on that desk of yours."

"We all can't be a neat freak like you." He gave her a wry grin. It wasn't the first time the chief's assistant had given him a hard time about the state of his desk. Given that Carolyn was a master of efficiency, he had no doubt it offended her sense of order. The funny thing was, even though it looked like a mess, he never had a problem finding what he needed when he needed it.

"I'm not a neat freak. I like things a certain way." She brushed her long braids over her shoulder. "How do you get anything done with all that mess?"

"I manage." He leaned back in the chair, wincing as it squeaked like an old rusty gate. No matter how many times he oiled the blasted thing, he couldn't get rid of the annoying sound. He made a mental note to requisition a new ergonomic chair. "Did you need something?"

"I haven't seen you all morning. I'm making sure you didn't decide to fly the coop like Cora Jean."

"What?" He bolted into an upright position. "She quit? When?"

"Don't get too excited, Sarge." The corners of her mouth twitched with amusement. "She didn't quit. She's taking some time off to deal with a family issue."

Ben's shoulders slumped. "That's...that's—"

"Not what you wanted to hear?" Carolyn's all-knowing smile made him suspect she was a mind reader. "It's okay. You're not alone. While Cora Jean's a sweet lady, we both know she's not exactly a go-getter. I'm not too sure about her temporary replacement, but I'll reserve judgment until the end of the day."

"Who's her replacement? Whoever it is has to be better than Cora Jean."

Sorry, Cora Jean. I love you like a grandmother, but it's the truth.

Carolyn didn't argue with him. "The chief's daughter. The actress, not the baker."

His stomach did a one-eighty. "Maddie? You're kidding?" *Well, hell.* Carolyn was two for two when it came to surprises today.

She narrowed her eyes, giving him what he called

the "look." The "look" was stern and always made him feel like he was being reprimanded for talking back to the teacher in grade school.

"Do I ever kid?" she asked, but before he could answer, she continued, "I'm surprised you haven't seen her. She's been here since eight."

"I haven't left my office since I finished my morning briefing." He glanced at his watch. It was almost ten. "I should have known something was up when I didn't get any calls from Cora Jean asking me to come up to the front and answer a simple question. You know, like where city hall is, or who to call if someone needs to report a barking dog."

Carolyn made a *tsking* sound. "Poor Cora Jean. She never could figure out how to use the—" She stopped mid-sentence and tilted her head. "That's my phone. Gotta run," she said and disappeared, the heels of her shoes clicking furiously on the linoleum as she hustled to her office.

Turning back to his computer, Ben focused on the screen, but the data blurred in front of him. How did Maddie end up at the front desk? She'd told him she was in town for a week. That meant she should be going back to Hollywood tomorrow. He thought he'd seen her for the last time at the football game, and although he'd tried to convince himself it was for the best, the adrenaline pumping through his veins told a different story.

Unable to stop himself or question why he had to see her, he left his office and made his way to the front reception area, the part of the building open to the public. Although the SPD was a twenty-four-hour operation, the reception area was staffed by a civilian employee only during regular business hours. After hours, anyone needing assistance could press the call button outside the entrance, and the evening shift sergeant would help them.

When he walked into the reception area, his footsteps alerted Maddie to his presence. Turning away from the computer screen, she acknowledged him with a curt nod. "Good morning." She tugged at the collar of her red turtleneck sweater before lowering her hands and clasping them together in her lap. "Cora Jean is taking some time off if you're wondering why I'm here."

"Yeah, I just found out."

"I'll be here for three weeks."

He stared at her, trying to process that he would see her almost daily for the next three weeks.

"Dad vouched for me with human resources," she said, filling the silence.

That made sense. Since she was the chief's daughter, they probably wouldn't squawk too much about not being able to vet her thoroughly beforehand.

The radio attached to his epaulet crackled, echoing loudly in the room. He was used to it, but Maddie started at the sound, so he lowered the volume after ascertaining the transmission wasn't directed to him. "Do you need anything?" he asked, noting the desk now looked much neater than how Cora Jean kept it. It was certainly more organized than his. Carolyn would, no doubt, approve.

"No. Thanks." She tucked several loose strands of hair behind her ear. "Carolyn was able to set me up on the computer. I have access to the department's intranet, and I've familiarized myself with the org chart and list of services. Other than a few calls and a couple of walk-ins, it's been quiet." She gave him a tight smile. "Nothing I can't handle," she assured him and reached for the visitor logbook on the counter above her desk. "I noticed no one has signed the visitor's log for the past two months. Did protocol change?"

"No." Exasperated, he shook his head. *Damn Cora Jean.* He'd specifically pointed out the importance of the log. "Any individual who comes in for an appointment with any staff must sign in. And unless you know them personally, they need to show their ID."

"Got it." She returned the logbook to the counter. "Thanks."

"Oh, and any records requests need to go to April." He hooked his thumbs in his utility belt, reluctant to leave. Not because he liked looking at her, but because it was her first day, and she probably had questions.

"Yes, Carolyn told me."

"Did you get a tour? The kitchen and restrooms are—"

"I've been here before. I know where everything is." Her tone was polite yet firm.

"Okay." He shifted uncomfortably under her direct gaze. "Sounds like you've got it under control, but let me know if you need anything or have any questions."

"I will. Thank you." She turned her attention toward the computer screen, dismissing him.

He stared at the back of her head for several seconds and then returned to his office, more unsettled by her presence than he cared to admit. Considering how he'd left things with her at the football field, he shouldn't be surprised by her cool demeanor. He'd stewed about his behavior all weekend, trying to assuage his guilt by reminding himself that she'd walked away from him first. She'd blindsided him on what he thought would be the happiest night of their lives, and he still had no clue why. But now that Maddie was staying in town longer, maybe that mystery could be solved, and he could finally put it behind him.

****

Early Tuesday afternoon, with a day and a half of work behind her, Maddie was confident enough to send an email to Carolyn, her father's administrative assistant, offering to help her with any tasks—even menial ones—that needed to be done.

From what she'd gleaned so far, Carolyn was overworked, and other than April, the records technician, who was busy in her own right, the department had no other administrative employees in the building to assist her. It didn't seem fair, but when she asked him about it, her father had said he'd long been trying to approve another administrative position but was denied due to budget constraints.

Although Summerwood was far from a sprawling metropolis, she had handled a steady flow of citizens since yesterday. The majority of their questions were easily answered. Though, in the age of internet search engines, the fact that most people didn't bother doing a simple search of the SPD's website before coming in or calling was amazing.

Even with the calls and the walk-ins, she had experienced extended periods of downtime. Time she could have spent doing something productive—another reason why she'd sent the email to Carolyn. Today, though, she'd anticipated the same scenario and planned accordingly. In her spare time, she'd tidied the rack displaying SPD informational pamphlets, tossed out old magazines in the seating area, packed Cora Jean's vast collection of knickknacks in a cardboard box, and shoved it out of sight under the desk. She'd put them back the Friday before Cora Jean's return.

Cora Jean's box wasn't the only thing out of sight. Maddie had only come into contact with Ben once today. A couple of hours ago, he'd stopped by the front desk to let her know he was leaving the building to assist his officers with a domestic call. He didn't come right out and say it, but his troubled expression and rigid posture indicated he was worried. When they'd been together, he'd often told her how much he hated responding to domestic violence calls—primarily because of the volatile nature of the situation *and* the participants. She'd worried about him then, and now, even though they weren't together, she couldn't help but still be worried about him.

A cold blast of air hit her as the front door opened. "So it *is* true. My favorite student is back in town."

Recognizing the husky feminine voice, Maddie looked up from her computer screen. "Stevie! I'm so happy to see you," she exclaimed and rose from her chair as her former drama teacher sailed across the lobby and halted with a dramatic flourish in front of the reception desk.

"Ditto, darling." Stevie gave her a thorough once-over. "You look marvelous."

"So do you. You never age." Maddie was in awe of the older woman's barely lined porcelain complexion and luxurious sable-brown hair, still styled in a timeless shoulder-length bob. Stevie Pepper's actual age was a mystery to everyone except Stevie herself, but she'd been teaching at Summerwood high school long before Maddie was a freshman. Stevie also founded the Summerwood Community Theater and still served as its theater director as far as Maddie knew. Rumor had it she'd once gone to New York City to fulfill her dream of starring on Broadway, but had returned to Summerwood ten years later, never saying one word about her time there.

"Oh, I'm aging." The corners of her crimson lips quirked up as she adjusted the watercolor-inspired silk scarf she'd tied artfully around her neck and tucked into the collar of her pink woolen coat. "One can only stave off Father Time for so long," she added dryly.

"Well, whatever you're doing, it's working." Maddie smiled. "Are you still teaching at the high school?"

"No. After my grandmother passed and left me a rather large inheritance, I retired from teaching. So now I'm focusing all of my creative energy on the community theater. Are you in town long? I'd love for you to come by and see what we've done with the place. The interior has been completely remodeled, and the acoustics are fabulous."

"I'm sorry to hear about your grandmother," Maddie said. "I'll be here for a few weeks, and I'd love to see it."

"Wonderful. My number hasn't changed. Call me, and we'll set it up. I can't wait to hear all about your life in Los Angeles."

As she leaned forward to air kiss Maddie's cheek, Maddie caught a whiff of Stevie's perfume. The rich scent with notes of jasmine and clove brought back happy memories of not only her drama class but rehearsals at the community theater.

"Ta, darling. I must go. I'm sure you remember putting on the annual holiday play is quite challenging."

Maddie nodded. "Oh, yes. I remember," she said,

looking forward to seeing the theater again but dreading talking about her life in LA. How would Stevie react when she found out her favorite student was barely making ends meet?

Stevie's gaze swung from hers as footsteps sounded behind Maddie. "Good morning, Carolyn. It's good to see you." She gave Carolyn a warm smile before redirecting her attention toward Maddie. "I expect to hear from you soon."

"You will." Maddie watched her glide toward the lobby doors with all the grace of a beauty pageant queen.

After the door shut behind Stevie, Carolyn leaned her hip against the edge of the desk. "Thanks for your email. Do you know anything about spreadsheets?" Carolyn asked as Maddie sat down.

"Yes." Maddie looked up at her. "Do you need help?"

"You have no idea how much help I need," she said with a wry smile. "I'll be back in a minute to show you what I need you to do."

At five, after locking the front doors, Maddie gathered her things and turned out the lights before leaving the reception area.

As she walked toward the employee exit, Maddie stopped short in front of Ben's office, surprised to see him hunched over in the chair at his desk, staring at his computer screen. The day-shift officers had clocked out at four, as had Carolyn, who'd left earlier than usual for a doctor's appointment.

So engrossed in whatever he was looking at, he seemed completely unaware of his surroundings. Maddie studied his classically handsome profile for several seconds, unable to stop the memories of the first time they'd met from flooding her brain. After one of her community theater performances, he'd come into Callie's Diner, walked right up to the table where she and her fellow actors were sitting, and introduced himself. When the diner closed, they were alone at the table, and when he asked her out, she'd said yes. What followed was like something out of a romance novel—wonderful and exciting—but they'd never gotten their happily ever after because of her actions. She stared at him, pain and regret merging into a tight knot in the pit of her stomach.

As if sensing her presence, Ben shifted in his chair. He turned toward her, and for a moment, she thought she glimpsed a flash of happiness in his eyes. But it was gone so quickly she must have imagined it.

"What are you still doing here?" she asked. "Your shift was over an hour ago."

"I've been reviewing the officers' reports from the DV incident earlier today." Swiveling his chair around, he scrubbed his hand over his jaw, the faint shadows under his eyes telltale signs of a few sleepless nights. "The whole thing was a cluster fuck. The husband and wife were so out of control one of their kids called 911."

Alarm pinged in her chest. "Oh, no. What happened?"

"Dodd and Anders responded and were first on the scene. When they attempted to break up the fight between the couple, the husband assaulted Dodd, and the wife jumped on Anders and started punching her. They were either high or drunk. In any event, we transported both of them to the county jail and placed the children in protective custody."

"Those poor kids." She moved to stand in front of his desk, which was covered with assorted papers and folders. She'd always teased him about his "organized mess," and for some reason, she was comforted to see he hadn't changed. "Will they be put into foster care?"

He nodded. "Yes, unless they can locate any relatives willing to take them in. The couple is looking at some jail time for sure. After they're released, family court will decide whether or not they can retain custody."

"It's a no-win situation either way, isn't it?" Her heart broke for the children. Innocent victims in a situation they had no control over. Her heart also ached for Ben. He'd had his share of family drama when he was younger. Cases like this one had to bring back unpleasant memories.

"Unfortunately, yes." He glanced at his watch. "I should get out of here now, or I'll be here all night." He stood and rolled his shoulders to get the kinks out.

Her gaze wandered over his broad chest and strong shoulders. Heat ignited in her belly and moved downward as memories swamped her. There was a time when she'd worked the kinks out of his back and neck. He'd always loved her massages. His were pretty good too. He had the best hands, and boy did he know how to use—

"Maddie?"

She blinked and found Ben's puzzled gaze on her. "You okay?"

"Um…yeah," she stammered as her cheeks flushed with heat. "Sorry. I'm a little light-headed. I haven't eaten since this morning."

"I can help you with that. I'd planned to stop by Callie's for dinner before going home. Would you like to join me?" The surprise must have shown on her face. The corner of his mouth lifted in a half-smile as he rounded his desk and grabbed a set of keys from the top of his file cabinet. "I don't like how we left things after the football game. Let me make it up to you. Dinner's on me."

Her knees trembled, and she wasn't sure why. Or maybe she did know and didn't want to admit it. "All right," she said softly. "I'll meet you at Callie's."

Chapter Six

Maddie snagged a table next to the big picture window at the front of the diner and tried to ignore the fluttering in her stomach as she waited for Ben to arrive. Callie's, a Summerwood institution since before she was born, was exactly as she remembered it. The comfortable upholstered chairs, chunky handcrafted tables, and the delicious aroma of homemade soups and other comfort foods created a down-to-earth ambiance that was hard to find in LA.

It was also the location of many of her fondest memories. Ben was a big part of those memories and why her stomach was tied in knots. Hopefully, in the time it would take for him to change into his civilian clothes and drive to the diner, she'd have a chance to settle her nerves. Opening the laminated menu, she studied the selections, tapping her foot to the upbeat holiday music that filled the room and muted the chatter of her fellow customers.

"Maddie?"

Maddie looked up at the waitress she'd only caught a glimpse of when she entered the diner. Her sandy-blonde hair was now the color of dark chocolate, but the dimples and the beauty mark on her right cheek were a dead giveaway. Peyton Troy had been a fellow drama geek in high school. But unfortunately, they'd lost touch a year after graduation when Peyton had gotten married.

"Peyton. Wow." She smiled, thrilled to see her old friend. "It's so good to see you. I thought you moved to Portland after the wedding."

"I did, but I moved back to Summerwood a few months ago, after the divorce." Peyton tucked what looked like tip money into the front pocket of her black pants. "I'm staying with my parents while I get back on my feet."

"Oh, I'm sorry it didn't work out." Maddie was surprised the marriage hadn't lasted. Peyton had been radiantly happy on her wedding day.

"Don't be," she replied with an airy wave of her hand. "I'm better off, and so is my daughter."

"Daughter?" Eagerly, Maddie shifted in her chair. "Tell me more."

Peyton's wide smile lit up her whiskey-colored eyes. "Her name is Hayley. She's five years old, smart as a whip, and the best thing that ever happened to me." She pulled a notepad and a pen out of her other pocket. "Can I get you something to drink? Or are you ready to order?"

Maddie shot a glance toward the entrance. Still no Ben. "I'm waiting for my…a friend. But water's fine until he gets here."

"You got it," Peyton said with a nod. "You must be home for the holidays. My mom told me you're acting full-time now and living in Los Angeles. It must be exciting."

Exciting? Yeah. Not so much.

Maddie smiled. "It has its moments."

After she exchanged phone numbers with Peyton and promised to catch up before she left town, Maddie's stomach did a deep dive when Ben walked into the diner.

69

He'd changed into faded jeans that showcased his slim hips and muscular thighs and a royal-blue V-neck sweater that set off his gorgeous eyes. The result was a mixture of wholesome good looks and raw sexuality that made a few heads turn in his direction as he stood in the doorway searching for her. She lifted a hand to catch his attention and tried not to devour him with her eyes as he headed toward her.

"Sorry to keep you waiting." He settled in the chair across from her. "Cora Jean called right after you left."

"Is she coming home sooner than planned?"

"No." An amused grin crinkled the corners of his eyes. "She asked me to tell you to call her if you have any questions. I didn't have the heart to tell her that you've already mastered the reception desk and reached out to Carolyn to see if she needs help. Of course, Cora Jean never offers to help."

His praise warmed her cheeks as she smiled. "I like to keep busy."

"Carolyn was impressed you were able to finish the project she gave you so quickly. She doesn't impress easily."

"I was happy to help. I can't believe the department doesn't have more administrative personnel. From what I've seen, you could use it."

"The city manager and the budget committee may approve a new position after the first of the year. So there's some hope." He lifted his gaze as Peyton returned to their table.

"Here's your water." Peyton set the glass in front of Maddie and turned her attention to Ben. "Hey, Ben. Can I get you something to drink?"

"Coffee's fine," he replied. "Black."

After Peyton left them alone, he rested his forearms on the table. "So tell me about Hollywood. What's it like?"

Meeting his curious gaze, she debated how much to share with him. Should she tell him the unvarnished truth or gloss over the difficulties of her life in LA? "Different than I imagined it would be." She reached for her water glass and slid it toward her. "There are so many people, and most of them want to be in the entertainment industry."

"Acting is a tough business," he commented. "Or so I imagine."

He didn't know the half of it. "Yes. It's very competitive." Maddie lifted her chin. "But I'm not giving up."

"So you're going back to Hollywood?"

"Yes," she said as she picked up her glass. Suddenly, the thought of returning to her small apartment was depressing. Even auditioning didn't hold any appeal. The joy she'd gotten from acting had evaporated somewhere along the way. Maybe that would change once she landed a more challenging role. She sipped her water, wishing it was something more potent.

"You don't look happy about it," he said. "Why is that?"

Before she could formulate an answer, Peyton came by again. "Here you go." She set the steaming cup of coffee in front of Ben. The interruption was timely. Examining her feelings about going back to LA wasn't something Maddie wanted to delve into.

After Peyton took their order and they were alone again, Maddie steered the conversation in a different direction. If Ben noticed, he didn't say anything and seemed happy to answer her questions about his family and catch her up on the latest goings-on in Summerwood. It was almost like old times. *Almost*, because back then, they would have been sitting side by side, and he would have had his arm around her and his knee pressed intimately against hers. *Almost*, because he didn't love her anymore.

A short while later, she finished the last of her chicken Caesar wrap and sighed with contentment. Leaning back, she wiped the corners of her mouth with her napkin and grinned at Ben. "I remember when you were thinking about going vegetarian. It looks like it was just a thought."

"A passing one." He pointed his fork at his plate. "I can't give up this pot roast."

"Callie's always had the best comfort food. Remember when we were craving homemade mac and cheese and tried to make it at your house because we were too lazy to get in the car and drive over here?"

His face twisted with a grimace. "That was some nasty stuff. I'm not sure how you can ruin mac and cheese, but we managed to do it."

"I know." Maddie laughed. "And we ended up here anyway." Her gaze wandered around the diner. Holiday decorations, including a Christmas tree decked out in a teddy bear theme, were potent reminders of the past. "There are so many wonderful memories in this place." Out of the blue, tears pricked the backs of her eyes. Surprised and mortified, she blinked to keep them at bay. "I'm sorry, Ben," she whispered, not sure why she'd gone from laughing to teary-eyed in seconds. Maybe it was the memories the diner evoked. "I'm *so* sorry I hurt you."

Something she couldn't decipher flickered in his eyes, and for several long seconds, silence hung in the air between them before he finally spoke. "I wasn't expecting to have this conversation tonight." He pushed his plate to the side and slid his coffee cup in front of him. "But since you brought it up, I'd like to know why you never talked about pursuing an acting career in Hollywood before the night you broke up with me."

"I—I must have," she stammered, guilt causing her to pluck at the fabric of her napkin in her lap with her fingers. She should have known Ben would want more than an apology.

"You didn't," he said emphatically. "Not once. That's why it surprised the hell out of me."

"But...but you knew how much I enjoyed performing at the community theater. Acting is the one thing I've ever done well."

Lifting his cup, he peered at her over the rim. "Why do you always do that?"

"Do what?" she asked, puzzled.

He took a quick sip of his coffee and then set his cup on the table. "Underestimate yourself. You're good at a lot of things."

"I appreciate you saying that, but you don't understand."

His brows knit together in a frown. "Understand what?"

Relaxing her death grip on the napkin, she leaned forward and met his perplexed gaze. "I have to be better than good. In my family, expectations run high."

Ben searched her face, his gaze thoughtful. "So you went to Hollywood to try to prove something to your family?"

"Yes. No." She let out a frustrated sigh. "I went to LA for myself. I needed to prove I could be successful at something. It certainly wasn't going to happen here."

Wrapping his fingers around his cup, he narrowed his gaze slightly and shook his head after several long seconds. "I'm not buying it."

"What do you mean you're not buying it?" she demanded.

"I'll concede that trying to prove something to yourself may be part of the reason why you suddenly decided to move nine hundred miles away and pursue acting, but it's not the only reason. There's more to it than that."

"Like what?"

"I don't know," he said with a shrug. "That's something only you can answer."

"I've already explained." She closed her fingers over the napkin, crushing it against her palm. "I've apologized, *and* I've explained. What more do you want?"

"The truth." His terse tone revealed his exasperation.

"I *am* telling the truth," she insisted.

No, you're not.

"Not completely." He shifted and pulled his wallet from his back pocket. "You've offered a reasonable explanation for why you decided to pursue your career, and you've apologized for the shitty way you broke up with me. But you still haven't told me why you never once discussed any of this with me beforehand or why you blindsided me that night. The woman I loved would never deliberately hurt someone she cared about. So either you're not telling me something, or you haven't figured it out for yourself yet."

"There's nothing to figure out." With a sigh, she plucked at the napkin again. She'd forgotten how perceptive he was. But she'd hurt him again if she told him the other reason why she left. "Did you tell me everything going on in your mind when we were together?"

"No, but I told you the important stuff." He pulled two twenties from his wallet and set them on the table. "How would you have felt if I had accepted a job with another law enforcement agency out of state and didn't bother to tell you?" A scowl marred his handsome face. "You know what?" He got to his feet and stared down at her. "Forget I asked." He slid his wallet into his back pocket. "I'll see you at work tomorrow."

Maddie's chest tightened as she watched Ben's long strides carry him out of the diner. Sagging against the back of her chair, she turned toward the window and stared at her reflection. She didn't care much for what she saw. Picking and choosing which of her actions to apologize for wasn't being honest. Until she could be completely truthful with Ben, she didn't deserve his forgiveness.

After saying goodbye to Peyton, she climbed into her car and slammed the door so hard the glove compartment dropped open. She reached across the passenger seat, flipped it closed, and swore under her breath as the ringtone on her phone filled the car with its catchy beat. Talking to anyone right now was the last thing she wanted to do, but after filming *LA Crime*, she started worrying about missing emergency calls from her family. She dug through her purse and pulled out her phone, surprised to see the M on the screen.

"Hi, Margo," she answered the call, sounding more upbeat than she felt.

"Hello, Maddie. Did I catch you at a bad time?"

My ex rightly accused me of lying, but other than that, I'm fine.

"No. What's going on?" She crossed her fingers. Maybe the casting directors had changed their minds, and she'd gotten one of the parts. Or maybe Margo had a new list of upcoming pilots being cast.

"I have some news, and I thought I should call before you hear it from anyone else," Margo said, her tone more formal than usual.

Maddie's skin prickled with unease. "What news?"

"I received an offer to join the Lifkin Agency."

She gasped. Lifkin was one of the top three talent management agencies in LA and, as rumor had it, were picky about whom they hired. "That's wonderful, Margo. I'm so happy for you."

"Thank you. I'm over the moon, as you'd expect." Margo paused, clearing her throat. "There's no easy way to say this, but Lifkin is opening a new office in New York City. So that's where I'll be located."

Apprehension shimmied down her spine. "New York City?"

"Yes. I'll be relocating in February. They wanted me in January, but there's so much involved in a cross-country move. So I asked for an extension, and they gave it to me. I'm sure you must be wondering about your status," Margo continued before Maddie could speak. "I've contacted several agents here in LA, and I'm sure I can convince one of them to take you on."

Maddie's head began to throb. She lifted her free hand and rubbed her temple. "But we have a contract."

"Yes, but if you read the fine print, you'll see that either party has the right to terminate the contract as long as they provide thirty days' notice. This is that notice, and I'll follow up with a written notice tomorrow," Margo said, her tone firm but not unkind.

"What if the agents you speak to don't want to sign me?"

"I doubt that will happen. Several of them owe me favors."

Margo sounded confident, but that didn't make her feel any better. If Margo had to rely on favors, she must not have much faith in her talent. "But what if they still don't want to sign me?"

"In that case, it would be up to you to find representation," she said gently. "At that point, I'll have done my due diligence."

Tears welled in Maddie's eyes. She shut them tightly to prevent them from spilling down her cheeks.

"I'll still be working on your behalf for the next thirty days. I'll let you know if anything comes up. I've been in contact with the casting director at *A New Dawn*. If anything pans out, I'll contact you immediately. I know this is a shock, but I'm sure you're aware that things change quickly in the entertainment field, and one must take advantage of every opportunity. It's not personal; it's business."

"Right. Business." Maddie kept her tone professional. Being temperamental was never a good look in Hollywood.

"I'll let you go now. I'm sure you're busy," Margo said, no doubt eager to end the call. "Have a Merry Christmas."

"Thanks. Same to you," she said, then flung her

phone onto the passenger seat, leaned forward, and rested her forehead on the steering wheel. In the space of a week, she'd been passed over for two lead roles *and* lost her agent. Even worse, she'd been confronted with the real-world consequences of what she'd done to Ben. Of how badly she'd hurt him. Her heart ached, and as much as she wanted to place the blame on Ben, her parents, or Margo, she couldn't. This pain, this hollowness inside of her, was her own doing. Four years ago, she'd set it into motion when she took the coward's way out of Summerwood.

A dry sob burned like fire in her throat. She fought to contain it, but she couldn't. Clutching the steering wheel, she let the dam break, and her tears began to fall.

Chapter Seven

The next morning Ben's mood wasn't as dark as the rain clouds drifting toward Summerwood from the north, but it was damn close. He walked into Callie's and headed toward Sam, who was sitting alone at the counter, and claimed the stool next to him. Meeting for coffee wasn't a ritual for them, but his shift didn't start for another half hour, and when he saw his brother's truck parked in front of the diner, he'd decided to join him.

Sam acknowledged him with a genial nod. "Rough night?" He lifted a hand to brush his hair out of his eyes. Unlike Ben, who was required to keep his hair cut short because of department regulations, Sam was one to let a lot of time pass in between haircuts.

"Yeah." Ben set his keys and phone on the counter. "For some reason, I had a helluva time falling asleep last night," he said as the server manning the counter delivered Sam's coffee and a glazed doughnut. Actually, he did know the reason. It was Maddie, but Sam didn't need to know that.

"What can I get for you?" the server, a new guy he didn't recognize, asked him with a pleasant smile.

"Just coffee. Black," he replied. "Thanks."

Sam grabbed a sugar packet and ripped it open. "I heard Cora Jean is off for a couple of weeks, and Maddie's filling in for her." He dumped the sugar into his coffee and blended it with a spoon. "How's that going?"

"Fine."

"Must be weird working with her."

"It's not." Working with Maddie hadn't been weird at all. It had only been two days, but she'd already shown she was a much better worker than Cora Jean, and the other day-shift sergeant had commented on how seamlessly she'd picked up the front desk duties.

Sam set the spoon on a napkin on the counter. "Have you guys talked about what went down in the past?" he asked before taking a sip of coffee.

"It came up last night." He paused as their server returned with his coffee. "We had dinner here," he said, sliding his cup in front of him.

"How'd it go?"

"It went." Ben shrugged.

"Did you tell her you were going to ask her to marry you that night?"

"No," he said sharply. "You're the only one who knows, and I'd like to keep it that way."

"Chill out, bro. It's in the vault." Sam grinned, set his cup on the counter, and picked up his doughnut. "Does she know you still have a thing for her?"

"Where'd you get that idea?" Ben asked, shooting him a glance. Sometimes Sam's directness was irritating.

"Hmmm." Sam's exaggerated frown scrunched his brow. "I don't know. Maybe because you haven't had a girlfriend—serious or otherwise—since she left town, you have one of the hottest women in Summerwood throwing herself at you, and you never take advantage of it, *and* you have a couple of TV shows that Maddie's been in saved on your DVR."

"How do you know what's on my DVR?"

"Remember last month when you asked me to replace the shelves in your closet?" Sam took a huge bite of his doughnut but didn't let the food in his mouth stop him from talking. "I took a short break to check the score of the basketball game and accidentally saw your saved programs list."

"Accidentally?"

Sam shrugged. "I was nosey. Sue me."

Ben took a tentative sip of his coffee. "You need a hobby."

"I have a hobby." A sly smile quirked Sam's mouth. "She lives in Portland."

"Does she know you don't do relationships?"

"Yep. She's only interested in hooking up." His brother grinned. "Something we have in common."

"Sounds like a match made in heaven," Ben said dryly.

"Don't knock it. Uncomplicated banging has its advantages," he said and finished his doughnut.

Ben didn't bother replying. He and Sam were different animals when it came to women and relationships. Or, in Sam's case, lack of relationships. He took another sip of coffee and tried not to think about the day ahead. Being around Maddie was conflicting as hell. As much as he didn't want to admit it, she still stirred powerful feelings in him. Part of him wanted her to leave Summerwood as soon as possible. But, on the other hand, the thought of never seeing her again twisted his gut into a tight knot.

"I got another letter from Mom yesterday," Sam said, his voice low.

Ben froze, and dread pooled in the pit of his gut. "Did you open it?"

"No way." Sam wrapped his fingers around his cup. "I read the first one, and that was enough." He shot Ben a curious glance. "Have you gotten any?"

"No, and I doubt I ever will. In Mom's warped mind, I betrayed her." Ben's fingers tightened on his cup. His innocent exploration of the attic had turned his entire family's life upside down. Afterward he'd wished he'd never gone up there, but it didn't take long for him to realize he had saved his father and siblings even more pain.

Sam's brows slanted downward in a frown. "I still wonder, you know? Why she did what she did."

Unlike Sam, who still bore the emotional scars from their mother's betrayal, Ben no longer wondered why their mother, along with her lover, had embezzled money from her employer. But then he and his mother hadn't been close. Sam was her favorite child, and he'd been devastated when the truth came out.

"Who knows why? She was damn good at living a lie, that's for sure," Ben said. "Even her friends were surprised."

"I guess you're right." He heaved a sigh and shook his head. "But it makes you wonder if you can ever really trust someone, doesn't it?"

Ben shifted on his stool and met Sam's wounded gaze levelly. "You can't base the trustworthiness of other people on what Mom did."

"I know, but it still freaks me out that someone can appear to be warm and caring and claim to love you, but underneath they're a liar and don't give a shit about you at all."

Ben silently cursed his mother. It was her fault Sam had trust issues. He'd never forgive her for that. "I understand why you feel that way, but not everyone has a hidden agenda. If you ever want someone in your life who isn't just a fuck-buddy, you're going to have to start trusting people."

Sam scowled. "Stop trying to analyze me. I got enough of that from the therapist Dad sent me to after Mom left."

"I'm sorry." Ben held up a hand. "I'm only trying to help."

After a prolonged silence, Sam sighed. "I appreciate that, but I don't need help. I like my life the way it is."

Ben wasn't so sure, but he'd said enough for today. "Got it."

****

Maddie thanked the officer who'd volunteered to sit up front while she took her morning break and made her way to her father's office. She couldn't imagine why he wanted to see her. So far, everything was going well at the front desk.

Last night, after pulling herself together and returning to her parents' house, she'd spent a sleepless night figuring out what to do about her plummeting career. Giving up the one thing that could bring her success wasn't an option; she needed to develop an action plan quickly.

Her first thought had been to go back to LA as soon as Cora Jean returned and immediately get to work finding a new agent. Initially, it seemed like her best option, but it hadn't taken long for her to rethink that idea. Margo *had* promised to call in a few favors, and since Margo had a lot of clout in LA and had always looked out for Maddie's best interests, she might be shooting herself in the foot if she didn't wait to see the outcome of her agent's efforts.

With no auditions on the horizon and no other pressing reasons to return to Los Angeles, the most sensible decision was to remain in Summerwood until after the holidays. If another agent was interested in representing her, they probably wouldn't want to meet with her until after then, anyway. If Margo's plan failed and she had to find an agent herself, she could start her search in January. She'd found an agent once; there wasn't any reason she couldn't do it again. However, this time, with several television and commercial credits to her name, she was one step ahead of the game.

Staying in Summerwood for the holidays had an upside. She'd be able to spend Christmas with her family.

And you can still see Ben.

No. She shushed her inner voice. Her decision had nothing to do with Ben. Besides, once Cora Jean came back, and Maddie was no longer filling in for her, the odds of her running into Ben were minimal, at best.

At the end of the hallway, she halted outside her father's office, knocked on the partially open door, and stuck her head inside. "You wanted to see me?"

Her father looked up from his computer screen, his frown dissolving as he met her gaze. "I know it's your break, but could you do me a favor and take a quick look at my email inbox? I think I screwed it up. I can see my emails, but I can't see the senders' names anymore."

"Sure, I'll check it out." She rounded his weathered oak desk and bent over to check the screen as he scooted his chair aside. She quickly discovered the problem. "You accidentally deleted the senders' column from your inbox view," she said, using the mouse to go to the settings and fix it. "There you go."

"It's that simple? I've been trying to figure it out for the past hour." He shook his head and chuckled. "My computer skills leave a lot to be desired. Most of the time, I muddle my way through it; I hate to bother Carolyn when she's so busy."

Not that she had ever doubted her father was a good man, but her heart warmed to see how considerate he was of his administrative assistant. "I'm glad I could help."

"I had no idea you were so knowledgeable about computers. Don't be surprised if I call on you for help while you're still filling in."

Now seemed like a good time to tell him about her change in plans. It would make him happy, and hopefully, he wouldn't ask too many questions. The last thing she wanted was for him to know her career was stalling. It would only prove he was right to doubt her ability to find success in Hollywood. "You can call me even after Cora Jean gets back. I've decided to stay in town through the holidays."

His eyebrows rose in surprise. "I thought you needed to get back to Los Angeles for auditions."

She waved her hand. "There's not much happening around the holidays."

"Well, whatever the reason, you'll be home for Christmas." He beamed at her. "I know your mother will be beside herself. We've missed you, Maddie."

"I've missed you too, Dad," she said, returning his smile.

After leaving her father's office, she took a detour into the kitchen and chuckled at the sight of Carolyn eyeing the large box of chocolate-covered macadamia nuts someone had left on the counter. Her long braids were arranged in a sophisticated updo, drawing attention to the beautiful crystal drop earrings dangling from her earlobes.

"I'd say it's a little early for candy, but there's never a bad time for chocolate." Maddie moved past her to the refrigerator.

Carolyn looked up and gave her a sheepish grin. "All right, you caught me, and I confess. I have a sweet tooth. Ben put these in here to torture me. I'm sure of it."

Maddie opened the fridge and pulled a bottle of water out of the multipack case on the shelf. "It's nice of Ben to share them. But then, other than lemon meringue pie, he's not into sweets," she said, then clamped her mouth shut as her face turned warm. "Or so I've heard."

Carolyn's eyes flickered with amusement. "It's okay, Maddie. Unlike Cora Jean and Traci, I don't gossip, but I do keep my ears open, and the word around the department is that you and Ben were an item before I started working for the chief."

Maddie wasn't surprised. The smaller the town, the more the gossip. "What are they saying?"

"It's more speculation than anything. Ben doesn't talk about his personal life." Carolyn gave her a wry smile. "A trait I wish was more prevalent around here."

She chuckled, grateful Carolyn didn't press her for details. "I was going to stop by your office. Is there anything I can help you with? I'm all caught up, and I'd rather be busy than bored."

"I do have something you can do to help Ben, and it's something that will benefit all the sergeants in the future." Carolyn reached for a piece of candy. "Since he's in charge of all the monthly reports, he spends a lot of time working on them. I know the process can be simplified, but I'm spread pretty thin now and can't help him. That's where you come in. I'll let him know you'll be assisting him. Why don't you stop by his office sometime after lunch, and he can fill you in on what he needs?"

"I'd be happy to." She hoped the incident at the diner didn't make things awkward between her and Ben. If so, working together could be uncomfortable for both of them.

After lunch, she hesitated outside of Ben's office. The door was slightly ajar, and once again, he was engrossed by something on his computer screen. Taking a deep breath, she squared her shoulders, tapped lightly on the door, and waited.

"Come on in." He swiveled his chair around, his expression revealing nothing as she stepped inside his office and moved to stand behind his visitor chair. Behind him, on a low credenza, she spied a framed picture of him with his father, Sam, and Sierra taken on what looked like a ski trip. They looked happy.

She braced her hands on the back of the chair. "Have you talked to Carolyn?"

He shook his head. "I left around nine to go to the courthouse. I was called to testify on an assault arrest I handled before being promoted. Afterward, I stopped for a quick bite to eat and just got back." He leaned forward, his expression curious. "Is there something I should know?"

"She suggested I might be able to help you with your monthly reports. So I've been thinking about it, and depending on your data sources, I may be able to create a pivot table with a macro to cut down the time you spend compiling them."

"Pivot table? Macro? What are those?" Shaking his head, he put his hand up. "Never mind. I don't care what the hell they are. I'm all for it if it can save me time." He regarded her with an inscrutable expression. If he was still irritated about last night, there was no sign of it. "I'll be in a strategic goals meeting most of the afternoon. Let's get together tomorrow morning. I'll go over the report with you, and then you can work your magic."

"Will do." She gave him a firm nod and turned to leave.

"Hold up."

Maddie stopped short and turned to face him. "Yes?"

"Thank you," he said solemnly. "I appreciate your help."

"It's nothing. I'm glad to be of assistance." She cleared her throat and took a step back. "I should get back to my—" She broke off with a surprised yelp as the heel of her shoe caught on something, and she pitched violently backward, hitting the hard floor with a loud thump.

Her lungs froze, and panic filled her as she gulped for breath. Unable to move, she whimpered as he bolted from behind his desk and crouched beside her. Tears swam in her eyes, and his face blurred. *Air.* She needed air. Why couldn't she breathe? Desperate for breath, she fought to scream, but no sound came out.

"Don't panic." Ben's soothing voice washed over her. "You've had the wind knocked out of you. Try to breathe in through your nose and out through your mouth. Stay calm, and you'll be able to do it."

Stay calm? How could she stay calm when she was about to die? This was *so* not the way she wanted to go out. Then, suddenly, her paralyzed lungs began to function. She drew in a deep gulp of air and coughed.

"Just lie still and breathe," Ben said as she continued to cough. "I'll get you some water."

Closing her eyes, she forced herself to take deep, measured breaths. In through the nose, out through the mouth. Seconds later, the pain in her diaphragm subsided, and her heart rate slowed to almost normal. Unfortunately, her mortification level was off the charts.

"Feeling better? Did your head hit the floor?"

She opened her eyes and found Ben once again crouched beside her. He had a bottle of water in his hand and concern shading his blue eyes.

"Yes. And no, my head is okay. I landed on my back."

"Think you can sit up?"

She nodded and, with his assistance, managed to maneuver herself into a sitting position. Ben handed her the uncapped bottle. "Thank you," she said, then took a long sip.

"There's a divot in the linoleum. Your heel must have gotten stuck."

Lowering the bottle to her lap, she tried to smile, but she was still a bit shaken, and her mouth twisted into a grimace instead. "Don't worry. I won't sue the department."

He chuckled. "That's the least of my worries. How are you feeling?"

She became aware of his hand on her back, rubbing in a gentle, circular motion. The gesture was meant to be soothing, but it was the first time he had touched her in four years, and until this moment, she hadn't realized how much she missed it. *Really* missed it.

Maddie looked up to meet his gaze, and just like that, she couldn't breathe again. This time it wasn't because she'd had the wind knocked out of her. No, this time, the heated look in his eyes and his clean male scent stole the breath from her lungs. The air seemed to electrify between them, and every nerve in her body screamed for her to lean forward, bridge the short distance between them, and press her lips to his. But before she could give in to the powerful instinct, the sound of footsteps jarred her back to sanity.

"I'm fine," she whispered, pulling back, breaking the spell between them.

He quickly got to his feet and offered her his hand. "Let me help you up," he said as Carolyn appeared in the doorway.

"What's going on?" she asked, her tone filled with alarm. "I heard a scream. Are you all right?"

Maddie let Ben pull her up. Brushing off the back of her pants with her free hand, she managed an embarrassed smile. "Nothing's broken or sprained. I tripped and fell. I'm more embarrassed than anything."

"She got the wind knocked out of her," Ben said gruffly, letting go of her hand and stepping back to put some distance between them. He propped his hands on his utility belt, a frown marring his handsome face. "That floor's a safety hazard."

"A work order to repair it was placed last week." Carolyn swung her gaze toward Maddie. "Are you sure you're okay? Do you need to go home?"

"What I need to do is get back to my desk," Maddie reassured her with a smile. "I'm fine."

Her assurance eased Carolyn's worried expression. "All right. I'll call facilities management and check on the work order."

"I can do that for you." She followed Carolyn out of Ben's office. As Carolyn continued down the hall, Maddie stopped and turned to look at Ben. "Thank you," she said softly.

"You're welcome," he said, his voice slightly husky. "I'm glad you're okay."

As she returned to her desk, Maddie wasn't okay. Hot and bothered was more like it. With one touch, Ben had awoken something inside of her that had lain dormant for a good long while.

Desire.

Chapter Eight

On Friday afternoon, Maddie paid a visit to Sweet Temptations. She chatted with Mallory's assistant for a few minutes and then made her way to the kitchen to find her sister bent over the metal counter, piping royal icing onto one of the many Christmas cookies laid out in neat rows in front of her.

Mallory looked up from her task. "I thought you'd still be at the police station."

"I left early to take the mandatory drug test. Even though I'm working there temporarily, human resources still needs a completed test for their records." Maddie hung her coat and purse on a hook near the door. Sliding onto the stool across from her sister, she admired Mallory's handiwork. Although she was working on Christmas tree cookies, Mallory had already iced and beautifully decorated snowflakes, snowmen, stars, and candy cane cookies.

On the rack behind her, a baking sheet with Santa faces appeared to be next in line for icing. "Carolyn said I didn't have to come back afterward, so I thought I'd stop by and say hi." She leaned forward, resting her elbows on the counter. "Guess what holiday movie they're showing at the theater."

"*Christmas Vacation*?" Mallory guessed and resumed her piping.

"That was last Friday. Guess again."

"*Love Actually*?"

"Nope. I'll give you a hint," she said, unable to contain her smile. "It's my favorite Christmas movie of all time."

Mallory straightened, and if the phrase "what the hell" had a look, her sister was giving it to her right now. "*Die Hard* is not a Christmas movie."

"The whole movie takes place on Christmas Eve," Maddie countered, more than ready to do battle over this issue.

"That doesn't make it a Christmas movie, and I read online that most of the actors in the film agree," Mallory said as she set down the piping bag and rubbed her palms down the front of the *Bakers Do it Better* apron Maddie had given her for Christmas several years ago.

"They're wrong."

"They're in the movie."

"Still wrong," Maddie said stubbornly.

Mallory threw up her hands and let out a frustrated sigh. "I don't know why I bother to argue with you."

"I don't know why you do either. You think you would have learned by now," she said, her grin smug. "Mom and Dad are hosting bunco tonight, so I thought I'd go see it. Do you want to come with me?"

"Sorry, I can't." Mallory flashed an apologetic smile. "After I get done here, I have plans with Tanner."

"Oh." Maddie scrunched her nose. "Tanner."

Mallory put her hands on her hips, her face set in a scowl. "Why did you say his name like that?"

"Like what?"

"Like he's some horrible disease you're afraid you'll catch."

"Was that how I sounded? Sorry." She reached for a

cookie with a repentant smile, jerking her hand back as her sister playfully swatted at it.

"What don't you like about him?" Mallory asked, pulling up a stool and perching on it.

She didn't have a problem sharing, remembering the hostile stare Tanner had directed at Mallory and Sam at the football game last week. "I know I've only been around him a couple of times, but he seems like the jealous, possessive type."

Mallory's expression relaxed, and she seemed almost relieved. "So you noticed it too," she said glumly.

"Let's just say when you talked to Sam at the sports complex on Thanksgiving, he didn't look happy about it." She was relieved Mallory hadn't turned a blind eye to Tanner's behavior.

"He asked me about Sam after the game, and even after I told him we're just friends, he wouldn't let it go." A worried frown creased Mallory's forehead. "That bothered me. A lot."

"Then why are you going out with him tonight?"

"To tell him I don't think we should see each other anymore. He's showing some of the same personality traits as Brandon. I'm not interested in putting up with verbally abusive behavior again." Her expression darkened. "I learned the hard way that it's best to end it before it gets worse."

"Couldn't you call or text him instead?" Apprehension worked its way up Maddie's spine. "I mean, what do you know about him? What if he loses it and gets rough with you?"

"You've done too many true crime shows," Mallory scoffed, brushing off Maddie's trepidation with casual indifference.

"You know the thing about those shows?" She leaned forward and held Mallory's unconcerned gaze with a steely one of her own. "They're true stories. Bad things happen, Mal. Especially to women."

Mallory averted her gaze and pulled at a loose thread on her apron. "If it makes you feel better, we're meeting at Callie's," she said after a few seconds.

"The public break-up." Slightly relieved, Maddie nodded in approval. "That's smart." She paused, frowning as another scenario presented itself. "But what if he does something afterward? What if he follows you back here and—"

"Stop it," Mallory said sharply. "Nothing bad is going to happen."

Maddie wanted to reach across the counter, slap Mallory—lightly, of course—and yell, *snap the hell out of it*. "Have you done an online search on him?"

"Yes, Detective Hart, I did." Mallory's tone was laced with irritation. "All I found was a bunch of stuff related to his job. He's a web developer, not a deranged killer."

"Do you have a security system? I don't remember seeing one the last time I was upstairs in your apartment." Mallory lived above the shop in a cozy one-bedroom apartment. In addition to an entrance inside the shop's kitchen, another entrance was located in the back alley.

"Sam put one in for me two years ago," Mallory said. "And I have one of those doorbell thingies too."

"Well, that's something, I guess." She drummed her fingertips on the counter. Maybe she was overreacting, but online search or not, what did Mallory really know about this guy? She'd read a bio and swiped right on a

95

dating app. Sure, his profession checked out, and he was attractive in a hipster sort of way, but after a mere handful of dates, he was raising red flags. "Wait." Her fingers stilled on the counter. "What time are you meeting him?"

"Late. About eight thirty. I have to finish this special order of cookies for the Girl Scout troop. They're having a Christmas event tomorrow afternoon."

"You're making cookies for Girl Scouts?" Maddie asked with an incredulous laugh. "That's ironic." As Mallory rolled her eyes and picked up her piping bag with a deadpan expression, Maddie checked her watch. "I know you think I'm nuts, but I'll feel better if I'm sure you're okay. I'll still go to the movie, but afterward, I'll stop by the diner for coffee, wait until Tanner leaves, and walk back here with you. The first showing starts in about twenty minutes. That'll give me plenty of time to get to the diner after the movie is over." She slid off the stool to retrieve her coat and purse. "Don't dump him until I get there."

Fifteen minutes later, with a bag of popcorn in one hand and a soft drink in the other, Maddie walked into the movie theater and almost squealed with happiness. The remodel included replacing the dumpy old seats with recliner seating. Not only did the new seats recline, but they also had a sliding tray table to hold snacks.

Welcome to the twenty-first century, Summerwood Cinema.

The lights hadn't dimmed, and she quickly found a section near the front with several open seats. Considering the affection for the movie, she was surprised the theater wasn't packed. But then again, it was the early showing; the later one would probably be more popular with the after-work crowd.

Once she'd settled into the seat and stowed her drink in the cup holder, she adjusted the seat to a comfortable position and munched on popcorn while watching the ads showing on the screen. Finally, a stern warning appeared on the screen advising everyone in the theater to turn their phones off, and the lights dimmed. Maddie scooped another handful of popcorn from the bag, giddy with anticipation. She hadn't seen *Die Hard* in a theater in years, and as far as she was concerned, it was the best way to see John McClane in all of his ass-kicking glory.

Just as she was about to shovel a handful of popcorn into her mouth, a large, strong hand gripped her shoulder. She let out a startled gasp, and popcorn went flying everywhere. Heart slamming in her chest, she jerked around in her seat and found Ben leaning forward in the seat behind her with a self-satisfied smile on his face.

"Small world, isn't it?"

"You scared the crap out of me," she said, her voice low and accusing.

"Sorry." His expression indicated the exact opposite.

"No, you're not. You enjoyed that."

"It *was* pretty funny when you tossed your popcorn in the air," he said, not bothering to deny it.

"What are you doing here?"

"Where else would I be?" he shot back. "You know I love this movie."

"Shhhh." Someone sitting nearby shushed them.

Ben glanced over his shoulder. "If we're going to talk, I should sit by you," he said, looking back at her.

"We're not going to—" She broke off as he got up from his seat and headed for the aisle. Seconds later, he settled himself into the seat next to hers.

"These seats are amazing." He reclined his seat until it was even with hers. "Don't you agree?"

"The movie's starting." She stared at the screen and trying to ignore the familiar scent of his cologne. Damn, he smelled good. Better than popcorn.

He crossed one long denim-clad leg over the other, and she was aware of him looking at her out of the corner of her eye. "It's the coming attractions," he said, keeping his voice low.

"I like the coming attractions." Too aware of him by far, she kept her eyes on the screen.

"You've got popcorn on your chest."

She jerked her gaze down. "Damn it," she muttered, picking popcorn off her sweater and depositing it on the tray in front of her.

"Did you turn off your phone?" he asked a few seconds later.

Maddie sighed. "Yes."

"They've got some new rules," he said affably. "If you talk or text on your phone, they'll kick you out."

Exasperated, she turned in her seat and met his amused gaze. "Oh my God, I can't believe you *still* talk this much in the movie theater."

"What can I say?" A smile slowly tipped up one corner of his mouth. "Some habits are hard to break."

"Do *not* talk during the movie." She tried not to get sucked in by that sexy smile. But it was hard. Really hard.

"Yes, ma'am." He gave her a mock salute. "Do you know what this reminds me of?"

"No, but I'm sure you'll tell me," she said wryly.

"Old times." He pointed at her bag of popcorn.

"Hey, since you got the extra-large bag, do you mind if I have some?"

Grudgingly, she moved the bag so it was between them. "Do you know what this reminds *me* of?"

"No."

"How you always hogged the popcorn," she said, his innocent expression not fooling her for one second.

"Yeah." Grinning, Ben scooped out a large handful of popcorn. "I do love popcorn."

She shook her head and looked back at the screen, but she couldn't ignore how her pulse was suddenly racing at a dizzying speed as she watched the preview. Or the way her whole body tingled with awareness. Actually, it had been tingling ever since Wednesday when she'd fallen in his office, and she'd had the overwhelming urge to kiss him. Her reaction didn't surprise her. From the first moment she met him, she'd been wildly attracted to him. And that attraction had grown stronger as she'd gotten to know him.

"Maddie," he said softly. She turned her head to meet his gaze, and their eyes clung for several heart-stopping seconds. "I've missed doing this with you."

Her breath caught in her throat as her body flushed with heat. "I've missed it too," she whispered, and to cover the effect of Ben's words, she flashed him a wry smile. "No one irritates me in a movie theater like you do."

****

After sitting through the movie's closing credits, Ben walked beside Maddie as they filed out of the theater. In the past, he'd always grown impatient when Maddie insisted they stay and watch the credits roll, but tonight he didn't mind it at all.

He had to be losing his mind. Maddie had hurt him more than anyone ever had. Even his mother. Yet he was still attracted to her, still wanted to be around her, and still wanted to kiss her. When she'd fallen in his office, he feared she'd been knocked unconscious, and the thought of her being seriously injured had scared him to death. In those brief moments, he'd flashed back to a heartbreaking incident last summer. A young boy had fallen at the skate park, hit his head on the concrete, and died. Tragedy could happen that easily, that quickly.

When it turned out she only had the wind knocked out of her, he'd been relieved and thankful. But then, the simple gesture of comforting her had turned into something more. The attraction he'd fought to extinguish for four long years had returned full force, and it wasn't one-sided. He'd kissed Maddie hundreds of times. The softening of her eyes, the slight parting of her lips, and the way she'd leaned slightly toward him as if seeking his mouth had given her away. If Carolyn hadn't interrupted them, he would have kissed her. And she would have kissed him back.

He couldn't stop thinking about it. That's why he'd decided to go to the early movie, to get his mind off Maddie. He'd invited Sam to join him, but the second he'd seen her sitting in the seat in front of him, he was glad his brother had declined his offer. After he'd finagled his way into sitting next to her, Ben wondered if, knowing how much she loved *Die Hard,* he had subconsciously hoped to run into her at the theater. All motivations aside, he now wished it had been a double feature so he could spend more time with her.

"I love it when Holly punches that reporter in the face." Maddie tossed her cup and crumpled popcorn bag into the trash can near the door leading to the lobby. "He was a douche bag," she said as Ben held the door open for her. "And I'm still unbelievably sad that Alan Rickman died. He was such a good actor. I can't imagine anyone else in the role, can you?"

"No. It wouldn't be the same movie, that's for sure," Ben said as they crossed the carpeted lobby and wove their way around the line of people waiting at the snack bar. "Where'd you park?" he asked once they were standing on the sidewalk in front of the theater.

"Across the street, but I'm not going home." Shivering in the cold air, Maddie buttoned her coat. "I'm going over to Callie's to make sure Mallory's okay."

"Why wouldn't she be?" he asked, his breath visible in the air.

"She's breaking up with this guy she's been seeing." Maddie rubbed her hands together to warm them. "I'm not sure how he'll take it, so afterward, I'll follow her back to the shop to make sure she gets there safely."

Suddenly uneasy, he frowned. This didn't sound good. "Do you believe he's dangerous?"

"I don't know." She shrugged. "But I don't want to take any chances. Mallory thinks I'm overreacting. Maybe she's right, but better safe than sorry."

Ben couldn't agree more. He'd handled his fair share of volatile incidents involving spurned lovers, both male and female. "I'm coming with you."

"You don't have to," she said, but her words contradicted the concern in her eyes.

"Yes, I do," he said firmly. Too many women didn't have anyone to help them in these situations. There was no way he would let Maddie or Mallory deal with potential danger alone. "If this guy's a nut job and goes off on her, I can diffuse the situation."

"True. You *are* trained to handle stuff like this." She shoved her hands into her coat pockets. "All right, let's go."

As they walked in the direction of the diner, old-fashioned gas lamps wrapped with festive red ribbons lit their way. In addition, several downtown merchants had decorated their windows with twinkling lights, snowmen, and artfully decorated wreaths. Soon the entire downtown corridor would be a holiday lover's paradise, attracting visitors from all over the Willamette Valley.

Across the street from the diner, a majestic Norwood spruce had been placed in the center of the plaza. The tree was only partially decorated, but next week, at the annual tree lighting ceremony, it would be blanketed with hundreds of lights and ornaments, making it the focal point of downtown Summerwood.

Having her beside him conjured memories. Good ones. It wasn't unusual for them to spend time downtown when they were together. Dinner at Callie's, drinks and darts at the pub, seeing a double feature at the movie theater on Saturday afternoons, or sitting on a bench in the town square talking about nothing and everything. It didn't matter what they did as long as they were together. After she left town, he'd forced himself to go to all the places they'd gone to together, but it hadn't been the same. Nothing was the same without Maddie.

Don't go there.

He shook his head to clear his thoughts.

"How's it going at the front desk? Do you have enough work to keep you busy?" he asked, nodding at an elderly couple walking in the opposite direction.

"Yes. Plenty. I've been working on that project for you, and Carolyn needed help with a media request. The local paper requested a detailed report listing all the overtime paid out for the past three years, and I was able to finish it by the time I left this afternoon."

He wasn't surprised by the overtime request. The local newspaper kept a close eye on the city's public safety budget. "I hate those last-minute media requests, but we have to be transparent."

"That's exactly what Carolyn said." She smiled. "Do you like being a sergeant?"

"I miss being out in the field, but I'm enjoying the supervisory aspect of it. I've learned a lot."

"What's the most important thing you've learned?"

He could write a book on what he'd learned since being promoted. When he'd been an officer, he'd been fairly cocky, thinking he knew everything about the sergeant position. He'd been wrong. There were nuances to the job he'd never even considered. "That I've been entrusted with not only the safety of our citizens, but also my officers. I have to make decisions with the utmost caution and never put their lives at risk unjustifiably."

"I've never thought about it like that," she said thoughtfully. "On any given day, a decision you make could affect their lives."

"And in turn, the lives of their families," he said, thinking of that responsibility. It could be overwhelming, but it came with the job, and instead of a burden, he considered it an honor. "We haven't lost an officer since I've been on the force. I hope we never do."

"Mom told me once that she was relieved when my dad moved up the ranks and spent less time in the field. She spent years worrying about him every time he left for work." She paused and hesitated before continuing. "I used to worry about you when we were together. I knew violent crime wasn't a huge problem in Summerwood, but it takes only one random incident. Like someone drunk or high with a gun. Or one of those domestic violence calls that escalates after the police show up."

Ben lifted his brows. She was a better actress than he thought; he'd never known she had worried about him. "You never said anything," he said. "Why?"

"I'm the daughter of a cop. I'm used to keeping worry bottled up inside of me."

"I'm surprised you agreed to go out with me once you found out I was on the force."

"Just a sucker for blue eyes, I guess." Maddie stopped and looked up at him as they reached the diner. "And it didn't hurt that you told me I was the best actress you'd ever laid eyes on."

"Did I say that?" He halted beside her.

"You did." The smile that broke across her face made her even more beautiful.

He swallowed. Hard. And like the first time he saw her, his chest constricted, and words couldn't get past his throat.

"Flattery got you everywhere." Before he could reply, she turned and peered in the window. "Good, we're not too late. They're sitting at a booth in the corner."

A few minutes later, after they'd divested themselves of their coats and sat next to each other at the counter, Maddie leaned back, craning her head to observe the booth where Mallory and her boyfriend were sitting. "Neither of them looks happy."

"If she's breaking up with him, that's not surprising." He grabbed a menu and opened it. "Are you hungry?"

"No. But I'd love some coffee."

"Two coffees and a piece of your lemon meringue pie," he said to their server. When they were alone again, he glanced at Maddie and shook his head. "Pro tip—if you're going to surveil someone, don't be so obvious."

"Got it. Act natural." She averted her gaze to meet his. "I auditioned for a cop show last year. I read for the detective, but they thought I was better suited for something else."

Their server returned with the coffee and Ben's pie.

"Thank you," she said to the young woman and reached for the creamer.

"What was the role?"

"The victim. A prostitute killed by her john," she said with a wry grin as she poured the creamer into her coffee and stirred it with a spoon. "I was murdered in the first scene, so I had to lie on the cold hard ground for a couple of hours while they filmed the other actors discussing my death." She set her spoon on her saucer and sighed. "I was stiff and sore for days after that."

Ben had seen the show she was referring to. Not that he'd admit it to anyone, but he watched everything she'd been in since she left. The scene had been disturbing. Maddie had looked like she was dead. "Isn't that what they call suffering for your art?" He picked up his fork and dug into his pie.

"If art is portraying a dead hooker, then yes, it is." She sipped her coffee and lowered a covetous gaze to his pie.

"No." He held up his fork as if to ward her off. "You

105

can't have any."

"Just one bite?" she asked, her eyes wide and pleading. "I shared my popcorn with you."

He couldn't argue with that logic. "Fine." He nudged his plate in her direction as he discreetly shot a glance toward Mallory's table. So far, no raised voices or angry gestures. "But just one bite."

"Thank you." A smile flitted across her lips as she put her cup on the saucer and picked up her fork. "Speaking of acting, how is Sierra doing with the play?"

"In her words, nervous but ready."

"The play is on Sunday, right?" Maddie asked, sectioning off a small piece of pie with her fork.

"Yes. At the high school." As he took another bite, savoring the tart lemon on his tongue, something Sierra had said to him popped into his head. "If you don't have plans, I know Sierra would be thrilled to have you in the audience. She idolizes you."

"She does?" A becoming blush stained her cheeks. "She's such a sweetheart. I'd love to see the play, and I'm sure she'll be wonderful in it." She popped the small piece of pie into her mouth and let out a low moan of pleasure that sent a spark of arousal straight to his groin. "Oh, wow. They still make a great lemon meringue pie. It's almost as delicious as Mallory's."

Shifting on his stool, Ben pushed the plate closer to her. "Have the rest," he said, not because he wanted to hear her moan again. He just liked to share.

As he and Maddie nursed their second cups of coffee, Mallory's boyfriend abruptly left their table and stalked toward the exit. Once the door closed behind him, Mallory slipped out of the booth and hurried toward him and Maddie.

"I'm glad that's over. And…" She held up the check with a grimace. "It looks like I'm paying for dinner." The contrast between her joking tone and her grim expression would be evident to anyone looking at her.

"How did he take it?" Maddie asked.

"Not well. Tanner thinks I dumped him for Sam."

Ben's brows shot up. "Sam? What does he have to do with this?"

"Nothing. Tanner saw me talking to him last week, and now he's got it in his head that something is going on between us."

"Do you think he's upset enough to hurt you?" he asked.

Mallory shook her head adamantly. "No. He was angry, but he never said anything threatening."

"I'm still walking you back to Sweet Temptations," Maddie declared, almost daring Mallory to argue with her.

As expected, Mallory opened her mouth to protest, but Ben plucked the check from her fingers before she could get a word out. "After I pay the checks, *I'll* walk you to the shop. And for the foreseeable future, you should probably access your apartment from inside the shop whenever possible. Just as a precaution."

Mallory's gaze moved between them for several seconds, and then her shoulders slumped. "Okay. You win, but I'm sure you guys are worrying for nothing. And you don't have to pay for my dinner," she said, a bit of her spirit returning as she looked at him pointedly.

"I insist, but I wouldn't say no to one of your lemon meringue pies." He grinned, and shifting on the stool, he pulled his wallet from the back pocket of his jeans.

"You've got a deal," Mallory conceded. "I'm going

to use the restroom. Be right back."

Maddie watched her go before turning toward him. "Thank you," she said softly, giving him a warm smile.

Something in Ben's chest shifted. "It's nothing," he said, averting his gaze before he drowned in those blue eyes of hers.

"It's something." She put her hand on his forearm and squeezed. She searched his face for several seconds, her eyes flickering with something he couldn't decipher. "May I sit with you and your family at the play on Sunday?"

"Of course," he said as Maddie's warm touch played havoc with his pulse. "I'll save you a seat."

Chapter Nine

Inside the lobby of Summerwood high school's auditorium, Maddie studied the framed theater poster hanging on the wall, impressed by its professional quality. The school must have created a graphic arts program since she'd graduated. They'd made do with homemade construction paper posters and muslin banners hand-painted by the drama class back then. Not that she or her classmates minded the extra work. Promoting school productions had been part of their class curriculum, and they'd spent many after-school hours together listening to music and eating pizza while they had created the posters and banners. It was the only time in high school she had ever fit in.

"I was hoping to run into you."

She whirled around at the sound of Stevie Pepper's voice. "I promise I haven't forgotten to call you," Maddie said with an apologetic smile. "It's been busy at the police station."

"Don't worry, darling." A smile widened Stevie's red lips. "I haven't had a spare moment since I last saw you. My theater assistant quit, and I've been wearing two hats." She put a hand to the chunky silver necklace at her throat. "It's *exhausting*," she added with a dramatic flourish.

"I can imagine." She gave Stevie a sympathetic smile. "Why were you hoping to run into me?"

"Because I wanted to introduce you to my current paramour, Lorenzo." Stevie scanned the room. "But I seem to have misplaced him."

Maddie frowned. When she'd left town, Stevie had been in a serious relationship with one of Summerwood's city council members. "Lorenzo?"

"He's a vintner. I met him at a wine tasting event in Newberg last year. He appreciates balance and character in wine as much as I do." One perfectly arched brow rose as she gave Maddie a suggestive smile. "He also appreciates the certain skills a more mature woman can bring into the bedroom."

"Sounds like a keeper," Maddie said before Stevie could elaborate on those skills. She hadn't been able to look at that city councilman in the same way after the last time Stevie had spilled all the details on her sex life.

"Oh, he is, darling," Stevie said with a throaty laugh. "If I locate him before the play starts, I'll introduce you. You're going to love him. He's delicious."

After Stevie wandered off to search for Lorenzo, Maddie took off her coat, and as she draped it over her arm, she spotted Clarice Worley standing next to the doors to the auditorium. As their gazes met across the lobby, Clarice's expression brightened, and she left her post to quickly head in Maddie's direction, her curly cap of auburn hair bouncing merrily with each step.

"Are the rumors true? Are you staying in town until the first of the year?" Clarice, never one to mince words, asked as she halted in front of her.

"Wow." Maddie let out an amused chuckle. "News travels fast around here."

"Doesn't it, though?" Clarice said wryly. "I was over at the beauty shop this morning, and your name came up before I even got my tushie in the chair."

Maddie wasn't surprised. But she didn't much care for being the day's topic of discussion at the beauty salon. "That doesn't sound good."

"Don't worry, hon. They know I don't tolerate mean-spirited gossip," Clarice assured her. "One of the gals said she'd seen you on television recently, and we got to talking about how brave it was of you to go to Hollywood like you did."

Now *that* surprised her. "Brave?"

"Yes. Brave," Clarice said with a firm nod. "Not many people would move so far away from home without having a job lined up. In my mind, that takes some courage. Anyway, that's when Kay—you know, April's mother—said you were filling in for Cora Jean." She leaned forward and lowered her voice. "Though from what I hear, she doesn't do much other than spread gossip. Not to speak ill of Cora Jean, mind you, but I imagine you're a definite improvement at the front desk, even if it's temporary."

Her heart swelled at Clarice's praise. "I'm doing my best."

"Of course, you are. I'm sure you'll have the front desk running like a finely oiled machine in no time. And mark my words." Clarice pointed a finger at her. "They'll be as sad as I was when you're gone. You were a wonderful employee."

The unexpected compliment warmed Maddie's cheeks. "That's kind of you to say."

"Kind. Schmind." Clarice waved a dismissive hand. "It's the truth. Having you take care of things at the office freed up a lot of my time. Time I used to cultivate new clients. And it paid off in spades."

For the life of her, Maddie couldn't imagine what she'd done that was so impressive. Running the small office hadn't been hard. "I'm glad I made a difference, but I was only doing the job you hired me for."

"Exactly. Do you know how many assistants I've had that couldn't even manage that?" Clarice let out a derisive snort. "More than I can shake a stick at." She lifted her gaze to the poster on the wall behind Maddie. "This must bring back wonderful memories. I remember watching you on stage in this very auditorium. Every time I see your commercials on TV, I remind Bert that you got your start right here at the high school. By the way, he swears by that medication. If they ever need a real-life testimonial, you should have them give him a call. He used to be on the radio, you know. They said he had the smoothest voice in Portland." Clarice's expression softened. "I always tell him that I fell in love with his voice first. And as it turned out, he was as wonderful as his voice. Still is."

"You're a lucky woman." She envied Clarice's happiness with Bert. Maybe if she hadn't left Summerwood, she would be as happy as Clarice. With Ben.

"You're darn right, I am. And now I'd better find that wonderful husband of mine. The play's due to start soon." Clarice patted Maddie's arm. "It was nice seeing you, dear."

"You too," she said as Clarice bustled away.

Maddie glanced at her watch and then scanned the crowded lobby, not overly concerned that Ben hadn't yet arrived. They'd agreed to meet twenty minutes before the start of the play, and he still had five minutes to spare. He'd called her this morning, and when his name popped up on her screen, her heart had skipped more than a few beats. Especially when she realized she could still be on his contact list. But if she was, did it mean anything? She'd never removed him from hers. Although she had never called him while she was in Los Angeles, she couldn't bring herself to delete him. It was much too final. Had he felt the same way?

Oh, for the love of Meryl Streep. Why was she questioning if it meant anything? Yes, she and Ben were getting along much better, but that didn't mean he'd ever forgive her for hurting him. And even if he did forgive her, she was going back to LA in January. Her life was there. Her career was there.

But what about your heart?

"Maddie."

She pivoted in the direction of the familiar voice, and the welcoming expression on Ben's father's face eased her fears he might not be too thrilled to have her back in town. With Ben trailing behind him, Russ Ashford halted in front of her and wrapped her in a bear hug. Crushed against his chest, she breathed in the scent of Old Spice.

"Hi, Russ. It's wonderful to see you," she said after he'd released her. Russ was still a handsome man with blue eyes and brown hair lightly peppered with silver strands that gave him a distinguished air. It was easy to see where Ben and Sam had gotten their good looks.

"Same here, kiddo," he said with a smile. "I appreciate you being here tonight. Sierra's talked of nothing else since she found out you were joining us."

"I'm looking forward to it. I'm sure she'll turn in a great performance."

"She should, considering she's been walking around

the house in character all week." Cocking his head, Russ turned and squinted at Ben. "What'd she call it again?"

"Method acting." Ben rolled eyes.

"Hey, don't knock it. It works for some people." She defended the practice even though it wasn't one of the acting tools she utilized.

Ben pulled off his coat and shot her a wise-ass grin. "Yeah, maybe for Christian Bale or Daniel Day-Lewis, but this is high school, not Hollywood."

"So you *were* listening when I talked about famous method actors," she said, appreciating how delicious he looked in his dark wash jeans and black pullover sweater.

"It was so crazy I couldn't help but listen. Tell me again how Daniel Day-Lewis texting as Abraham Lincoln helped his performance in the movie? There were no cell phones back then; if he was going to stay in character, he should have sent handwritten letters."

She laughed. "Good point," she said, marveling that Ben remembered one of what must have been hundreds of times she'd talked about acting.

"Okay, now that we've settled that, we should probably head into the auditorium." Russ's mouth quirked with an amused smile. "Sam texted me while we were on our way. He got here early to save our seats."

Maddie greeted Sam before settling into the aisle seat next to Ben. As the auditorium filled, she gazed at the stage, welcoming the fond memories it evoked. She imagined the young cast was nervously awaiting their first scene behind that same royal-blue velvet curtain. Just as she had during her school days.

Those days had been magical. Performing on the stage was different than acting on television. On television, whether it was in a commercial or a series, the actors waited around for long periods of time. And with no audience except the director and crew, the performers received minimal feedback. What she'd missed most about performing on stage was the crowd reaction. A collective gasp, shared boisterous laughter, or even the sound of sniffles if the scene was sad.

"I can't believe I've never asked you this, but what was the first school play you were in?" Ben's question pulled her from her thoughts.

She shifted in her seat and met his curious gaze. "In my freshman year, I played Frenchy in *Grease*."

"That's a musical, right?"

She nodded. "The one musical I've ever been in. I can barely carry a tune."

"I know. I've heard you sing in the shower."

His tone was matter-of-fact, but the reminder of how intimate they'd once been sent a flush of heat over her skin.

"How'd you get the part?"

"All of the other female roles had been cast, and I was the last girl standing. So I guess you could say I got the part by default." Her singing hadn't wowed anyone, but she'd gotten praise for her acting, giving her the confidence to continue.

Before he could reply, a girl about Sierra's age rushed up the aisle toward them, and after catching sight of Ben, she crouched in the aisle next to Maddie's seat. "Ben. Please, I need your help." Her voice was low but agitated. "You have to come quick."

"Faith?" Ben's shoulder pressed against Maddie's as he leaned toward the girl. "What's going on?" he asked calmly.

Concerned, Maddie waited for Faith to continue.

"It's Sierra," Faith whispered. "She's freaking out in the bathroom. She says she can't go on stage."

"Why?" Ben's expression turned serious. "Is she sick?"

"She's scared she won't remember her lines." Faith brushed at the choppily cut pink and blonde bangs that almost covered her eyes. "I think it's nerves, but nothing I say calms her down. I didn't know what else to do except come and find you."

Both Russ and Sam leaned forward, peering at Ben with concern. "Is Sierra okay?" Russ asked.

"Just pre-show jitters," he reassured them and then turned to Faith. "Take me to Sierra. I'll talk to her."

"I'll come with you." Maddie rose from her seat in unison with Ben. "I've been through this myself. I might be able to help."

"Good idea," he said, lightly touching her arm.

The theater hadn't changed since Maddie had been a student. Even the wallpaper was the same. An odd shade she and her friends had laughingly called puke green. She followed Ben and Faith to the bathrooms at the foot of the stairs leading up to the stage and tried the handle on the women's room door. It was locked.

Ben rapped on the door with his knuckles. "Sierra. Open the door."

"No!" Sierra said, her voice slightly muffled. "Go away."

Maddie met his worried gaze. "Let me try," she whispered, and he nodded. "Sierra." She rapped on the door with her knuckles. "Sweetie, it's Maddie. Please come out."

"I don't want to go on stage."

"We're not here to force you to go on stage," she

said soothingly. "We only want to talk." She exchanged a concerned glance with Ben and tried again. "Please, open the door. Everything will be all right. I promise."

Seconds later, the lock popped as Sierra opened the door. With her dramatic makeup and the ethereal, ghostly white gown, she had been transformed into the Ghost of Christmas Past, but her kohl-rimmed eyes were filled with anxiety. "I threw up. Twice," she confessed, blinking back tears.

Maddie was quick to recognize Sierra had stage fright. She hadn't met an actor who, at some point in their career, hadn't been afflicted with it. She swung her gaze toward Faith, standing next to Ben and seeming about to burst into tears herself. "Do you still keep water and ginger ale backstage?"

Faith nodded vigorously. "It's my job to stock the cooler. I'll go get some." She shot up the short flight of stairs with a quick pivot and disappeared.

"Listen to me." Maddie lifted her arms and gently rested her palms on Sierra's slim shoulders. "What you're feeling right now is perfectly normal."

Sierra lifted a skeptical brow. "It is?"

"Yes. Even seasoned performers deal with stage fright when they do live theater."

"Did you?"

"Oh, honey." She chuckled softly. "I can't tell you how many times I thought I would toss my cookies in front of a live audience, but I never did. Not once."

"What if I forget my lines?" Sierra asked tremulously.

The trepidation in Sierra's eyes tugged at Maddie's heart, triggering the need to comfort her. "You won't."

"How can you be sure?"

"Because when we were running lines last weekend, you didn't have to look at your script. You had already memorized all of your dialogue. And your dad says you've been in character all week. You're prepared and ready for tonight."

Sierra shook her head. "That's not the same as doing it on stage."

"You had dress rehearsal yesterday," Ben said. "You said it went great."

"It did. But there weren't a ton of people sitting in the auditorium watching us."

"Remember, you're the Ghost of Christmas Past. Try to focus on your interaction with Scrooge and nothing else," Maddie said firmly, holding Sierra's gaze. "Trust me when I say that once the scene begins, the fear will disappear, and you'll be fine."

Hope flickered in Sierra's eyes. "Are you sure?"

"Yes." Maddie squeezed Sierra's shoulders. "I'm absolutely sure."

Faith returned, rushing down the stairs with a bottle of water in one hand and a can of ginger ale in the other. "I brought both." She almost plowed into Ben as she came to a sudden halt.

"I'll go with water. Ginger ale always makes me burp," Sierra said with a sheepish grin.

Maddie lowered her arms and stepped back as Sierra accepted the water from Faith. "I have another idea that might help."

Sierra's eyes widened. "What is it?"

"When you go backstage, peek out at the audience and look for us. We're sitting in the second row, center aisle. If you feel nervous when you're on stage, make eye contact with one of us, and you'll know you're not alone, and we believe in you."

"Does that really work?" Sierra's brow arched in question.

Maddie gave her a reassuring smile. "You'd be surprised at what the sight of a friendly face can do. But I'm betting you'll be fine once you get out there and won't need us at all."

"Okay." Sierra inhaled deeply, and the tightness around her mouth eased. "I can do this."

"Yes, you can." Maddie glanced at the stairs. "You should go before your director sends out a search party to look for you."

"Break a leg, Skittles," Ben said, giving Sierra a wry grin.

"Don't call me that." Sierra wrinkled her pert nose at him. "C'mon, Faith, let's go."

As Sierra and Faith hurried up the stairs, Ben lowered his gaze to hers. "Thank you. I'm not sure I could have talked her down."

"It helps that I've been in her shoes." She smiled up at him. "Now, let's get back to our seats. The play is starting in a few minutes."

After the play, Maddie stood with Ben and Russ outside the auditorium. The production had gone off without a hitch, and as she expected, Sierra had conquered her stage fright as soon as she uttered her first line. After the final curtain call, a jubilant Sierra had given her a big hug and asked her father for permission to join the rest of the cast at Callie's Diner to celebrate. Russ had agreed as long as she was home by eleven. As for Sam, he'd already said his goodbyes and headed for home.

As cars started streaming out of the nearby parking

lot, Russ zipped his coat to ward off the cold night air and focused his friendly gaze on her. "Are you attending the tree lighting ceremony on Wednesday night?"

"Probably. I haven't made definite plans yet, though."

"You should join us."

Aware of Ben's gaze on her and unsure of how he'd feel if she crashed his family's outing, she gave Russ an apologetic smile. "Thanks, but I wouldn't want to intrude on your family time."

"It wouldn't be an intrusion." Russ slanted a questioning look toward Ben. "Would it?"

"Not at all," he said, his unreadable eyes giving nothing away.

Glancing from Ben to Russ, she nodded. "Well then, it sounds like fun. I'd love to join you."

"Extend the invitation to Mallory and your parents. The more, the merrier."

"I'll do that." Maddie pulled her keys from her purse. "It was good to see you again, Russ."

"Same here, Maddie." He gave her shoulder a paternal pat. "You're a sight for sore eyes."

"I'll walk you to your car." Ben's expression was neutral. She still couldn't tell how he felt about her joining his family at the ceremony.

"You don't—"

"I insist." Russ cut her off as he extended his hand toward Ben. "If you give me your keys, I'll warm up the car."

After Ben gave Russ the keys, Maddie walked beside him in the direction of her car.

"I'm sorry Dad put you on the spot. About the tree lighting ceremony."

"It's fine. I'm looking forward to it. Do you still go over to Callie's for hot chocolate afterward?"

Ben nodded. "We didn't have much in the way of holiday traditions after what happened with my mother, so Dad made sure we started some when we moved here. It's important to him."

"Traditions are nice." She thought of her family's rowdy board games on Christmas Day. The nostalgic memory made her smile. "I've missed them."

"It's too bad you're leaving right after Cora Jean gets back. I remember how much you always enjoyed Summerwood's holiday events."

So he hadn't heard. Maybe because he didn't frequent Tresses, the hot spot for hair *and* juicy town gossip.

"I'm not leaving."

"I thought you couldn't wait to get back to Hollywood." He shot her a surprised glance.

"I'm extending my vacation. I'll be in town until the first of the year." Surreptitiously, she studied his profile, and again, his expression gave nothing away. Maybe he didn't care one way or the other.

"Your family must be happy about that," he said as they reached her car. "Since you're staying in town, you might be interested in signing up for the Santa Claus 5k Fun Run/Walk. All proceeds go to the Summerwood Animal Rescue."

Maddie didn't care for running, but she did care about animals. The people who worked in animal rescue were angels on earth. If participating in the event would enable them to take care of more animals, she would sign up and do her part to help them. "That's a great cause."

"I agree. And they need the funds to expand.

They're running out of room."

"Sounds like fun. I'll mention it to Mallory." She pressed the button on her key fob to unlock the car. "Although she may have already signed up. She adores animals. When we were in high school, she volunteered at the shelter."

"Fair warning. You'll have to dress up as Santa." He grinned. "Or at least wear a Santa hat."

"I think I can scrounge one up." She opened the door. "Will you be decked out in full Santa gear?"

"Yep. Beard, belly, and all."

"Well, now I *have* to participate. Just to see that." She tossed her purse onto the passenger seat.

"Thank you again for your help with Sierra," he said as she was about to get into the car. The golden glow from a nearby light fixture illuminated his face, and the gratitude in his eyes warmed her. It was a million times better than the cold indifference he'd displayed when she first returned to town.

"You're welcome," she said softly, holding his gaze as the vibe between them shifted and turned into something familiar. Something intimate. A surge of longing shot through her, almost robbing her of her breath.

A car drove by, and the moment passed. He took a step back and ran his fingers through his short hair. "I'll see you at work tomorrow," he said gruffly, then turned and walked toward the other side of the parking lot.

Maddie stared at his retreating back and, not for the first time, wished she had the power to turn back time.

****

When Ben reached his car, the engine was running, and his father was sitting patiently in the passenger seat.

Trudging to the driver's side door, he opened it and climbed inside.

"You all right?"

"I'm fine." A lie. He wasn't quite sure what the hell was happening to him.

"Do you want to talk about it?" His father lowered the volume on the radio, which he'd changed from Ben's favorite sports channel to a classic rock station.

Ben buckled his seat belt. "Talk about what?"

"About what's bothering you?" he asked as Ben shifted into reverse. "I assume it's Maddie."

"I'd rather not discuss it," Ben said, mostly because he was still trying to figure it out. A couple of weeks ago, his life had been uneventful, predictable even. But then Maddie had come back to town and stirred up emotions he thought he was done with. He shifted into reverse, checked behind him, and backed out of the parking space.

"You sure about that?"

"I'm sure." His reply was sharper than he intended, and he instantly regretted it. It wasn't his father's fault he was mixed up.

His father shrugged. "Okay. But if you ever need to hash it out, I'm available."

"I know, Dad," he said, softening his tone. "Thanks."

As they left the high school behind, his father hummed along to an old Eagles tune, and Ben, out of force of habit, scanned the streets for anything that looked suspicious. There wasn't much to see other than a few people walking their dogs. A typical Sunday evening in Summerwood, or so it appeared. But unfortunately, a lot of things, bad things, could be going on behind those closed doors. He knew that from experience.

One of those bad things popped into his head. His mother. Did his father know she hadn't given up on getting back into Sam's good graces? If not, he should. Lucinda Ashford couldn't care less about her children. She was up to something, and he had to ensure they were ready for anything. "Did Sam tell you he got another letter from Mom?"

His father jerked his head in Ben's direction. "No. He doesn't discuss her with me much anymore." He hesitated for a few seconds before continuing. "Your brother still blames me for what happened."

Ben shifted in the leather seat and studied his father's profile. Even in the dim light of the car, he could make out the tightness of his jaw. "He doesn't blame you."

"Oh, he's never come out and said it, but deep down inside, he believes I should have figured it out." He ran a hand through his hair and sighed. "He's right. I should have been paying more attention."

"You were working two jobs."

"That's no excuse. You were fourteen, and you figured it out."

In his line of work, Ben had seen many people shoulder the blame for something that wasn't their fault. Mired in guilt, they convinced themselves they'd missed the signs, never realizing most perpetrators were highly skilled in deception. "I didn't figure it out. Mom got sloppy by hiding incriminating evidence in the attic. I just happened to find it." For a few years afterward, he'd felt guilty for accidentally discovering one of his mother's secrets, but he'd done the right thing in telling his father about it.

"Still, I should have known." He shook his head and let out a frustrated grunt. "Forget about all the money she stole. How could I have not have known she'd been cheating on me for years?"

Ben's chest constricted. Even after all these years, his mother still had a powerful hold on both his father and brother. His father had never remarried, and Sam had never let himself get too close to any woman. He was still surprised that Sam and Mallory had become such good friends. That was probably due more to Mallory than Sam, though. When they first moved to Summerwood, Mallory had befriended Sam on his first day at their new school, and they'd formed a close friendship. Ben suspected it was because Mallory had never once displayed any romantic interest in Sam. If she ever did, his brother would probably run for the hills.

"I don't want to talk about this anymore," his father grumbled.

"I'm sorry I brought it up," Ben said, then hesitated. "But if you don't stop blaming yourself, you're never going to be happy." As he said the words, he wondered if he'd overstepped. But he'd been worried about his father for some time, and it had to be said. Whatever the fallout.

"What does that mean?" His father's tone was edged with a hint of anger.

"It means you still have a lot of life ahead of you. Do you want to spend it alone?"

"I could ask the same of you," he said as Ben slowed the car to a stop at the intersection. "You haven't been serious about anyone since Maddie."

He waved a dismissive hand. "I haven't had time for

a relationship."

"That's bull, and you know it. You've had plenty of time. You haven't found anyone else because you're still in love with Maddie."

"That's crazy," he shot back, not sure if he was annoyed his father was analyzing him or that he might be right. "How can I still be in love with someone who blindsided me the way she did?"

"Because sometimes love isn't something you can control. No matter how much you want to."

"Is this your way of telling me you still love Mom?" Ben stepped on the gas as the light changed to green.

"God, no." His father fired him an incredulous look. "The love I had for your mother died when I found out what she'd been doing behind my back for five years."

Ben blew out a frustrated breath. "Then what's your point?"

"My point is that you'll never be happy with someone else until you deal with your feelings for Maddie."

"It doesn't matter what I feel for Maddie. She's leaving again in January."

"That didn't stop you from allowing her to join us tonight."

"I did it for Sierra."

His father snorted. "Yeah. Right," he said and then turned up the radio.

Ben opened his mouth but then snapped it shut. Arguing with his old man was useless when he got some wild idea into his head. He'd wanted Maddie to sit with them because Sierra wanted Maddie to be there.

Or had he? He'd been quick to second his father's invitation to the tree lighting ceremony. And what about casually dropping the 5k run into their conversation? If he was trying to keep his distance, why was he trying to spend more time with her?

Was his father right? Was he still in love with Maddie?

No. He couldn't be, not after what she'd done. It was plain old lust. Maddie was beautiful and sexy. What he was feeling for her had everything to do with his body and nothing to do with love.

Nothing at all.

Chapter Ten

The plaza in downtown Summerwood bustled with holiday cheer. Nearby intersections had been blocked off, allowing citizens and visitors to gather around the giant Norwood spruce that would soon twinkle with thousands of colorful lights.

Maddie stood between Ben and Sierra, not far from the growing crowd, but the only thing she was aware of was Ben. It wasn't the first time she'd been affected by his presence that day. At the police station, she'd sat next to him at his desk, demonstrating how to compile his monthly reports by running the macro and pivot table she created for him.

Between the subtle scent of whatever soap he was using these days and the way her shoulder was pressed against his, she'd found it difficult to keep her mind on work. And when their fingers accidentally brushed over the keyboard, a ripple of excitement had ricocheted through her entire body, reminding her of the times they'd made love. Thankfully, Ben didn't seem to notice. He was all business.

"Where are Sam and your dad?" Maddie asked as she fastened the top button of her coat.

Sierra nodded in the direction of Sweet Temptations. "Mallory texted Sam, and he and my dad went over to the bakery."

"I hope everything's okay." As far as she knew,

Tanner hadn't contacted Mallory since she'd broken up with him, but Maddie couldn't shake the feeling that Tanner was trouble. Maybe not stalker trouble, but trouble all the same.

"They're probably discussing the renovation in the back of the shop," Ben said. "Sam told me he's been working on the blueprints."

"I hope they don't miss the tree lighting." Sierra shot a worried glance at her phone. "The ceremony starts in twenty minutes."

"I'm sure they won't," Maddie reassured her. "Mallory's closing the bakery for the ceremony and opening it again afterward. She would never miss the tree lighting. She's loved it since we were kids."

"Are your parents here?" Ben asked.

Maddie scanned the crowd. "They're around here somewhere. They usually make the rounds with the city council members and chamber of commerce folks."

He grimaced. "I'd rather walk on broken glass."

She laughed. "Wait until you're the chief of police. It comes with the territory."

"If that's the case, I'll pass on being chief."

"You'd be a good chief," Sierra chimed in. "You're always bossing me around."

She and Ben exchanged an amused glance. "Thanks for the vote of confidence," he said affectionately.

Sierra looked up from her phone. "Faith texted me. She needs help with her mom's craft booth. Do you mind if I go help them?"

"No. It's fine." Ben nodded.

"I'll see you later at Callie's for hot chocolate," Sierra called over her shoulder.

Maddie watched as Sierra disappeared into the

129

crowd of people on the perimeter of the plaza. "I can't believe she's going to college next year. It seems like yesterday we were at her eighth-grade graduation."

Ben let out a snort of laughter. "Remember how she accidentally tripped and took down Mrs. Griffiths when she went up on the stage to receive her certificate?"

"Accidentally?" She cocked her head and waggled her brows. "I'm surprised no one tried it before that night."

His eyes widened. "Sierra did that on purpose?"

She shrugged. "Who's to say? Mrs. Griffiths terrorized the students of Summerwood Junior High for years before she retired. Maybe it was a karmic accident."

"Maybe. I do believe in karma." A flicker of anger flashed in his eyes. "It finally caught up to my mother," he said harshly.

The tone of his voice reminded her of how much damage his mother had done. "Does Sierra ever ask about your mom?"

"No. Not since she was old enough to understand what happened." Ben let out an annoyed sigh. "Speaking of my mother, she's been writing to Sam."

"How did she get Sam's address?" she asked, surprised he was sharing information about his mom with her. She hoped it was a sign the barriers between them were crumbling. "When she was sentenced, you guys were still in Ohio."

"I'm not sure. It's not hard to find someone these days."

"Do you think she'll show up in Summerwood?" she asked, thinking of the turmoil that could cause the Ashford family. She wasn't sure about Russ, Sam, or

Sierra, but she didn't think Ben would ever be able to forgive his mother for what she'd done to their family.

A scowl darkened his face. "I hope not, but I wouldn't put it past her. Sam worshipped her, and out of the three of us, he was her favorite. I'm sure it's bothering the hell out of her that he's not responding to her letters."

She studied Ben's profile, noting the tension in his jaw. "And you're worried about him if she shows up in Summerwood."

"I don't believe he's fully processed what happened."

Her heart clenched. The Ashford children had been dealt a cruel blow. She sent a silent thank you out to the universe for the parents she'd been blessed with. "I thought the therapy he had afterward helped."

"To an extent. But other than a few select people, he keeps everyone at arm's length." Ben paused. "I'm glad he let Mallory in, though. She's been a good friend to him."

She chuckled. "Like Mallory gave him a choice. Once she decided to be his friend, she didn't give up until he caved. She's tenacious like that."

"I'd say tenacity runs in your family," he said with a hint of admiration in his tone.

Maddie's cheeks warmed. "I think you mean stubborn."

"That too." His amused gaze turned somber. "Thanks for letting me vent about my mother. There aren't many people I'm comfortable talking to about her."

His words gave her hope the rift between them was healing. She put her hand on his arm. "I'm glad you feel you can still talk to me." She paused, uncertain if she should vocalize that hope. "Maybe that means you don't hate me anymore."

For several long seconds, his enigmatic gaze roamed over her face. "I don't hate you, Maddie," he said, his voice low and husky. "I was angry, but I never hated you."

Her heart skipped a beat, and her stomach fluttered. "I didn't realize until right now how much I needed to hear you say that," she said, giving him a tremulous smile.

"And I didn't realize until you came back how much I missed you," he said softly.

"I've missed you too." She squeezed his arm as the fluttering in her stomach intensified, and her knees got a little wobbly.

His gaze lowered to her mouth. Heat suffused her body, and she parted her lips, waiting and wanting his kiss so desperately. The atmosphere around them filled with electric energy, and as he leaned in close, the only sound she heard was the furious beating of her heart.

Ben's lips were a breath away from hers when the high-pitched whine of a microphone somewhere in the plaza shattered the charged moment. Immediately, he pulled away. She took a step back and fought to rein in the desire thrumming through her body and the disappointment that they'd been interrupted.

Before either of them could speak, Traci tapped Ben on the shoulder. "I've been looking for you," she said, her smile directed solely at Ben. "Sierra was amazing in the Christmas play. You must be so proud."

"We all are." Ben's tone was pleasant, but Maddie didn't miss the annoyance flickering in his eyes. "She did a great job."

"What are you doing after the tree lighting ceremony?" Traci asked. "A few of us are going to JD's. You're welcome to join us." Finally, she swung her gaze to Maddie and gave her a thin smile. "You're welcome too, of course."

Maddie fought not to roll her eyes. Traci would rather walk on hot coals than spend time with her. And the feeling was mutual.

"Thanks for the offer, but I've got plans with my family. And Maddie's joining us."

Traci's eyes flashed with annoyance, but her smile remained intact. "Well, maybe another time." She adjusted the plaid scarf around her neck. "Enjoy your evening," she said and headed off down the sidewalk.

"For a few seconds, I thought I'd become invisible." Maddie grinned.

Ben chuckled as Stevie Pepper, arm in arm with a tall, distinguished man with jet-black hair and equally dark eyes, stopped beside them. "I'm so glad I ran into you, darling." Stevie's luminous smile and her shining dark hair the perfect contrast to her cherry-red wool coat. "I wanted to introduce you to Lorenzo." She gazed adoringly up at him. "Lorenzo Lucci, this is Maddie Hart. One of my most talented students." Stevie gestured a gloved hand toward Ben. "And this is Ben Ashford; he works for the police department."

"It's an honor to meet you." Lorenzo reached for Maddie's hand, a charming smile curving his lips. "Stevie has spoken highly of you."

"It's nice to meet you too." Maddie returned his smile as they shook hands. If she was casting a role for an Italian-lover type in a movie, Lorenzo, with his smoldering good looks and European accent, would get the role. "I understand you're a vintner."

"Yes." Lorenzo nodded. "I'm thinking of opening a wine bar in town. Featuring my finest wines, of course. I've done quite a bit of research, and I believe it would do well here."

"A wine bar?" Ben's voice held a hint of incredulity. "In Summerwood? You've got to be…" He stopped mid-sentence as Maddie discreetly elbowed him in the side. "Well, a wine bar would be a first for Summerwood," he continued after glancing at her. "And a welcome one for many of our residents, I'm sure."

Maddie bit back a laugh. Ben wasn't into wine at all. He'd always been more of a beer man. She couldn't imagine him stepping one foot into a wine bar unless it was to arrest someone.

"I suspect it would be a refreshing change from pubs and sports bars, would it not?" Lorenzo returned with an amused glint in his eyes that said he had a good idea what Ben thought of wine bars.

"I think it's a fabulous idea," Stevie said, smiling at Lorenzo. "If Summerwood is to prosper, it must be open-minded when it comes to new businesses." She inclined her head toward Ben. "Don't you agree, Ben?"

"Sure, but didn't you protest against the proposal for a gentleman's club in town last year?"

Maddie stifled a laugh.

Stevie's eyes flashed with annoyance. "Oh, for goodness's sake, a wine bar and a…a strip club are two entirely different things."

"Gentleman's club," Ben corrected her with a pleasant grin.

"Whatever." Stevie let out a soft huff and tugged at

Lorenzo's arm. "Let's go, my love. I want to introduce you to the mayor before the ceremony starts." She swung her gaze to Maddie. "Don't forget to come by the theater for a chat."

"I won't forget," Maddie called after her. Once Stevie and Lorenzo were out of earshot, she turned to Ben and gently swatted his arm.

"What?" He gave her a devilish grin. "You'd think as an advocate for the arts she'd be more supportive of artistic dance."

She burst out laughing. "You're so bad."

****

Ben enjoyed the tree lighting ceremony. To his surprise, the usually wordy mayor gave a short but eloquent speech about the true meaning of the holidays before proceeding with a theatrical flourish to the giant light switch hooked up next to the Christmas tree. Then, when she flipped the switch and thousands of tiny colorful lights illuminated the tree, the boisterous crowd collectively cheered before breaking out into an impromptu version of "Winter Wonderland." He'd never been much for singing, but standing next to Maddie, who was singing with gusto, he joined in.

It seemed like old times when Maddie walked beside him as they headed to Callie's. As was their tradition, they each had a mug of Callie's famous hot chocolate. This wasn't just any mug. It was huge, almost as big as a soup bowl, and topped with four small skewers of marshmallows crisscrossed over the rim and a large dollop of whipped cream with chocolate sprinkles on top. He didn't care much for sweets, but he had to admit it was delicious except for the marshmallows. Those were disgusting.

The diner was packed. Mallory had joined them for the tree lighting ceremony. Afterward, she had returned to Sweet Temptations to reopen, hoping to capitalize on the good-sized crowd still milling around the plaza and the downtown corridor.

As subtly as he could, Ben drank in the sight of Maddie, who was in deep conversation with Sam about the remodel at Sweet Temptations. His gaze roamed over the curve of her cheekbones and the fullness of her lips. Her silky hair fell loose around her shoulders, and he wished he could run his fingers through it like he had when they were together.

Tonight something had changed between them. He hadn't planned on telling Maddie he missed her, but at that moment, he couldn't have stopped himself if he'd tried. She said she missed him too. He wasn't sure what it meant or if it meant anything. She was still leaving town in January.

"Ben, can I have your marshmallows?" Sierra's question interrupted his thoughts. It was just as well; those thoughts could only lead him down a road already traveled.

"You bet." He picked up one of the skewers and passed it to her. "I don't know how you can eat those things. They're pure sugar."

"That's why I like them." Sierra pulled one gooey marshmallow off the skewer and popped it into her mouth.

"So, Maddie. What's this I hear about you staying in town?" his father asked. "Is it true?"

Maddie shifted in her chair, directing her attention toward his father. "You must get your hair cut at Tresses."

"Yep." He nodded. "Kay's been cutting my hair for years. She's better than any barber I've ever been to. Really knows her stuff. She said she heard you were sticking around for a while. I'm glad to hear it."

"Thanks, Russ." Maddie gave him a warm smile. "I'll be here until after Christmas."

"What else did Kay tell you?" Sam leaned forward, resting his forearms on the table. "I saw a sold sign on the Bateman property. Does she know who bought it? And what's going on with the Davidsons? Are they getting divorced or what?" He quickly scanned the diner, his eyes resting briefly on their server. "Does she have the scoop on why Peyton Troy is back in town? And what about Coach O'Brien? Did the high school renew his contract?"

"A veterinarian from Portland bought the house. The Davidsons have started seeing a marriage counselor, and as for Peyton Troy, well, it seems she's back living with her folks because she got a divorce and sole custody of her daughter," his father said matter-of-factly. "As for O'Brien, they'll give him a couple of more seasons to get the baseball team out of the dungeon. But Kay said they might try to hire someone with more experience after that. Maybe a former minor league player or coach. If they can get one looking to settle in a small town."

"Kay seems to know a helluva lot about what's going on in town," Ben said and met Maddie's amused gaze across the table. And here he'd thought Cora Jean was the biggest gossip in town. But evidently, the competition was stiff for the number one spot.

"Duh, Benjy." Sierra looked at him like he was dense. "Didn't you know Tresses is gossip central?"

"Oh, I knew they gossiped. I just didn't realize the

scope of it."

"They don't talk about me," Sam said confidently.

His father let out a snort. "Oh, they talk about you plenty."

"Really?" Sam cocked his head. "What do they say?"

"You don't want to know."

As Sam attempted to coax their father into spilling the beans, Ben noticed Maddie checking her phone. Seconds later, she looked up, her relaxed expression changing into concern.

"What's wrong?"

"Tanner's hanging around outside the bakery. Mallory said he's been there for almost ten minutes." She got to her feet and, with jerky movements, grabbed her coat and purse from the back of her chair and headed for the exit. "I'm going over there."

Ben's adrenaline kicked in, and he immediately went into cop mode. No way was Maddie going to the bakery alone.

"Isn't Tanner the guy Mallory's dating?" Sam asked as Ben slid his chair back.

"She broke up with him, and he wasn't happy about it. Hold up, Maddie. I'm going with you." He grabbed his jacket, rose from his chair, and high-tailed it after her as she disappeared outside.

"I'm coming too," Sam called after him, but Ben didn't wait for his brother. If Tanner was a threat, he needed to get there as quickly as possible to diffuse the situation.

Along the way to Sweet Temptations, he scanned the area, but there was no sign of Tanner. Mallory was inside when they reached the bakery, pacing in front of the main display case. When she saw them standing outside, she rushed to the door, unlocked it, and pulled it open.

"Where is he?" Maddie asked after they'd entered. "He wasn't outside."

"He left when he saw me texting." Mallory's voice trembled.

"Did he threaten you?" Ben asked in a calm tone even though his stomach was roiling. Only the worst kind of men threatened or intimidated a woman. He'd seen it many times in his career, yet it still made him see red.

"No. He never came inside." Mallory put a hand to her chest and took a deep breath. "He stood in front of the window and stared at me. He had a strange look on his face." She shivered. "It weirded me out."

"Where does this prick live?" Sam demanded. "Someone needs to talk to him, and by talk, I mean kick his ass."

Ben noted Sam's clenched fists and tight jaw. He'd never seen his brother in this state. Even the letters from their mother hadn't elicited this type of anger.

He shot Sam a look of warning. "That's not going to happen."

"He fucking scared Mallory," Sam declared. "He can't get away with that. You need to arrest him. Now."

"I can't arrest him. It's not a crime to stand on a public sidewalk."

"Ben's right," Mallory said. "Maybe I overreacted."

"No." Maddie's sharp tone sliced through the air. "Don't do that. Don't make excuses for him."

"You didn't overreact," Ben quickly assured her. He placed his hand on Mallory's shoulder, giving it a brief squeeze. "I can't arrest him, but I can have a little chat with him when I'm on duty tomorrow."

"Do you think it will help?" Maddie's worried gaze bobbed between him and Mallory.

"It'll let him know he's on my radar and that I'm watching out for Mallory," he said, frustrated by his limited options.

The pinched expression on Maddie's face indicated she wanted to say more, but she pressed her lips together into a firm line and kept silent. He knew exactly what she was thinking. He was thinking it too. A little chat might not be enough if Tanner had turned from ex-boyfriend to stalker. Even a small, peaceful town like Summerwood had its share of abusive men. He'd arrested a few of them.

Sam moved toward the window and peered outside. "I'm staying here until you close up for the night."

Mallory breathed a sigh of relief. "I'd like that, but are you sure it won't be an imposition?"

Sam turned from the window. "It's not an imposition. You're my best friend, and I'm not going to let anyone hurt you." His tone had softened, but Ben knew his brother well. The stubborn intensity in Sam's eyes meant he would not be dissuaded.

"Okay. Thank you." She rubbed her palms down the crisp pink-and-white apron she wore. "All of you." Her solemn gaze traveled over each of them, and after a moment, she gave them a shaky smile. "How about some pie? And coffee? I have some brewing in the back."

An hour later, Ben walked next to Maddie as they headed toward the off-street parking lot where she'd left her car. She had barely spoken since they left the bakery, and knowing her as well as he did, he had no doubt she was running through countless scenarios—none of them good—about Tanner and what type of threat he could be to Mallory.

As the daughter of a cop, she was well aware of the darker side of humanity. As the sister of a woman who might be in danger, she had to be scared to death. He wished he could assure her Mallory was safe, but he'd never lied to her in the past, and he wasn't about to start now. All he could do was pay a visit to Tanner Gates—Mallory had supplied his last name and address—and hope once Tanner was aware he was on law enforcement's radar, he'd back off and leave Mallory alone.

"What's your plan?" Maddie asked as they passed by the plaza. The Christmas tree glittered with colorful lights, and despite the lateness of the hour, many people were still braving the frosty evening to admire its grandeur. "With Tanner."

"I'll inform him there's been a complaint of him loitering outside of a local business. At this point, that's all I can do."

"I hope it's enough. But we both know if Tanner intends to hurt Mallory, a stern warning or even a restraining order won't stop him."

He couldn't argue with that. Just as he knew nothing he said would stop her from worrying about her sister. "I'll get a feel for his state of mind when I talk to him tomorrow. After that, we can regroup and plan our next step. If I know Sam, he'll insist on bunking on Mallory's sofa until he believes she's safe."

"I wish he would. It would take a load off my mind." She pulled her keys out of her purse as they approached the parking lot. "Should we tell my dad about Tanner?"

Ben didn't usually inform the chief about incidents of this nature, but since it involved his daughter, Eli would not take kindly to being kept out of the loop. "Yes. I'll brief him in the morning."

Maddie's car was one of the few left in the lot. She turned toward him, and his breath jammed in his throat. The streetlight bathed her face in a soft ethereal glow that enhanced her delicate features. She was still the most beautiful woman he'd ever seen, and he wanted so badly to kiss her.

Instead of unlocking her door, she gazed up at him and gave him a tremulous smile. "Thank you," she said, and lifting her head, she leaned toward him.

His heart pounded like a jackhammer in his chest. Her soft lips touched his, and it was all he could do not to pull her to him and deepen the kiss. Her mouth on his was gentle, and her kiss so brief it might have been considered nothing more than a peck. But to him, it was much more than that. A mixture of emotions surged inside of him. Emotions that brought up questions he didn't have the answers to. The one thing he *did* know was the attraction between them was still powerful.

When she pulled back, he opened his eyes and met her unreadable gaze.

"That's something else I've missed," she said in a husky voice. She hit the button on the key fob to unlock the door, and before he could say a word, she opened the car door and slid inside. "I'll see you tomorrow."

"Drive safe," he said, still surprised by her unexpected kiss. After closing her door, he watched until she pulled out of the parking lot.

"Drive safe? That's all you've got?" He shook his head in exasperation. "Good one, dumb ass."

Chapter Eleven

Late Thursday morning, Maddie checked her watch for the third time in five minutes. Ben had left the police station over an hour ago to visit Tanner Gates and still hadn't returned. After a mostly sleepless night, she'd been relieved to get a text from Mallory early this morning telling her Sam had insisted on sleeping on her pull-out sofa in case Tanner decided to pay her a late-night visit. He hadn't, and once again, Mallory wondered if she'd made too much of the incident. Maddie assured her she wasn't and made her promise to keep her guard up.

Another reason for her restless night was the kiss she'd laid on Ben. Granted, the kiss had been chaste. Nothing more than the light touch of her mouth against his. But hours later, she could still feel its imprint on her lips. Just thinking about it had her longing for more. Was he thinking about it at all? Or was she the only one obsessing over a peck on the lips?

The lobby door opened. Maddie looked up, hoping it was Ben, but instead, it was Kay Yoffee who stepped inside and headed straight for the reception desk, the soles of her shoes squeaking on the linoleum.

"Hi, Maddie. It's good to see you." Kay smiled, revealing a row of perfectly straight and blindingly white teeth. "It's so thoughtful of you to help out your dad by filling in for Cora Jean."

"Thanks, Kay. It's good to see you too," she said, bracing herself for what could be an inquisition. Kay wasn't the queen of gossip for nothing. "How are things at the salon?"

"Oh, the same as usual." Kay drew off her gloves and stuffed them into her coat pocket. "I've been busy."

"I bet you have," Maddie muttered under her breath.

"Beg pardon?" Creases traced thin lines across Kay's forehead.

She cleared her throat. "Umm, I bet everyone wants to look their best for the holidays. I'm sure you're drowning in appointments."

Kay's forehead smoothed. "It's been a madhouse." She rummaged through her oversized tote bag branded with the Tresses logo and pulled out a covered plastic container. "I'm between clients and thought I'd drop this by for April. I made lasagna last night, and it's her favorite. So I thought she could have it for lunch. Do you mind if I go back to her office?"

"Not at all." She pointed to the visitor's log on the counter. "Just sign in, and you're good to go."

"You betcha." Kay picked up the pen sitting on top of the clipboard. "Will you be in town long?" she asked as she signed the log.

"A few more weeks."

"What's new on the career front? Will we see you at the movies or on television soon?" she asked, setting the pen down. Her questions were innocent enough, but Maddie wasn't fooled. Kay was in full-on snoop mode. The woman thrived on the attention she received from ferreting out personal information about people who lived in Summerwood.

"I'll be auditioning when I get back, so it's

possible."

Kay flashed a sly smile. "So how's your love life? Are you seeing anyone special?"

Whoa. Kay hadn't wasted any time getting personal, and judging by the eager gleam in her eyes, she was hoping to hit the motherlode. Curious to see how quickly Kay worked, Maddie inched forward, resting her forearms on the desk, and met Kay's rapt gaze. "There is someone I've been seeing, but I can't tell you his name," she said, intentionally lowering her voice.

Kay's eyes widened as she instinctively mirrored Maddie's posture and leaned over the counter. "Why? Is he married?"

"No," Maddie said, more than a bit insulted that Kay assumed she would date a married man. "But he's recently divorced, and he hates the tabloid press. If they found out we were seeing each other, the paparazzi would go into a feeding frenzy."

"Oh, my," Kay murmured, her expression practically giddy. "He must be very famous."

She nodded. "Trust me. If I told you his name, you'd know who he is."

"He's a big star?"

"Huge." She tried not to laugh as Kay's mouth fell open. No doubt she was compiling a mental list of the most famous actors in Hollywood. The beauty shop would be abuzz before she started shampooing her next client.

"Ah, sorry to interrupt."

Forgetting Kay, she swiveled her chair around. Ben stood behind her desk, his expression inscrutable.

"What happened?" she asked. "Did you talk to Tanner?"

Ben looked behind her and zeroed in on Kay. "Hey, Kay. Are you here to see April?"

"Yes."

He inclined his head. "You can go on back." After Kay rounded the counter and disappeared, he peeked surreptitiously around the doorframe.

Maddie let out a short laugh and shook her head in amusement.

"What?" he said, looking at her with exasperation.

"Nothing."

He let out an aggrieved sigh. "She's a known eavesdropper."

"I believe you. So did you talk to Tanner?" she asked as he perched on the low file cabinet behind her desk. She tried not to notice how the fabric of his pants stretched over his muscular thighs, but how could she not? He was right in front of her, and the view was glorious.

"He wasn't home." He folded his arms over his broad chest. "At first, I thought he purposely wasn't answering the door. But as I was about to leave, his neighbor pulled into the adjoining driveway—he lives in a duplex—and when I talked to him, he said Tanner asked him to keep an eye on his place and check his mail because he was going out of town."

"Where?"

"Home to visit his family for the holidays."

"I wonder where home is."

"Somewhere in the San Francisco Bay Area, according to the neighbor."

Maddie breathed a sigh of relief. "Well, that's good news. At least we know he won't be bothering Mallory for a while." She hesitated before giving voice to an alternate theory. One she didn't necessarily believe, but one to consider before condemning Tanner without any proof. "Is there any possibility Tanner's visit to the bakery was nothing more than he misses Mallory and wants to see her? Maybe he wanted to talk to her but wasn't sure how to approach her?"

"Anything's possible, but I'd rather err on the side of caution. I'll have Dodd keep an eye on the duplex. It's on his regular patrol route. At least we'll know when Gates is back in town." He regarded her thoughtfully for a few seconds. "You and Kay looked like you were in the middle of a serious conversation when I came in."

"Oh, it was nothing." She waved a dismissive hand. "She was fishing for personal information, and I decided to give her something juicy."

His brows rose. "Like what?"

"Like I'm dating a famous actor."

Something she couldn't decipher flared in his eyes. "*Are* you dating someone?"

"No," she said, unable to keep from smiling. "But I bet by the end of the day, almost everyone in Summerwood will be trying to figure out who my fictitious mystery man is."

Amusement quirked the corners of his mouth. "Oh, there'll be a betting pool on it before then."

"Why am I not surprised?" she said with a shake of her head. "You know, even though almost everyone in town knows everyone else's business, there's a sense of community here that's comforting. I've missed being a part of that."

His eyes flickered with curiosity. "What about the acting community in Los Angeles?"

"I've made a few friends, but we're all so busy with

different things we don't get together often."

"Sounds lonely."

It was. She hadn't realized how much until she came home. "It can be," Maddie said as Carolyn appeared in the doorway.

"The chief wants to see us in his office. Bring your year-to-date patrol stats," Carolyn said to Ben and gave Maddie a quick smile before disappearing down the hallway.

"This will probably take a while." Ben stood. "Do you have plans after work? If not, do you want to grab some dinner?"

Her heart skipped a beat. "I'd love to, but I promised Stevie I'd come by the community theater for our long-overdue chat." She hoped he didn't think she was making an excuse to avoid him.

"How about Saturday night?" A smile quirked his mouth.

"That sounds…wonderful." Her pulse accelerated as his gaze locked with hers, and suddenly, intimacy sparked between them.

The moment was shattered when the lobby door flew open, and the postal carrier cursed loudly as she maneuvered herself through the doorway with a large box in her grasp. Immediately, he crossed the lobby to assist her.

While Ben helped the woman, Maddie tried to tamp down her emotions. Emotions that ran the gamut from nervous to excited. It was ridiculous. Ben's invitation was probably nothing more than a renewal of their friendship. Or was it? They *had* shared a kiss, and the heated look in his eyes just now and last night before the tree lighting ceremony wasn't how one friend looked at another. Unless that friend wanted a lot more than friendship.

After work, Maddie drove straight to the community center, and as she walked through the doors of the theater, her breath caught in her throat as dozens of memories washed over her.

Stevie rose from one of the seats near the stage and made a sweeping gesture with one arm. "Isn't it beautiful?"

Maddie moved slowly down the aisle, taking it in. The theater's footprint hadn't changed, but the old vinyl-covered benches had been replaced with beautiful deep-red leather seats that looked comfortable. The aging flocked wallpaper peeling off the walls had been replaced with acoustic panels, and the aisle was now covered with a subdued red-and-gold patterned carpet.

"It's amazing," she said, stunned over the transformation.

"Come sit with me." Stevie beckoned her with a waving motion. "Rehearsal doesn't start until seven, so we have plenty of time to chat."

Maddie shrugged off her coat, draped it over the back of the seat, and sat down next to Stevie. "I see you're doing *Miracle on 34th Street* this year."

"You can't go wrong with the classics." Stevie brushed back her hair and crossed a slim leg over her knee. "Now tell me *everything*, darling."

Everything? *Oh, hell no.* She couldn't tell her mentor, the woman who had believed in her and encouraged her to pursue her career, that said career was circling the drain. Disappointing Stevie was almost as bad as disappointing her father.

"Well, it's tough. Like you said it would be,"

Maddie began. "But I audition as much as I can, and I take as many acting classes as I can afford. Luckily, the residuals from that series of commercials I did helped the last couple of years."

Stevie nodded. "Commercials can be lucrative."

"My agent is working on getting me an audition for *A New Dawn*. The soap opera."

"These days, you're lucky to get a job on a soap. There aren't many left, so I imagine the competition is fierce." Stevie reached out and covered Maddie's hand with hers. "Tell me the truth, darling. Are you happy?"

Maddie met Stevie's empathetic gaze and bit her lower lip to keep it from trembling. She swung her suddenly blurry gaze to the stage. The stage where she'd felt free and safe. Where her confidence had soared, and she'd felt accepted. She'd gone to Los Angeles brimming with that confidence, but over time it had ebbed. Hollywood could wear down even the most confident person and was far from the nurturing environment Stevie had created. "The happiest time of my life was when I was on that stage. I loved everything about it. It wasn't just acting; it was the whole collaborative effort. Helping with the costumes, the props, and the set design."

Stevie chuckled. "You always were a jack of all trades."

She turned back to Stevie and gave her a wry smile. "As evidenced by my many different jobs."

"Listen to me." Stevie lifted her hand and brushed a lone tear from Maddie's cheek. "If acting is no longer fulfilling for you, I don't recommend continuing to pursue it as a profession. I've been there, so I feel qualified to give you advice."

Maddie stared at her, momentarily speechless. "What do you mean you've been there?" she asked as her brain kicked into gear.

Stevie settled back in her seat, her expression morphing into melancholy. "Like you, I had talent. But after college, when I got to New York, I discovered quickly that I was a small fish in a vast ocean. So for ten years, I worked my butt off. I auditioned for anything and everything. I worked as a waitress in the evenings so I could audition and take acting classes during the day. I booked a lot of small parts, but the closest I ever got to Broadway, which was my dream, was a starring role in an off-Broadway play. I thought that was it—my big break. The show would do so well it would move to Broadway, and I'd be a star. Maybe even win a Tony Award." A heavy sigh escaped her lips. "It closed after one week."

Maddie's heart constricted at the underlying sadness in Stevie's voice. Now she understood why Stevie never talked about New York. It was a painful time in her life. "That must have been so disappointing," she said, touched Stevie had opened up to her.

"I was crushed." Stevie let out a hollow laugh. "That supposed big break? It took years. Years of waiting on tables. Years of sharing a small, cramped apartment with a rotating crop of roommates, who were also my competition. Most of them as talented, if not more so, than me. After the play closed, I realized I had a choice to make. I could stay in New York and continue to hope for that elusive big break, or I could try to find something to make use of my skills, but in a different way."

Maddie tilted her head, curious about Stevie's path to becoming Summerwood High School's drama

151

teacher. "Is that when you decided to become a teacher?"

"In a roundabout way. During one of my weekly calls with my grandmother, she mentioned she was going to the retirement party for the high school's drama teacher. Gran worked at the school. I think she somehow sensed I was at a crossroads in my life, and she asked me if I had any interest in applying for the job." Stevie laughed. "And the rest is history."

"Do you ever regret leaving New York?"

"Never," Stevie said with an adamant shake of her head. "Teaching and now running the community theater group has been far more satisfying."

"I don't know what I'd do if I didn't act." Maddie stared at the stage where she'd brought so many different characters to life. What could be better than that? Yes, maybe acting wasn't as satisfying as it had been back then, but she couldn't imagine her life without it.

"You don't have to give it up. There's a thriving theater community here in Summerwood and the entire valley. You could work and still do theater. With your administrative and computer skills, you'd be an asset anywhere. If you were staying in town, I'd hire you as my theater assistant in a hot second."

"That's sweet of you to say," Maddie said, suddenly a bit light-headed. That Stevie thought she was assistant material was a huge compliment. Her mentor had high expectations and didn't suffer fools. Being Stevie's assistant wouldn't have crossed her mind four years ago. At that time, she had focused solely on finding success as an actor. Now the idea sounded exciting.

"Sweet?" Stevie scoffed. "I don't have the time or the patience to be sweet. Running the theater is a tough job. I wouldn't hire just anyone."

Maddie grinned. "Deny it all you want; you have a heart of gold."

After she watched the cast run through the play, Stevie gave her a tour of the refurbished dressing rooms and the costume and prop areas behind the stage. The whole experience filled her with memories. Wonderful memories she'd kept at bay because it was easier than owning up to her rash decision to leave Summerwood. Ben was right. Proving something to her parents wasn't the only reason why she'd left town. And if he found out, she wouldn't blame him if he never wanted to speak to her again.

****

One of the busiest spots in Summerwood was JD's Pub on half-price rib night. As he wound his way across the crowded restaurant, Ben spotted Sam sitting at a table in the corner not far from the bar. With no plans for the evening, he'd texted his brother from work and asked him if he wanted to grab some dinner.

"Sorry, I'm late." He removed his jacket and draped it over the back of his chair. "I stopped by the bakery to update Mallory on the Tanner situation," he said, sitting down across from Sam.

"Did you tell him to stay the hell away from her?" Sam said, his tone hard.

"I didn't get the chance to tell him anything, but that wouldn't have been my opening gambit if I had."

Sam's brows lowered in a quizzical frown. "Why didn't you talk to him?"

"He's left town for the holidays."

"Are you sure?"

"Reasonably. Gates left his neighbor in charge of checking the mail and putting out his trash and recycle bins on Monday."

"Did you run his name?" Sam set his phone on the table.

"Came back clean. Not even a speeding ticket."

"That could mean he just hasn't been caught." Sam's expression darkened. "Mom's the perfect example of that."

"No argument there," he said, hoping that would be the last mention of their mother. He wanted to enjoy the evening, not dredge up painful memories. "What's going on with that auction property you bought outside of town last year? Are you planning to flip it?" He pushed the menu aside. He already knew what he wanted.

"Maybe." Sam averted his gaze. "I haven't decided."

"What about the Rosebud reno? What's up with that?"

"About the same as the last time we talked." He looked over the menu. "The Californians can't make up their minds about anything. Even the name of the place."

"What type of business is it?"

"A dog boutique."

"A dog boutique?" He shook his head. "I don't even want to know what that is."

"It's a business catering to dog owners. They sell specialty dog treats, clothes, leashes, and collars." Sam looked up from his menu. "The whole nine yards."

"Dog clothes?"

"Yeah. It's a thing." Sam grinned. "My friend in Portland dresses her dog in a Trail Blazers dog jersey."

"Friend?"

"With excellent benefits." Sam gave him a knowing smile. "You should try it."

"No, thanks."

His brother narrowed his gaze. "You and Maddie seemed pretty chummy at the tree lighting ceremony last night. And I saw how you were looking at her at Callie's before she got that text from Mallory."

"How was I looking at her?" he asked, annoyed at his brother's observation skills.

"Like you used to when you were together. You need to be careful."

"What do you mean?"

"Unless she's recently changed her mind, she's out of here after Christmas. If you get involved with her again, it can only end one way. Not good."

Ben bristled. "Don't worry about me. I can take care of myself. Besides, Maddie and I are just friends."

Sam snorted. "Famous last words."

"You and Mallory are just friends," he retorted.

"That's *all* we are. Mallory and I aren't in love with each other. And I would never ruin our friendship by sleeping with her." Sam glowered at him. "This isn't about me; it's about you. Look, I like Maddie, but her career will always come first."

Their server arrived to take their order before he could respond. While Sam exchanged flirty small talk with the attractive blonde, his brother's words echoed in his head. He wasn't naïve. In a few weeks, Maddie would be gone. Again. He knew this, and yet he couldn't seem to stop thinking about her or wanting to spend time with her. Sam had warned him to be careful, but he didn't want to be careful.

He wanted Maddie.

Chapter Twelve

"Mom! Where's the box with the Christmas stockings and Santa hats?" Maddie called out from the top of the stairs. "I looked in the attic, but I can't find it."

"It's in the garage," her mother's muffled voice drifted up from the kitchen.

She hurried down the stairs and made her way to the kitchen. "Is the box marked?" she asked as she pulled on the red fleece hoodie she'd borrowed from Mallory.

"Of course. You know your father." Her mom turned from the counter with a *World's Best Dentist* mug cradled between her palms. "Everything in the garage has a label on it."

She grinned. "How could I forget? When are you and Dad getting the tree? Christmas is in less than three weeks." She was looking forward to helping to decorate the tree and the house. It was a family tradition and one she'd missed.

"We're going out to the tree farm this afternoon." She sipped her coffee. "I've invited Mallory over tomorrow morning for brunch. I thought we could all decorate the tree together."

"What about Lauren? I thought you wanted to wait for her to get here before decorating."

"She's not coming home."

"What? Why not?"

"Her vacation was canceled. They're shorthanded at

the hospital. She called last night to let us know."

"I'm sorry, Mom. I know you were looking forward to all of us being together," she said as a seed of doubt sprang to life in her mind. Something seemed off about the situation. Was Lauren's absence due to her job, or was she avoiding her family?

"It is what it is." Her mother shrugged, but disappointment was etched on her face. "Lauren has a critical job, and they need her. However, she did say she may be able to visit early next year." She nodded toward the coffee maker. "Do you want some coffee before you leave?"

"No, thanks," Maddie said, zipping the hoodie. "I need to find those hats and get going. I don't want to be late for the 5k. Mallory's meeting me there."

Vertical worry lines creased her mother's brow. "Your father told me about Tanner. When I met him at the football game on Thanksgiving, he seemed polite. Do you believe he's a threat to Mallory?"

Did she? His actions could be calculated or completely innocent. He hadn't made any overt threats. "I'm not sure."

"Maybe Mallory should move home for a while."

"I don't think that's necessary. And I doubt Mallory would agree. But I can mention it to her if you'd like."

"No. You're right. Mallory has a good head on her shoulders, and she knows she can stay here if she needs to." Her mother patted Maddie's arm. "Have fun today."

Due to her father's propensity to meticulously label every storage box in the garage, Maddie arrived not far from the starting line banner with ten minutes to spare. Mallory was easy to spot in the crowd. She'd dressed in several layers, the last being a neon-pink T-shirt with the

Sweet Temptations logo and address on the front and back. It didn't scream Santa or even Christmas, but it might attract customers to the bakery after the event.

Maddie headed for Mallory, dodging both humans and dogs dressed in Santa costumes of all variations. Judging by the number of people milling around, the event was shaping up to be a success. Next to a podium near the water station, Clarice and Bert Worley were talking to Traci Kemp. While Clarice and Traci had both gone the Mrs. Santa route, Clarice had opted for the traditional, more matronly Mrs. Claus look, whereas Traci, in her form-fitting red-and-white top and skirt paired with black leggings, had gone for a more modern version of Santa's wife.

As Maddie approached her sister, she stopped short and stared down at the cute dog that, with its fluffy gray-and-white fur, looked like it was part poodle, sitting next to Mallory. "When did you get a dog?"

"I didn't. This is Bailey. She belongs to Sam." Mallory gazed fondly at Bailey, who looked positively adorable in her Santa costume. A hood with small antlers attached to it partially covered her head, and a small stuffed Santa Claus had been sewn onto the back of the outfit, which made it appear he was riding on Bailey's back. "Sam had plans in Portland this weekend, so I offered to dog-sit."

"What's he doing in Portland?"

"Banging some chick." Mallory gave her a cheeky grin. "He thinks I don't know, but his friends-with-benefits situation has been discussed ad nauseam at Tresses."

"Are you okay with that?"

Mallory gave her a puzzled look. "Why wouldn't I

be?"

"Well, you did have a crush on him."

"That was ages ago." She waved a dismissive hand. "I was a child. Besides, Sam isn't one for long-term relationships. As soon as something starts to get serious, he bails."

"I guess that makes you his longest non-family relationship."

"Yep." Mallory nodded toward Bailey. "I am, however, madly in love with his dog. The rescue group said she's a poodle-terrier mix. And she's the best dog in the world. Aren't you, sweetie?" As if she knew she was being discussed, Bailey wagged her fluffy tail.

"Please tell me we aren't going to run the whole way." She handed Mallory the extra Santa hat. "You know I only exercise because I have to."

Mallory chuckled. "Almost everyone walks, and Bailey and I are fine with it. I scoped out the route, and the halfway mark is near Summerwood Slice. Since we're doing the 5k for fun and don't care how long it takes to finish, why don't we stop there for a break? I've been craving their pizza all week. And I brought treats for Bailey."

"Excellent idea, Mal." She crouched and gave Bailey's neck a playful scratch. "Do you want to take a lunch break during the walk?" Bailey's tail continued to wag as she licked Maddie's cheek. "I think that's a yes." She chuckled.

"It looks like someone made a new friend."

Maddie looked up and, for a second, almost didn't recognize Ben. He'd walked up to stand next to Mallory, dressed in an authentic Santa Claus costume. A snow-white mustache and bushy beard covered the lower portion of his face, but the old-timey wire-rimmed glasses couldn't disguise those mesmerizing blue eyes.

"Wow, way to commit." She stood and poked his fake belly. "I'm not sure what a bowl full of jelly feels like, but this is close."

Mallory turned and tilted her head, giving him the once-over. "Forget the belly. How are you going to run in those clunky boots?"

"I'm not." Ben hooked his thumbs into the wide black belt encircling his huge stomach. "The guy they hired to play Santa bailed, and I volunteered to take his place. I'll be taking pictures with the kids after the event."

Mallory's eyes widened. "Are you kidding? Do you know how tired and cranky those kids are going to be? And it won't be just pictures. They'll want to sit on your lap and tell you what they want for Christmas."

"It'll be fine." The tone of his voice wasn't nearly as confident as his words. He looked at Maddie with wide eyes. "Right?"

"First of all." She held up a hand. "Let me preface this by saying that this was strictly my own experience. Your mileage may vary. But last Christmas, I worked a seasonal gig at a mall in Glendale. I was one of Santa's elves, and it…" She shuddered at the memory. "It was hell on earth. One of the worst jobs I've ever had, and I wasn't even Santa." She shook her head, making a *tsking* sound. "*That* poor guy. I thought he would have a breakdown before our last day."

"You're joking." His eyes flickered with apprehension. "Aren't you?"

"I wish I was. But I've never seen or heard so many crying kids and obnoxious parents in my life. It was a madhouse."

Mallory patted Ben's arm and gave him an encouraging smile. "Good luck, man. You're going to need it."

Ben shot them both a dour look. "You're messing with me, and I'm not falling for it." He checked his watch. "I need to head over there and get ready." He swung his gaze toward Maddie. "I'll pick you up at your folks' house at seven if that works for you."

"Will you be wearing that outfit?" she asked with a cheeky grin. "If so, then yes, it works for me."

"Very funny." He grimaced. "I'll see you later."

"Picking you up for what?" Mallory asked after Ben was out of earshot.

"Dinner."

"You and Ben are having dinner?" She frowned. "The two of you?"

"Yes."

"So it's a date."

"It's dinner."

"Sounds like a date to me. Is that wise? You're leaving after Christmas." After a few silent seconds, Mallory's eyes narrowed. "Aren't you?"

Maddie bit her lower lip. "That was the plan." A few weeks ago, her answer would have been an unequivocal yes, but today she wasn't sure. Going back to LA and her lonely life there held little appeal.

"Was?" Mallory leveled her with an assessing gaze. "Are you thinking of staying in Summerwood?"

"Maybe," she said and hesitated. She had no clue how Mallory would react to her giving up her career in Hollywood. Would she be happy, disappointed, or worse, believe Maddie was a failure? "Being back home has made me realize how much I've missed it."

And Ben.

"What about your acting career?"

"Truthfully, Mal, it's barely paying the bills," she said, surprised at her relief after saying it aloud. It was as if a thousand-pound boulder had been lifted from her chest. "I don't know what I'm going to do. I've got a lot to think about."

As the event's emcee instructed all participants to report to the starting line, she searched her sister's face and found no trace of judgment. Just the opposite. Mallory's expression was beaming as she looped her arm through Maddie's and pulled her close as they shuffled forward. "I, for one, hope you decide to stay. I've missed you. A lot."

"I've missed you." She squeezed Mallory's arm, grateful for her sister's love and support. "And your cupcakes."

****

La Rambla was one of Ben's favorite restaurants, and he'd selected it for a couple of reasons. One, they served the best Spanish tapas he'd ever tasted, and two, it wasn't in Summerwood. The last thing he wanted was for him and Maddie to become the latest grist for the gossip mill at Tresses.

In a quiet corner of the restaurant, Maddie sat across from him. Although modest, the black sweater dress she wore clung to her curves, and her strawberry-blonde hair framed the creamy complexion of her face. In the diffused light of the dining room, her eyes sparkled like blue crystals. She was absolutely stunning.

The drive to McMinnville had been like stepping back in time. Any fear he might have had about awkward silences between them had been abated by the sound of Maddie's laughter as he gave her a blow-by-blow description of his experience as Santa at the 5k run. It reminded him of the many dates they'd gone on when they were together—relaxed and fun.

"So tell me the truth." He leaned back in his chair and got comfortable. "Is it wrong for me to wish Cora Jean would stay in Seattle with her daughter?"

"No." She shook her head as she picked up her wineglass. "It's not like you wish her harm."

"I wonder why your father keeps her on. He has to know she can barely do the job."

"I can tell you exactly why he keeps her," she said before sipping her wine.

His gaze was immediately drawn to her mouth, and he lost his train of thought for a moment. How many times had he kissed her lips? Too many to count.

"Why?" He forced himself to concentrate on their conversation, not on the memories of their past physical intimacy. He lifted his glass and took a drink of his sparkling water.

"She saved Lauren's life."

He nearly spit out his water. "How? When?"

"One summer when we were kids, Lauren, Mallory, and I went to The Candy Emporium—"

"The Candy Emporium?" He squinted, trying to place the business. "Never heard of it."

"It went out of business before your family moved to Summerwood." She set her glass on the table. "Anyway, we'd decided to use some of our allowance money to buy our favorite candy. I loved anything tart and sweet, Mallory favored malt balls, and Lauren loved any kind of gummy candy. Worms, bears, if it was gummy or super chewy, she'd eat it. Anyway, we walked over to the plaza and sat on one of the benches. Lauren shoved a huge handful of the gummies into her mouth, and a few seconds later, she started choking." A light shudder shook Maddie's shoulders. "It was terrifying. Both Mallory and I freaked out; we had no idea what to do. We started screaming for help. Cora Jean happened to be passing by and immediately ran over. When she got to us, Lauren couldn't breathe. Her face was bright red, and her eyes were bulging out of her head. Without missing a beat, Cora Jean performed the Heimlich and dislodged a huge wad of candy from Lauren's throat."

He couldn't imagine Cora Jean acting with such a sense of urgency. But, on the other hand, maybe he'd misjudged her. "That was quick thinking on her part."

"We were lucky she was nearby. My dad, of course, was beyond grateful, and I remember him telling Cora Jean that if she ever needed anything, all she had to do was ask."

"So when she needed a job, he hired her, and that's also why he won't fire her."

Maddie nodded. "Bingo."

He set his glass on the table and stared at Maddie for a good long moment as the implications of Cora Jean's heroic act sank in. "That means Cora Jean will be at the front desk until she's ready to leave on her terms."

"I'm afraid so." Her expression filled with empathy. "Sorry."

"So I'll only have fond memories of these few short weeks when we had someone competent." He heaved an annoyed sigh. "I foresee a lot of frustration in my future."

"Hey, look on the bright side." A winsome smile curved her lips.

"Bright side?" He cocked his head. "Is there one?"

"If you choke on something, she can save your life."

Ben laughed. "Somehow, that doesn't make it any easier. I wish we could clone you."

"Clone me?" She chuckled. "Isn't one of me enough?"

"More than enough." He grinned. "I meant you've done a great job filling in. If you were staying in Summerwood, I'd beg your father to replace Cora Jean with you. And I wouldn't be the only one begging. Carolyn and the other two sergeants would be in line right behind me."

Her cheeks turned a light shade of pink, and her eyes suddenly welled with tears. "Thank you for saying that."

"It's true. You'd be a huge asset to the department." He leaned forward, unprepared for the tears glistening in her eyes. "Hey, what's wrong?"

"Nothing." She reached up and wiped the corners of her eyes with her napkin. "I've gotten so many rejections lately. It's nice to hear something positive."

"I'm sorry. That must be rough."

"It's part of the job. I try not to take it personally because it isn't. The number of roles available at any given time versus the number of actors looking for work is minuscule." She lowered the napkin to her lap and stared at it. "When…when I went to see Stevie a few days ago, she asked me if I was happy."

"Are you?" His pulse spiked. He leaned forward, eager to hear her answer.

"When I was sitting in the theater with her, I realized the last time I was truly happy was when I was on that stage."

She lifted her gaze to his, and the emotion in her

eyes was like a tripwire to his heart. It started thudding.

"I had everything I wanted and didn't even know it."

Ben stared at her, the implication of her words hitting him like a truckload of bricks. "That's a coincidence," he said after several seconds. "The last time I was truly happy was when you were on that stage. I had everything I wanted, and I knew it."

She hesitated as if considering her words. "I know I've said this before, but I need to say it again. I'm sorry I hurt you," she said softly. "I mean it, Ben. I'm truly sorry."

This was the second time she'd apologized. The first time he had been wary of trusting she meant it, but this time, his gut told him she was being honest. "I believe you."

A soft sigh of relief escaped her lips. "But…but can you forgive me?"

A mixture of fear and hope shimmered in her eyes. She was a good actress, but he knew her well enough to know she wasn't faking. His breath caught in his throat, and his heart started to pound. Her emotional admission that she was genuinely sorry for her actions was something he hadn't realized he needed to hear until this moment. "Yes. I forgive you."

She gave him a tremulous smile. "Thank you. That means more than I can say."

As their waiter returned to take their order, he tore his gaze from hers and tried to remember what dish he'd decided on when he looked at the menu. Good thing the menu was still on the table; he couldn't think of anything but Maddie.

The atmosphere between him and Maddie on the drive back to Summerwood wasn't dramatically different. But in the confines of the car, an intimacy between them that hadn't been there before infused the air. He couldn't determine if La Rambla's excellent food had mellowed them or because they'd taken the first step in putting their past to rest without actually saying it aloud.

The beams of his headlights played upon Maddie's car and the chief's city-issued vehicle as he pulled into the driveway. It wasn't yet eleven, but other than the porch light, the house was dark.

After pulling his car behind Maddie's, he got out and rounded the front to open the passenger door. Maddie smiled her thanks as she slipped out and waited while he closed the door. Walking beside her toward the porch, Ben caught a hint of her perfume. The subtle floral scent swirled around him and heightened his senses.

"Thank you for dinner," she said as they halted at the front door. "I had a wonderful time."

"You're welcome. I did too." He rubbed his hands together to warm them. The temperature had dropped dramatically since they'd left for McMinnville. "I drove by the movie theater this morning, and they're showing *The Holiday* on Friday night."

"I love that movie, but then I love anything Kate Winslet is in."

"Would you like to go with me to see it?"

"I'd love to." Her radiant smile took his breath away. "But I'll have to meet you there. Carolyn is taking me out for drinks after work to thank me for filling in for Cora Jean. Next week is my last week, remember?"

"I remember." As if he could forget. He'd gotten used to seeing her at work and was trying hard not to think about her impending departure. "When are you going back to Hollywood?"

"I'm not sure I am."

He sucked in a breath. "You're thinking of staying in town?"

She tilted her head, regarding him solemnly. "I'm considering it."

"But what about acting?" he asked, trying to tamp down the kernel of hope ballooning inside of his chest. "You love it."

"I don't have to stop acting. There are plenty of theater productions in the valley."

Stunned, he ran a hand through his hair. When Maddie had first returned to Summerwood, she had been adamant about continuing her career. What had changed? And was he a fool to think it might have something to do with him? "I have to admit I'm surprised. What brought this on?"

"A combination of things." Her eyes were difficult to decipher in shadows. "But I'm taking my time with this decision." She took a step forward, placing her hand on his arm.

The intoxicating scent of her perfume again drifted into his senses, making him almost light-headed.

"It's too important not to."

"A lot of people would be happy if you decided to stay."

"Good to know," she said with a soft laugh. "I'd better go inside before we both freeze to death."

"Yes, you should." As his gaze roamed over her face, all he could think about was kissing her.

She leaned toward him. It was an almost imperceptible move, but one that made it clear she was feeling the same thing he was.

"Jesus, Maddie. You are *so* damn beautiful." Lowering his head, he heard the swift intake of her breath right before his mouth covered hers. After that, nothing else registered except her lips tasted as sweet as he remembered. And they were soft...so soft as they parted, and she returned his kiss with an urgency that surprised him.

She tasted like the Spanish wine she'd sipped at dinner. Plum and dark berries. He savored it, deepening their kiss until she placed her palm against his chest. With a low groan, he pulled back. Her eyelids fluttered open, and when their eyes met, he felt an instinctual tightening low in his gut.

"For the record, that kiss was in no way an attempt to sway your decision. I've wanted to do that since I picked you up tonight."

Her gaze lowered to his mouth, lingering long enough for him to yearn to kiss her again. "Would you have kissed me even if I wasn't considering staying?" she asked.

"Honestly? Yes." He lifted his hand and gently brushed the curve of her cheek with his thumb. "I tried, Maddie. I really did. But I've never gotten you out of my system."

"That's a coincidence. I haven't gotten you out of my system either." A sultry smile curved her lips. "Good night, Ben," she said softly and turned to open the door.

After she disappeared inside, Ben stood on the porch until she turned off the outside light. In the darkness, he allowed himself to hope that Maddie would return to Summerwood for good. Hope could be a dangerous thing, but now that it had sparked to life inside of him, he couldn't do a damn thing to extinguish it.

****

Maddie locked the door behind her, turned off the porch light, and for a moment stood in the darkened foyer, relishing the moment. Tonight she'd become keenly aware the attraction between her and Ben had never died. For either of them. That kiss had proved it. That kiss…oh boy…that kiss had melted her insides and left her wanting more. She was sure the possibility of more would keep her awake long after climbing into bed.

A high-pitched whistle from the kitchen cut through the silence and her increasingly erotic thoughts. Reluctantly shaking them off, she crossed the living room, entered the kitchen, and found her mom. "Hey," she said softly.

"Hi, honey." Her mother set the kettle on the stove, picked up her cup and a saucer, and moved to sit at the table in the breakfast nook.

"You always drink tea when you're worried about something." Maddie pulled off her coat, folded it over the back of the chair, and sat down across from her mother. "Or someone."

"That's something I inherited from my mother." She dunked the tea bag several times but left it in the cup to steep. "Whenever there was a crisis, Mom brewed a pot of tea. The night I told her and your grandpa that I wanted to go to a dental college instead of medical school, she made two pots."

"How could that be a crisis?" Maddie asked. "There's nothing wrong with being a dentist."

"You'd think so, right? But it wasn't good enough for my father. For as long as I can remember, he wanted me to be a medical doctor. It started when it became clear I had an aptitude for science and math. They were my favorite school courses." She laughed, but it was hollow. "While Dad was bragging about my excellent grades and proclaiming to anyone who would listen that I was going to medical school, I had already cultivated an interest in dentistry. I was that weird kid who enjoyed going to the dentist. I loved everything about it. Even the strange dentist office smell."

"But Grandpa has always seemed so proud of you. He was thrilled when you opened your practice. I remember the grand opening; he gave that corny speech and started crying."

"That's because long before then, I'd found the guts to tell him that his dreams weren't my dreams. And that I loved him and respected him, but I had to follow my own path." She reached across the table and patted Maddie's forearm. "Like you did by going to Hollywood."

Maddie tilted her head and frowned. "You think that's why I went?"

"Isn't it?" Her mom arched a brow. "Why else would you have gone?"

She stared at her mother, at a loss for words. For years she had convinced herself that she'd been following her own path. But in reality, she'd been running away. Away from her fear of failure and her fear of committing to Ben. Her actions were the exact opposite of her mother's brave stance.

"Maddie?"

She blinked, and her mother's concerned face came into focus. "I'm sorry. What?"

"Are you okay? You looked stricken."

"I'm fine, Mom." Despite the churning of her stomach, she managed a reassuring smile. "So tell me why you're having tea. What or who are you worried about? Is it Mallory?"

"The Tanner situation is troubling, but I'm more worried about Lauren tonight. She called me again this evening, very upset."

"Why?" she asked, once again thinking something was off with her sister. Lauren wasn't one to get upset easily. At least she hadn't in the past.

"A patient she's been caring for at the hospital passed away this morning. She'd grown attached to the young woman, and she's not taking it well."

Maddie's heart clenched. "That's awful," she said and instantly understood why Lauren would reach out to their mother.

"Yes. And Lauren's always had a soft heart." She sighed. "I wish she was coming home for Christmas. Call it a mother's instinct, but I think she needs us right now."

"I'll call Lauren tomorrow," she said, hoping to alleviate her mother's worry. "Maybe we can do a video chat with her on Christmas Day. It won't be the same as her being here, but it's close. When I talk to her, I'll ask her what her schedule is and set it up."

"That would be wonderful. I'm so happy you thought of it." Her expression brightened. She lifted the tea bag from the cup and placed it on the saucer. "So how was dinner?" She raised her cup, peering at Maddie over the rim. "Did you have a good time?"

"Yes." Maddie's stomach fluttered as the memory of Ben's kiss washed over her. The kiss was amazing, and the fact that he had finally forgiven her equally so. She was beginning to think that not getting either of the two roles she'd auditioned for had happened for a reason. It had given her the opportunity to reevaluate her priorities and the direction of her life, as well as a chance to reconnect with Ben.

Now all she had to do was make the most significant decision of her life.

Chapter Thirteen

A week later, on Friday morning, Maddie almost dropped her coffee cup when she noticed the bouquet sitting on the counter above her desk. The bouquet, a mixture of pink roses, red and white carnations, and another pink flower she didn't know the name of were artfully arranged in a clear glass vase and were gorgeous.

Setting her purse and cup on the desk, she plucked the attached envelope from the arrangement, quickly opened it, and read the enclosed card.

Maddie,

Words can't express how much we appreciate all you've done for us. You've become a part of the family in a few short weeks. To say we'll miss you is an understatement. Thank you for putting up with us and making our lives so much easier.

Fondly,

Carolyn and the sergeants

She blinked as tears welled in her eyes. She'd known her last day would be emotional, but she hadn't expected waterworks so early in the day. Gazing at the flowers, she wiped the corners of her eyes and carefully replaced the card in the envelope.

"Maddie."

The sound of her father's voice startled her. Whirling around, she found him standing in the doorway, still wearing his overcoat and carrying his briefcase.

He looked past her and flashed a wry smile. "Cora Jean has never gotten flowers from the staff."

"Not even for her birthday?" Maddie asked, feeling a bit sorry for Cora Jean.

"Oh, Carolyn usually gets her a cake for her birthday, and we all chip in for something for her at Christmas, but I've never seen the sergeants get together with Carolyn to discuss doing something special for her. But they did for you. That says something. You've made a difference here, Maddie. I'm proud of you."

"Thanks, Dad," she said with a tremulous smile. She couldn't remember her father ever saying those words to her before. She had always imagined she'd hear them if she ever landed a starring role in a film or television series, but not for doing what she'd always done at every job she'd ever held.

Not one for emotional conversations, he shifted and cleared his throat. "Well, I'd better get to my office. I have a conference call in a half hour, and I need to prep for it," he said and gave her a brisk nod before retreating down the hallway toward his office.

Ben appeared in the doorway before Maddie could fully absorb what had just happened. "Do you like the flowers?"

"I love them." Her heart fluttered at the sight of him. "I'm a sucker for pink roses."

"I remember." The intensity in his eyes caused her stomach to flip-flop.

"Did you pick them out?" she asked, her cheeks warming.

He lifted a shoulder in a nonchalant half shrug. "I may have given some input. But more importantly, I vetoed the fern idea."

She laughed. "That had to be Cooper's suggestion. He has three ferns in his office. Every time I walk by, he's spraying them with a plant mister."

"You should see his house." He cringed. "His living room looks like a jungle."

"I can hear you!" Sergeant Cooper yelled from his office next to the hallway. "And I happen to like the jungle."

Maddie stifled a giggle and met Ben's amused gaze. "Busted," she whispered.

He leaned against the doorway. "I'll be out in the field with my new officer this morning and in a training class after lunch, so I wanted to check in with you about the movie tonight. The second showing starts at eight. Will that work for you?"

"Definitely." She nodded. "Carolyn and I are going to JD's for drinks. That's not too far from the theater. I'll meet you there around seven forty-five."

"Sounds good." A smile quirked his mouth. "I'll spring for the popcorn."

"As you should. You always end up eating most of it, anyway," she shot back with a grin.

Before he could reply, the lobby door opened, and the cheerful expression on his face slowly faded. Maddie swung around and inwardly sighed. If there was one person she wouldn't miss seeing from the station, it was Traci. She assumed Traci felt the same way. Although Traci was never overtly rude, she only spoke to Maddie when she had to.

"Good morning," Traci said, her tone pleasant and her gaze quickly flitting from Maddie to Ben. "I was hoping to run into you. Can we talk?"

He pushed off the doorframe and checked his watch.

"I can spare a few minutes." He motioned to her with his hand. "Come on back to my office."

Traci glanced at the bouquet. "Nice flowers." Her wide smile seemed genuine. "I bet you can't wait to get back to Hollywood. I'm sure Summerwood seems dull in comparison. Good luck with your career."

"Thank you," Maddie said as they disappeared down the hallway.

The week since her dinner date with Ben had been a busy one. After brunch on Sunday, she and Mallory helped decorate the Christmas tree their parents had picked out, and afterward, while her dad put the lights on the house, they had fun going through all the boxes of holiday décor her parents had collected over the years. The entire house was a festive ode to Christmas when they were done.

She'd also touched base with Lauren and was able to set up a video chat for Christmas Day. After the phone call, she understood why her mother was worried. Lauren's monotone and short responses were entirely out of character. But she'd brushed off Maddie's concerns, saying she was busy and didn't have time to talk. Maddie didn't push her and couldn't help but wonder if dealing with life and death on a daily basis had taken its toll on her sister.

At work, she'd finished up a step-by-step guide for the sergeants detailing exactly how to use the pivot table and macro she'd created to run their monthly reports and helped Carolyn wrap up several projects. At the end of the day, she would unpack Cora Jean's knickknacks box and leave the desk exactly as she'd found it.

No. You'll leave it better than you found it.

She let a self-satisfied smile break free. Yes, she

would.

****

Ben's Spidey sense kicked in as Traci closed his office door behind her. Usually, when she dropped by his office, an invitation of some sort was involved. He hoped this wasn't one of those occasions.

"What did you want to talk about?" He moved behind his desk and sat down.

Traci loosened the red-and-black scarf around her neck and gave him a bright smile. "Are you going to the Jingle Ball next weekend?"

Ben frowned. The Jingle Ball? He'd forgotten all about the event. The annual benefit dance was sponsored by the chamber of commerce, and the money raised from ticket sales was used to beautify downtown Summerwood. The last time he'd gone was with Maddie. They'd ducked out early to spend the night alone together. They'd stopped on their way to his house to pick up a bottle of wine and then spent the rest of the evening sitting in front of the fire, sipping wine, talking, and making out like school kids.

"I hadn't planned on it."

"Why don't we go together? They have a live band this year." Her green eyes sparkled with excitement. "It should be fun."

"I don't think that's a good idea."

Her eyes lost a bit of their luster. "Why not?"

"Well, for one, we work together."

"We work for the SPD, but I'm in the ECC, which isn't in your chain of command." She tilted her head and narrowed her gaze. "You said for one. What's number two?"

Time to man up, buddy.

"I appreciate the invitation, and if I'm off base, I apologize." He picked up the pen on his desk and tapped it on a notepad several times. This was a moment to choose his words carefully. "But I'm not interested in anything more than a working relationship."

Traci's mouth pressed into a tight line, and for several long seconds, a taut silence reigned between them. "It's Maddie, isn't it? Ever since she came back to town, you've ignored me."

"That's not true," he said, wincing inside because she wasn't wrong. "We've spoken several times."

"You couldn't take your eyes off her the night we played darts," she said, her voice as cold as the Willamette River in January. "Why did you even come that night if you weren't interested?"

He ran a hand through his hair. Why hadn't he listened to the little voice inside his head telling him not to go to the pub that night? "Because my brother would be there, and…and I didn't want to hurt your feelings."

"I see." Her chin rose imperiously. "I feel sorry for you, Ben. You have a blind spot when it comes to Maddie. As soon as the holidays are over, she's going back to Hollywood and her precious career, and where will you be? In the same spot you were four years ago." She turned and marched to the door. "Alone," she fired her parting shot and stalked out of his office.

Blowing out a long breath, he leaned back in his chair. Staring at the detailed map of Summerwood on the wall across from his desk, he replayed Traci's scathing prediction in his head. Was she right about Maddie? About him? Did he have a blind spot when it came to Maddie? Sure, Maddie said she was considering staying in town, but that's all she was doing—considering it.

Maybe he was a fool, but a gut instinct told him Maddie would remain in Summerwood. He hoped his gut was right.

****

At a little past their appointed meeting time, Maddie found Ben waiting outside the Summerwood Cinema. When he caught sight of her and his mouth tipped in a lazy, sexy smile, her heart did a double somersault. "Sorry, I'm a few minutes late. A few of the officers joined us, and it took a bit longer than I expected to say my goodbyes."

"It's okay. I already bought our tickets." He motioned toward the glass doors. "Shall we?"

After a quick visit to the concession stand for popcorn and drinks, Maddie settled into her seat next to Ben and adjusted her reclining seat to the perfect position. Ben nestled the popcorn bag on his thigh next to their shared armrest and adjusted his seat in a similar position.

The usual advertisements had started playing on the movie screen. Maddie sipped her soda, acutely aware of Ben and the subtle scent of his cologne. Although her week had been busy, she'd had plenty of time to think about their kiss on the porch. And plenty of time to think about doing it again.

"I'm not sure *The Holiday* classifies as a Christmas movie." She placed her cup into the holder on her armrest.

Ben reached into the bag and snagged a handful of popcorn. "It's literally called *The Holiday*."

"Yes, and don't get me wrong, I love the movie, but there's barely any mention of Christmas other than the opening scene. But we do get that nice scene with Iris and Miles sharing a Hanukkah meal with Arthur and his friends." She shifted in her seat to study him as he munched on the popcorn. "This isn't your kind of movie. Why did you want to see it?"

"Because I knew you would," he said. "You have a crush on Kate Winslet. Or at least you used to."

"I still do," she said. "In my opinion, she's brilliant. And you're one to talk, Mr. I've Watched *Castaway* a Million Times."

"Hey, Tom Hanks made me care about a volleyball. Now, that's acting."

"I remember you shedding a tear or two after Wilson fell off the raft and floated away."

"I did." A smile crinkled the corners of his eyes. "And I'm not ashamed to admit it."

"That's brave. Not many men will admit they cried over a volleyball," she said as the lights dimmed. "The movie's starting so—"

"I know. No talking." He shook his head and chuckled. "You and your movie rules." He leaned closer. "Refresh my memory. Do you have a rule against making out during the movie?"

Her breath hitched. "It's on the list, but you know what they say. Some rules are meant to be broken."

His gaze lowered to her mouth, a wicked smile curving his lips. "I'll file that away for future reference."

After the credits rolled and they'd left the theater, she walked beside Ben, slightly disappointed they hadn't made out during the movie. But then again, they weren't teenagers, and anybody could have seen them. She could only imagine *that* discussion at Tresses.

Outside, she glimpsed a man with dirty blond hair. She tensed, then let out a sigh of relief when he turned, and it wasn't Tanner. "Is Officer Dodd still driving by Tanner's house?" she asked as they crossed the street and headed toward the parking lot.

"Yeah. There's been no indication Gates is back in town."

She buttoned her coat to ward off the cold air. "I hope we're wrong about him."

"Me too." He waved at a car's driver, who'd stopped at the crosswalk to let them pass. "I still plan to talk to him when he returns."

"I appreciate that, and I know Mallory does too."

He shot her a quick glance. "So now that your stint at the station is over, what do you plan to do next week?"

"Mom and I are going Christmas shopping, and I'm helping out Mallory at the bakery." She would also be thinking about her future and where she would be spending it. "She's got a ton of orders to fill. Sweet Temptations is doing well. I'm so happy for her."

"She's put a lot of heart into it." Suddenly, he stopped dead in his tracks. "Oh, hell no."

She jolted to a halt beside him. "What? What's wrong?"

"Kay Yoffee sighting. Directly ahead." He grabbed her hand. "C'mon. I'm not in the mood to talk to her. Let's go around the block. There's another entrance to the parking lot."

Maddie felt like a fugitive on the lam from the law as they hurriedly retraced their route and turned the corner. Halfway down the block, they slowed their steps, but he didn't let go of her hand, and she was more than okay with that. Being with Ben like this was at once both familiar and new. She didn't want the night to end.

"Do you think she saw us?" She glanced over her

shoulder and breathed a sigh of relief when the only other person on the street was a man walking his dog.

"I don't think so. She was talking to Daisy Connors."

"Is Daisy still working for your dad?"

He nodded. "She runs the office like a drill sergeant. Dad complains, but he'd be lost without her. I think they enjoy butting heads."

Still holding hands, they walked the rest of the way in companionable silence. Maddie tilted her face to the sky, marveling at the stars above. In Los Angeles, the stars weren't nearly as bright. She'd forgotten how brilliant and beautiful they could be.

As they approached her car, he let go of her hand, and immediately, she missed the warmth of his touch. "Thanks for walking me to my car." She pulled her keys from her coat pocket, and before she could hit the button to unlock the car door, he took a step forward to brush away a few errant strands of hair from her face. His gaze roamed over her, and the sensuality in his eyes seemed to suck the air out of her lungs.

"So tell me the truth. Did you want to make out during the movie?" The low husky tone of his voice sent a vibration of tingles throughout her body.

"Yes. Did you?"

He leaned in close. So close the warmth of his breath brushed against her cheeks; so close his clean male scent invaded her senses. Her pulse raced as his gaze lowered to linger on her lips, then lifted.

"It's all I thought about." He raised his fingertips to caress her cheek.

Her heart skipped a beat, and pleasurable goose bumps prickled her skin in response to the gentle touch.

"Ben," she whispered.

"What?" His eyes burned into hers.

She shivered in anticipation. "Kiss me."

He slid his hand to her nape with a low groan and pulled her forward. At first, he seemed content to brush his lips against hers. Teasing her, tempting her. Only a week had passed since he'd kissed her on the porch, but it seemed like years. She parted her lips with a faint moan and welcomed his hungry mouth.

Their deep, wet kiss sent waves of scorching desire through her body. All coherent thought left her as she slid her arms around Ben's waist and pulled him against her. His hard body against hers sent a thrill up her spine. She'd missed this. Missed him.

He slowly backed her up without breaking the kiss until she was pressed against her car. Bracing his palms on the windows, he pinned her against the frame with his body. Then he dragged his mouth from hers with a low growl and trailed his lips to her neck. Maddie gasped as he pressed warm kisses on her throat, concentrating on the particular spot near the hollow that had always been so sensitive.

Nearby, a car door slammed, but she didn't care. She was so completely immersed in Ben that nothing else mattered.

Much too soon, he pulled back, leaving them both breathless.

"If we'd done that in the theater, they probably would have kicked us out," she said and slipped her arms from around his waist.

"But it would have been worth it." He stepped back and scanned the parking lot. "I want to see you next week."

Butterflies danced in Maddie's stomach. "I want to see you too. I'll let you know what days I'm working. I still need to find out when Mallory needs me." She pointed the key fob toward the car and unlocked the door. "Are you going to the Jingle Ball next weekend?"

He cocked his head. "I hadn't planned on going. Are you?"

"No. I'm going to see *Miracle on 34th Street* at the community theater." She opened the car door. "Since you're not going to the Jingle Ball, would you be interested in seeing the play? Stevie's holding two tickets for me."

"Oh, I'm interested," he said, and judging by the sexy grin that slowly curved the corners of his mouth, she had this feeling he wasn't referring to the play.

Chapter Fourteen

The night of the play, Maddie surveyed her attempt at barrel curls in the mirror, pleased she'd finally mastered the art of getting the perfect curl. Turning off the curling iron, she cinched the belt of her satin robe around her waist and returned to the bedroom. Laid out on the bed was the red wrap dress she planned to wear to the play. She'd bought it during a mid-week shopping trip with her mother, especially for this evening.

During the past week, Ben had stopped by Sweet Temptations several times. Twice to take her to lunch and the other times just to talk. Each time he walked in and flashed his killer smile, her heart raced like it had when she was a lovestruck teenager crushing on a cute guy at school.

Ever since the night when she told him she was thinking about staying in Summerwood, he hadn't brought it up again. Neither had she. Even so, the looming decision had been there, unspoken, between them. Not in an uncomfortable way, but there, nonetheless.

She'd thought about her future and what she wanted it to look like all week. It hadn't been easy, but once she finally asked herself if going back to the hamster wheel that was life in Los Angeles would make her genuinely happy, she had to admit it wouldn't.

Even with that admission, though, she was still

struggling with her decision. Perhaps it was years of feeling like she had to prove something to her parents, or maybe it was a deep-seated fear of being labeled a failure holding her back. But whatever it was, she needed to come to terms with it. Her future happiness hung in the balance.

With an hour remaining before Ben was due to pick her up, she wandered down the hall to her parents' bedroom. At the doorway, she paused and, for a moment, silently watched her mother, who was sitting on a stool in front of her mirrored vanity table, applying mascara. The memory of her and her sisters doing this same thing when they were kids popped into her head. All three of them had loved to watch her transform herself for an evening out. To them, she had been the most beautiful woman in the world. And in the simple black velvet dress she wore, her classic beauty hadn't faded over time.

"You look beautiful, Mom."

"Thank you, honey." She smiled, replaced the wand in the mascara tube, and set it on the table. "Is your father pacing downstairs? Whenever we go anywhere, he's always worried we'll be late."

"I don't think so." Maddie padded to the foot of the bed and perched on the edge. "He's got the basketball game on."

"Good. That will keep him occupied." She met Maddie's gaze in the mirror. "Is Mallory going to the play with you?"

"No. Ben's joining me."

Her mother regarded her thoughtfully for a few seconds. "You two have been seeing a lot of each other since you came home. Don't get me wrong. I think it's wonderful that you've repaired your relationship. But I worry Ben could get hurt again when you go back to Los Angeles."

Maddie bit her lip, and grabbing the end of the satin belt around her waist, she twisted it with her fingers. She was worried too, which was why she had to be sure of her decision. "About that. I may not be going back to LA."

Her mother's eyes flickered with surprise. "Don't you have to be in Los Angeles for auditions?"

"Yes. At least *I* do. I'm not established enough to have the luxury of living so far away."

"Then I don't understand." A frown tugged at her brows. "Why would you stay in Summerwood?"

"Because I hate LA," she said, finally admitting the truth she'd kept inside for so long. "I know you and Dad will be disappointed if I decide not to go back, but I have to do what's right for me."

"Why would you think we'd be disappointed?" Her mother's frown deepened.

Fearing her mom's reaction, Maddie averted her gaze and continued to fidget with the belt. "Because disappointing you is all I've ever done."

"That's not true, Maddie," she said, her tone gentle but firm.

"Really?" Her gaze snapped to her mother. "What about when I was held back in the third grade because the teacher thought I was slow? And except for my drama classes, I floundered so badly in high school it's a miracle I graduated. Then came community college, and that was an even worse fiasco. I was never better than an average student, no matter how hard I tried. So how could you not be disappointed?"

Her mother slid off the stool and crossed the short

distance to sit beside her. "Listen to me. You are *not* a disappointment to either your father or me. We love you exactly as you are." Her eyes flashed with irritation. "And you weren't slow. That teacher didn't know what he was talking about. Nor did he ever attempt to help you or let us know you were struggling with the curriculum. There's a reason why he didn't last long at the elementary school."

Her mother's defense warmed her heart, but facts were facts. "But I didn't make it, Mom. I'm one of the large percentages of people barely earning a living as an actor." She sighed, more out of relief than anything else. Admitting it had been a struggle was actually freeing. Her entire life had revolved around trying to justify her impulsive decision to leave Summerwood. Justification she believed would only come from becoming a star. "I wanted to be as successful as Mallory and Lauren."

"Is that why you went to Los Angeles?"

"Honestly?" She met her mother's sympathetic gaze. "It's a big part of the reason. At the time, I thought the only thing I could do well was act, but since I've been home, I've realized it's not true. I know I've been a job-hopper, but I was an excellent employee at every place I worked. If I didn't know something, I researched it and figured it out. If I saw an overly complicated procedure, I streamlined it. If I had to deal with difficult people, I called on my acting skills to handle them. High school was demoralizing for me. But once it was over and I didn't feel so much pressure to do well, I found I could learn so much more on my own. And while I was working at those different jobs, I was able to do what I love. Acting."

She searched her mother's face in the silence,

relieved it was filled with compassion instead of disappointment.

"Do you still love it?"

That was the question she'd been asking herself all week. When she could answer that question, her decision became easier to make. "I believe the love of it is still there. But over the past four years, the joy it's always given me has disappeared. The more pressure I put on myself to succeed, the worse it got. The bottom line is I loved it more when it wasn't a career."

"So you don't want to go back to Los Angeles?"

"I don't think so." She lifted her chin. "But if I don't go back, I don't think it makes me a failure." The vehement tone of her voice surprised her. Was she trying to convince her mother or herself?

"Of course, it doesn't, honey." She reached for Maddie's hand, squeezing it gently. "People change careers all the time."

"So you're not disappointed in me?"

Her mom gave her a reassuring smile. "Not at all. I'm proud of you for following your heart."

Giddy relief washed over Maddie, but the respite was short lived. "What about Dad?"

"I'm proud of you too."

Startled, she swung her gaze toward the bedroom door where her father stood in the doorway, a somber expression etched on his face.

"I didn't intend to eavesdrop, but the door was open."

"How much did you hear?" Her knees trembled. This was the moment she'd been dreading. Meeting her father's gaze, she silently prayed he would be as supportive as her mother had been.

"Enough to know you must have been under a lot of pressure. And it pains me to know it's partly my fault. Just like my parents expected a lot of me, I expected it of my daughters. You're a wonderful actress, Maddie. I never suspected how much my expectations affected you."

"Lauren and Mallory never had a problem exceeding your expectations. I wanted to be like them."

"You don't need to be like them." Her father crossed the room, unbuttoning his dark suit jacket as he sat down beside her. "Do you think our family would have had as much fun if you weren't exactly who you are? Do you think your sisters would have turned the living room into a makeshift theater and put on plays and extravagant musical numbers for us?" He reached for her hand and gently squeezed it. "*You* did that. You've given us so much happiness, and I'm deeply sorry you ever felt less important than your sisters, because you're not."

Maddie blinked, trying to keep from crying, but a smattering of tears spilled from her eyes and rolled slowly down her cheeks. It had been ages since she thought about her early efforts to entertain her family. She'd had a blast preparing for those silly shows, but the best part had been performing them for her family. They were her favorite audience. "I loved putting on those plays," she said with a wobbly smile.

"You had quite the imagination." Her mother slipped an arm around Maddie's shoulders, enveloping her in the light floral scent of her perfume. "And you blossomed when you started taking those drama classes in high school. Finally, you'd found an outlet for your talents at long last. As parents, we couldn't have asked for more. We love you, Maddie. Just the way you are."

Maddie's heart swelled with emotion. She'd dreamed of hearing those words for years, but actually hearing them was so much better than any dream. "I…I love you too. That's why I wanted you to be proud of me," she said, absorbing the warmth of her parents' embrace.

"We are," she said softly, hugging Maddie tighter. "Don't ever doubt it."

"I won't. I promise." The tension she hadn't realized she was carrying eased from her body. "If I decide to stay, I'll still need to go back to LA to pack up my apartment. In that case, may I stay with you for a while? Until I get a job."

"This is your home. If you decide to move back to Summerwood, you can stay as long as you need to," her father said. "And if I get approval for another administrative position next year, I strongly encourage you to apply. If you're interested, that is. We could use a self-starter like you. You've certainly proven yourself more than capable."

"Thanks, Dad," she said, her voice still a bit shaky. "That means more than I can say."

He lifted his hand to brush the tears from her cheeks. "Don't you have a play to get to?"

She nodded. "I should go refresh my makeup. I'm probably a mess. I always was an ugly crier."

Her mom laughed and gave her another hug. "The ugly cry runs in our family."

****

Outside the Center for the Arts building, Ben slipped on his gloves and waited for Maddie to join him. After the play, she'd gone backstage to congratulate Stevie on a successful production.

192

Sitting next to her in the theater had done a number on his equilibrium. Instead of concentrating on the play, all he could focus on was Maddie. He'd picked her up at her parents' house, and as she'd gracefully walked down the stairs, he couldn't take his eyes off her. The red dress she'd chosen for the evening was as sexy as hell, and when he helped her with her coat, the alluring aroma of her perfume had filled his senses and sent heat coursing through his body.

All week he'd avoided the topic of her staying in Summerwood. As much as he wanted her to stay, he didn't want to influence her decision. So all he could do was wait, and the waiting was killing him.

But if she did stay, what then? Was there a future for them, or was he living in the past?

The sound of footsteps pulled him from his thoughts. His gaze landed on Maddie as she hurried toward him, buttoning her long black coat along the way.

"Sorry it took me so long," she said, halting next to him. She pulled a pair of gloves from her pocket and slipped them on. "I ran into a few people I hadn't seen in a while. Oh, and I chatted briefly with Lorenzo. It looks like the wine bar is happening."

He rolled his eyes. "I can hardly wait."

She laughed. "I know it's not your thing, but I think it will do well. Considering we're in wine country, I'm surprised Summerwood doesn't already have one."

"To tell you the truth, so am I." He checked his watch. It was still early. He wanted to spend more time with her and hoped she felt the same. "Would you like to get some coffee? There's a new place not far from here. We can walk."

"Are you working on Christmas?" she asked as they

headed toward the corner.

"Yeah. I'm a low man on the totem pole when it comes to seniority. But I'll get some overtime because it's a holiday, so I don't mind. And I'll still be able to have Christmas dinner at Dad's house."

"Oh, I've always loved that hotel. It's so elegant," she said when they stopped at the corner.

He followed her gaze toward the Hotel Evergreen, a Summerwood institution. Situated on the opposite corner, the four-story brick hotel was the oldest building in Summerwood, and while it was stately, it had a certain charm he found appealing. Now, in honor of the holidays, the trunks and branches of the trees planted on the block around the hotel were wrapped in festive white lights that added to the magical holiday atmosphere Summerwood exuded.

"It was recently named a historic landmark by the Summerwood Historical Committee," he said.

"I haven't been inside for years, but I remember it being very dark. There was a lot of wood paneling." She looked at him, a thoughtful frown pinching her brows. "I also seem to remember something about a murder there years ago, and now it's haunted by the dead woman's ghost."

He smiled, amused by how the old story had taken on a life of its own. "There was a mysterious disappearance there, but it's not haunted," he said as they stepped off the curb to cross the street. "That's an urban legend. As for the paneling, it's all gone. The owners wanted to increase revenue and decided to renovate the entire first floor. Dad's company bid on the job and was awarded the contract. Now there's a large ballroom and smaller meeting rooms available to the public."

"That was smart."

"I agree. Since the renovation, the hotel has been able to book larger events. The Jingle Ball is being held there tonight."

She gave him a surprised look. "But the Jingle Ball has always been held at the high school auditorium. It's a tradition."

"They moved it to the Evergreen two years ago. From what I heard, attendance was dropping, so the beautification committee thought moving it to a nicer venue would increase ticket sales."

"Did it work?"

"It appears so. At least that's what Cora Jean says. And she knows everything going on in this town."

She laughed. "Speaking of Cora Jean. How's it going now that she's back?"

"Like she never left." He grimaced. Having Cora Jean back at the front desk had been frustrating. "On her first day back, we got the lowdown on her daughter's divorce drama. I don't think she did any work at all."

Maddie shot him a sympathetic look. "I'm sorry."

"It's not your fault. Well, maybe it is. You spoiled us." He blew out an irritated breath. "Let's not talk about Cora Jean. Did I mention there's a garden terrace adjoining the ballroom?"

"A garden terrace? That sounds lovely."

"It is. Dad and Sam worked with Zaslow Landscaping on the project." He nodded to an older man waiting to cross opposite them. When they reached the corner, Maddie stopped, and he halted beside her.

"I remember the Zaslows." A fond smile curved her lips. "I went to school with Julie Zaslow. She started the garden club our freshman year."

"From what I've gleaned, Julie's been running the business for the last year. Unfortunately, Sid's not well."

"Oh no, I'm sorry to hear that. Dad hired him to redo the landscaping in the backyard about six years ago, and what I remember most about him is how upbeat and cheerful he was. He also liked to listen to classical music while he and his crew worked. He said it was soothing to the plants."

Ben chuckled. "I seem to recall Sam saying the same thing. The garden terrace is one of the last projects Sid worked on." He quickly checked out the foot traffic up and down the block. "The coast is clear," he said, lowering his voice. "We can sneak in through the back entrance to the garden."

Her eyes widened. "Isn't that trespassing?"

"Not if we're guests of the hotel or attending the dance."

"We're neither of those things."

"No one will know we're not attending the dance." He nodded in the direction of the alley. "C'mon. You really should see it. We won't stay long."

After a few seconds, she nodded. "Okay. But if we get busted, you're the one taking the fall. Not me."

"Way to have my back," he said, firing a sarcastic grin.

"Hey." She lightly poked his upper arm. "I'm not built for prison. I'd be someone's bitch two seconds after the cellblock door slammed behind me."

He let out a snort of amusement and grabbed her hand. "You do have a flair for drama. Let's go."

After they rounded the corner, he walked beside her until they reached the alley behind the hotel. Once they were out of sight from the street, he guided her along the dimly lit alleyway past a large trash dumpster and what looked like an area for deliveries until they reached the white stucco wall that enclosed the terrace.

"You sure know how to show a girl a good time," she whispered.

He chuckled under his breath as they approached the wrought iron door that would grant them entry. "Trust me. It'll be worth it," he said and reached for the handle on the door. "Damn it." He let out a groan of frustration when the handle didn't budge. "It's locked."

"A sure sign this is a bad idea."

"No, it's not." Ben stepped back and surveyed the white stucco wall next to the gate. "We just need to be creative. Wait here." He turned and jogged back to the dumpster.

"What are you doing?" she called after him in a loud whisper.

"Just wait there." At the dumpster, he grabbed a wooden vegetable crate sitting next to it and hurried back to where Maddie stood, wearing a puzzled expression on her face. After a furtive glance over his shoulder, he set the crate at the base of the wall. "I'll climb over and unlock the door."

"Are you serious?" she said, keeping her voice low. "Why don't we try to get inside the normal way?"

"Where's the fun in that?" He stepped on the box, which gave him enough height to pull himself up, swing his leg over the wall, and easily straddle the top. He grinned at her as he balanced himself.

"Sergeant Ashford?"

He froze as one of the hotel's security guards approached them. As the young man moved closer, Ben recognized him, and suddenly, his idea of harmless fun had turned into a colossal error in judgment. "Hey, Andre." He looked down at Andre with a sheepish grin. Then he glanced at Maddie, who had covered her mouth with her hand. Probably to hide a gloating smile. "Long time, no see."

Andre cocked his head and grinned. "It looks like the shoe's on the other foot. When you were a patrol officer, you came upon me and my buddies trying to jump the fence over at the skate park."

"Well, it was after hours. And the skate park was closed for the evening."

"The garden door is locked for a reason," Andre replied, using similar verbiage Ben used that night to Andre and his friends.

Under Andre's amused gaze, a knot tightened in Ben's stomach. He grimaced. Andre was enjoying this. And who could blame him?

"You're right," he acknowledged with an apologetic smile. "I shouldn't be climbing the wall."

"You don't have to break in. I'd be happy to open the door for you." Andre grinned. "You let me off with a warning at the skate park. So I guess I can return the favor and not call this in."

"Thanks, Andre," he said, exhaling in relief. He swung his leg back over the top of the wall and eased himself down onto the crate. "I appreciate that."

"No problem." Andre unhooked a key carabiner from his belt loop and unlocked the door with one of the keys. "But if I catch you doing this again, I'm not gonna go so easy on you."

Ben cleared his throat and nodded. "I understand. It won't happen again," he said as Maddie stifled a laugh.

"Have a nice evening." Andre opened the door and

motioned for Ben and Maddie to proceed.

"You too, Andre."

"Merry Christmas," Maddie called out to Andre as they entered the garden. Then, as Ben closed the door behind them, she burst out laughing. "The look on your face when Andre showed up was priceless. You're lucky it was him and not one of your officers."

"Oh, don't worry," he said. "I'll be hearing about this at the station. Andre is Carolyn's nephew."

She chuckled. "Small towns. You gotta love 'em."

****

As Ben made a sweeping motion with his hand, Maddie turned and let out a soft gasp at the scene in front of her. They stood in the secluded section of the terrace where a cobblestone path flanked with small trees led to a multitiered fountain. The trunks and bare branches of the trees were wrapped entirely in white lights and illuminated the pathway with a diffused glow. In contrast, blue lights had been placed in the fountain's base, making the water sprouting from the basin appear otherworldly.

"Oh, wow. The fountain is beautiful."

The whoosh of the water muted the sounds of music and chatter coming from the other side of the garden. In warmer months, the terrace and garden would probably be filled with people, but tonight only she and Ben had braved the cold.

"Are you warm enough?"

She nodded. "My toes are a little cold, but Mom's coat is keeping me warm."

He pointed to one of the benches placed in strategic spots along the pathway. "Let's sit for a few minutes." Together they moved toward the closest bench and sat down.

"Thank you for bringing me here. It's amazing."

"You're welcome." He leaned back, stretching his arm along the back of the bench. "I can't believe Christmas is three days away."

"I know. It seems like Thanksgiving was just yesterday." She slid back against the bench next to him, and just like at the theater, she was wholly aware of him. The subtle fresh scent of his cologne swirled around her, invading her senses and evoking memories she'd never been able to forget. "A lot has happened since then."

"Yeah. It has."

Nervously clasping her hands together, she took a deep breath. After the emotional discussion with her parents, it had become clear she had to be honest with him. Completely honest. He deserved to know the whole truth. "I had a long overdue talk with my parents earlier this evening."

"What about?"

"Expectations, perception, disappointment." She turned to meet his curious gaze. "I felt so inadequate compared to Lauren and Mallory that I assumed my parents had to be disappointed in me. I was wrong. And I was so used to focusing on attaining a certain kind of success that I discounted all the things I did well. I thought landing a starring role in a movie or television series would level the playing field, but I was the only one who thought the playing field was uneven." She paused, searching his face. "Does that make sense?"

"Perfect sense." He nodded. "You could never take a compliment when it came to anything other than acting. Everyone you've worked for thinks you're the best employee they've ever had, but it never seemed to register with you. I thought you were being modest. It never dawned on me you felt like you were standing in the shadow of your sisters."

"I hid it well," she said with a slight smile. "I am an actress, after all."

"Now it makes more sense why you went to Los Angeles." He shifted on the bench, confusion shadowing his eyes as he stared at her. "But I still don't understand why you sprang it on me last minute. I wish you had been able to confide in me. I love…loved you, Maddie. I would have understood."

"I wish I had," she whispered, her heart aching from the thought of the pain she'd caused him. "You don't know how much I wish I'd behaved differently." She turned toward him. "You said there was more to my leaving than I was willing to admit, and you were right." She took another deep breath, fortifying herself for what she was about to say. "The other reason why I left was because I was afraid."

His eyes widened. "Of what?"

She clasped her hands together to keep them from trembling. It was one thing to have cut and run because she was chasing success, but this—the other reason she'd left town—was the thing she was most ashamed of. "I had this feeling you wanted to get married and…and it scared me. But instead of talking to you about my fears, I ran away. Do you remember when Stevie's friend, the casting director, came to visit her?"

Ben nodded.

"He told me I'd be perfect for a part in a film he was casting, and he wanted me to go to Los Angeles and audition for the part. So I used it as an excuse to leave town." She bit her lower lip and held his gaze, silently praying he would be able to forgive her.

He sucked in a breath. "Why did the thought of marrying me scare you?"

"It wasn't because I didn't love you. I did. So much. But I wasn't ready for that kind of commitment, and I also didn't feel worthy of you. You had a solid plan for your life, and I was so lost at the time. I was afraid you'd meet someone else as time went on. Someone who had herself together. So I latched on to the idea of going to LA."

He stared at her for several seconds. "I never knew you felt so insecure."

"Why would you? I never told you, and I was pretty good at hiding my insecurities. I had a lot of practice," she said with a wry laugh. "I should have told you the entire truth the night we went to La Rambla when I asked you if you could forgive me. I won't blame you if this changes things between us now."

For several seconds silence reigned between them, and her nerves were stretched to the breaking point. What she'd just confessed could be the end of any future for them, but if she wasn't completely honest with him now, their relationship going forward would always be tainted. She didn't want that for either of them.

"Do I wish you'd said something?" he said, breaking the silence. "Yes, I do. You said you had a feeling I was going to ask you to marry me. But if it was only a feeling, I wasn't doing a good job of communicating either." A frown creased his forehead. "I assumed we were on the same page regarding marriage, but we never actually discussed it."

Maddie held up her hand. "Please, don't blame yourself. I was too afraid to talk about it," she said adamantly. "And if it means anything, I'm not the same person I was back then. I would never do something like that again. I hope you can believe me."

"I do believe you," he said, his expression softening. "The old Maddie would have brushed off a conversation like this."

She exhaled slowly as the tension eased from her body. "You're right. And from now on, I'm going to face things head-on instead of running away." She made a cross over her heart with her index finger. "I promise."

His mouth quirked with amusement. "It sounds like you've done a lot of soul searching this past week. I don't want to pressure you, but have you made your decision about returning to Hollywood?"

"Not a final one, but I'm ninety-nine percent sure my future residence won't be in LA."

His eyes widened. "That percentage sounds damn close to final if you ask me." A slow smile curved his firm mouth.

"It does, doesn't it?" she said, giving him a cheeky grin.

"Is there anything I can do to up the percentage?"

She nodded. "You could kiss me. If you're willing."

"Oh, I'm willing." He leaned forward and pulled her against him. "More than willing," he said, covering her mouth with his. Immediately, she parted her lips, and he kissed her, slow and deep like he was savoring the taste of her. Maddie couldn't formulate a coherent thought. Not that she cared. The one thing she cared about right now was kissing the only man she'd ever loved.

He slipped his arm around her waist, pulled her closer, and leaned back against the bench, so she was pressed against him. She moaned, and their kiss turned passionate and deeply intimate. Pure animal instinct had her yearning for more until she remembered they were in a public place where anyone could come upon them.

"Ben," she murmured against his mouth, then pulled back and stared into his eyes, trying to control her erratic breathing.

He loosened his arm from around her but didn't put any distance between them. Instead, he lowered his smoldering gaze to her mouth, sending a jolt of heat straight to her core.

"If we don't stop, we could get arrested for indecent exposure."

"You're right. We should go. The last thing I need is another run-in with Andre." He flashed a sexy grin that didn't do anything to cool her off. "Do you still want to get some coffee?"

"That depends." She smiled. "Do you have coffee at your house?"

His eyes darkened. "Coffee and tea. Whatever you want." His low husky voice prickled her skin with anticipation.

"Then what are we waiting for?" She held his burning gaze. "Let's go."

Chapter Fifteen

Maddie had always loved Ben's house. He'd purchased the craftsman bungalow before they started dating, and except for the night on his porch when she'd broken up with him, the times she spent with him here had been among her happiest.

As he pulled his car into the driveway, she could see the house hadn't changed. Even though the sun had set, the porch light and a nearby streetlight illuminated the light-green house and its white trim. In a word, it was adorable.

During the ten-minute drive from the Hotel Evergreen to Ben's house, she was filled with anticipation and nervousness about what would happen when they arrived.

She was certain he knew she wanted more than coffee. And she was also certain *he* wanted more than coffee. The hot kiss they'd shared and the heat in his eyes whenever he'd looked at her since then were proof of that. But it had been so long since they made love. Would it be as wonderful as she remembered?

After he parked in front of the detached garage, they walked to the back door and entered the kitchen. "You finally remodeled," she said, looking around the room. "I love these countertops. Are they marble?" She moved to the small but functional rectangular island and swept her hand over its smooth surface.

He closed the door behind him and began unbuttoning his coat. "Quartz. Dad had some slabs leftover from one of his jobs, so I got it at a good price."

"It's lovely. The gray veins running through it aren't too busy. I'm surprised you went with white cabinets, though. I thought you liked the darker ones that were in here before." She smiled. "I remember when you were first thinking about remodeling and asked for my opinion, we went a few rounds over the cabinet color."

"You made a good case for white. You said it would make the kitchen look brighter and larger. I thought about that when it was time to choose the cabinets." He shrugged out of his coat and draped it over the back of one of the chairs that surrounded the kitchen table. "Can I take your coat?"

She nodded and fumbled with the buttons as he moved toward her. It was a crime for any one man to be so gorgeous. Between the black slacks and a charcoal-gray sweater he'd probably thrown on without a second thought and his dark hair sexily tousled from the light breeze outside, he looked like he could be on the cover of one of those male-centric fashion and lifestyle magazines.

The lazy smile he gave her before she turned so he could help her ease out of her coat jumpstarted her pulse. As he removed her coat, he was so close the crisp scent of his cologne drifted into her senses and sent her pulse racing. His thumb lightly brushed against her neck. She shivered, but not because she was cold. If anything, it was the opposite.

"I'll make some coffee," he said after depositing her coat and purse on the same chair where he'd laid his. "Why don't you go into the living room and get comfortable. It won't take long. I have one of those pod coffee makers."

"Okay." She gave him a quick smile. "I remember the way."

The living room hadn't changed much. He had switched out the worn black leather sofa with a new one of chocolatey brown. The same patterned rug covered the hardwood floor, and the built-in bookcases flanking the gas fireplace were still filled with books. Probably mysteries and thrillers, his favorite genres.

"Hey, could you hit the switch next to the fireplace?"

She crossed the room and flipped the switch. After a low hiss, blue and gold-tinged flames shot up from the fake log, adding a romantic ambiance to the room.

"Are you hungry?"

"No." She turned from the fireplace and smoothed her palms over the fabric of her dress. Why was she suddenly so nervous? "Are you?"

"No. You still use milk or creamer in your coffee, right?"

"Yes." She sat down on the sofa and ran her fingertips over the smooth leather, surprised at its softness. "This is a great sofa."

"Thanks." He came into the room, holding two mugs. "I've fallen asleep on it watching television more than a few times." He handed her one of the mugs before sitting next to her.

"Thank you." She cupped the warm mug between her hands, hoping it would help steady them.

"You're welcome." He eased back on the cushion and took a tentative sip of his coffee. "Are you nervous?" He tilted his head, watching her with a thoughtful expression.

Was it that obvious? So much for her acting skills. "Do I look nervous?"

"A little bit, yeah." He edged forward to set his mug on the coffee table. "Nothing is going to happen you don't want to happen. I can take you home after you finish your coffee."

"I don't want to go home." She sipped her coffee, meeting his gaze over the rim of her mug.

"What *do* you want?" His gaze lowered and lingered on her mouth.

A little ball of need burst to life in the pit of her stomach, and she had the sudden urge to lick her lips. "To finish what we started on the terrace. As soon as possible."

"That's doable." He reached out and removed the mug from her hands. As he set it on the coffee table next to his, she caught another hint of his cologne. Lord, he smelled good. *So good.*

This time when he leaned back, he shifted closer to her. The heat from his thigh seemed to burn straight through the fabric of her dress. As their eyes locked, the intensity that shone in his caused her knees to tremble.

"You're so beautiful," he murmured, then leaned forward and kissed her. In a matter of seconds, he pulled her against his hard chest, his lips going from gentle to demanding. Fueled by the desire that had been simmering since they kissed on the terrace, she parted her mouth, deepening the kiss until she was longing for more.

Much too soon, he pulled back, leaving them both breathless. He gazed at her, his eyes blazing with heat. "I want you."

The huskiness of his voice sent a swift shot of desire straight to her core. "The feeling is *so* mutual," she said and angled her head to press her mouth to his neck. His pulse pounded against her lips. In no hurry, she trailed soft kisses up to his ear and gently nipped his earlobe.

"Maddie, I need you. Now." His aching whisper sent a delicious shiver up her spine.

She pulled back, her stomach clenching at the desire smoldering in his eyes. "I love this sofa, but I'd rather be in your bed."

A slow, sexy smile tilted his lips. "So would I." Rising from the sofa, Ben extended his hand. She grasped it and got to her feet. He lifted his other hand to her face and gently caressed her cheek. "Are you sure?" he asked softly.

Suddenly, the air in the room thickened, and a tingle of awareness prickled over Maddie's skin. She wanted him so badly she ached. Lightly biting her lower lip, she nodded. "Are you?"

"I'm sure I wanted you in my bed from the moment we first met. That hasn't changed," he said, and Maddie's heart skipped a beat as he led her out of the living room toward his bedroom.

"Wait." She stopped short. "Do you have—"

"Condoms?" Amusement flickered in his eyes. "There're some in the nightstand. At least there should be. Who knows what Sam pilfered when he replaced the shelves in my closet."

"If he did take them, I hope he at least had the courtesy of leaving you a few."

One of Ben's brows kicked up. "A few? Feeling ambitious?" he said with a husky laugh.

"And if I am?" she asked as they walked down the

dimly lit hallway. "Are you up for it?"

Pulling her to a stop, he turned and gazed down at her with raw hunger blazing in his eyes. "Oh, yeah. I'm more than up for it."

****

The rhythmic cadence of Ben's breathing was the first thing Maddie became aware of as she slowly stirred awake. She'd been in Summerwood for weeks, yet nestled here in his arms, with his warm body pressed snugly against hers, was the first time she felt like she'd truly come home.

Last night had been nothing short of amazing. Making love with Ben again had been both new and familiar. He'd always been a generous lover, and that hadn't changed. They hadn't quite used all the condoms in the box, but they'd used a few.

The loud ring of the doorbell startled her and jerked Ben awake.

"Who the hell is here this early?" he said hoarsely.

"Maybe it's Traci," she said, turning to face him. The scowl on his handsome face spoke volumes. The doorbell sounded again. This time longer. Whoever it was *really* wanted to see him.

"You should get that; it might be a neighborhood emergency. Everyone knows you're a cop."

"You're right." He flung the covers aside, sat up, and rubbed his eyes. "I'll handle it," he said and crawled off the bed. Maddie rolled to her back, appreciating his fit body as he pulled on a pair of sweatpants and an Oregon State University T-shirt.

After he left the bedroom, she slipped out of bed and quickly used the adjoining bathroom. She washed her hands and, for good measure, squeezed out some toothpaste from a tube sitting on the sink and rinsed her mouth with it.

Back in the bedroom, she was about to crawl under the covers when she heard voices. Familiar voices. Heart racing, she rushed to the dresser, pulled open a drawer, and snagged one of Ben's T-shirts. Pulling it on, she crept out of the room and moved slowly down the hall toward the living room.

"Do you know how worried my parents are?" Mallory said, her voice strident. "They've been calling you both for hours."

"They called me too." Maddie recognized Sam's voice, and he wasn't any happier than Mallory.

"Maddie's fine," Ben said patiently. "We're both fine."

"Why didn't you answer your phones?" Mallory asked as Maddie stepped into the living room.

Tugging at the hem of Ben's T-shirt, Maddie cleared her throat. "We were busy."

Both Mallory and Sam, who were facing the fireplace, turned around to look at her. Mallory's eyes widened while Sam's jaw dropped. Maddie's cheeks grew warm, but she lifted her chin and stared them down. Last night was wonderful, and she refused to be embarrassed about it.

Mallory recovered first. "Look, I know you're an adult, but couldn't you have at least returned their calls? You *are* staying in their house. And you know how Dad was whenever we stayed out later than planned."

Maddie winced. Her phone was in her purse. In the kitchen. "I'm sorry. I haven't been in the vicinity of my phone since last night. I didn't hear it ringing."

"Same here," Ben added, running a hand through his

hair. "As Maddie said, we were busy."

"I bet you were," Sam said and exchanged a knowing grin with Mallory, who didn't bother to hide her amusement.

Ben crossed his arms across his chest and glowered at his brother. "Now that you've verified we're alive and well, you can leave."

"That's not very hospitable." Sam unbuttoned his coat. "How about I mosey on into the kitchen and make us all some breakfast? How do pancakes sound? Or waffles. I make a mean waffle."

"How about you mosey on outta here?" Ben retorted.

"Sam, I think we should go." Mallory looped her arm through his. "We can stop by Callie's for breakfast." She glanced at Maddie. "I'll let Mom and Dad know you're okay."

"Thanks, Mal." Maddie suppressed a smile when Mallory winked at her. "I'll talk to you later."

"Oh, yes, you will," she said with a knowing look and tugged on Sam's arm. "C'mon. I'm hungry."

"You're always hungry," Sam grumbled but allowed Mallory to lead him to the front door. "Don't do anything I wouldn't do," he called out before closing the door.

Maddie met Ben's irritated gaze and shrugged. "At least it wasn't my parents."

"True." His expression relaxed, and his gaze roamed over her with frank appreciation. "Nice shirt."

She shrugged a shoulder. "This old thing? I found it in the drawer and couldn't resist it."

With a chuckle, he moved toward her and slipped his arms around her waist, pulling her against him. "You always did look good wearing my T-shirts." He dipped his head and kissed her hungrily until they were both breathless. "Do you have any plans for today?" he asked when they came up for air.

His erection pressed against her, and her body's response was immediate. A frisson of desire ignited low in her belly. "No, but I think *you* have plans for me," she said with a teasing smile.

Amusement flickered in his eyes. "How about after that?"

"No."

"Come with me to get a Christmas tree."

She tilted her head back to scan the room. "How did I not notice you don't have a tree? You're cutting it pretty close, you know. Christmas is the day after tomorrow."

"I wasn't going to get one at all." He lowered his hands to her bottom, pulling her even more tightly against him. "But suddenly, I'm chock-full of holiday spirit. How about it? Will you come with me?"

"I'd love to, but we'll have to stop by my parents' house so I can change."

"All right, but I'm staying in the car."

She chuckled. "It's okay, Ben. My parents are worrywarts, not overreactive jerks. We'll be fine."

"If you say so." He squeezed her bottom with both hands. "It's still early. Want to go back to bed?"

She smiled up at him. "I thought you'd never ask."

Chapter Sixteen

On the day before Christmas, Maddie absently wiped the gleaming metal counter in the kitchen at Sweet Temptations and listened to Mallory chatting with her final customer of the day. This morning when Mallory informed her she was closing the bakery early, Maddie was thrilled. They'd been busy from the moment the bakery opened, and she had the aching feet to prove it.

Christmas Eve had always meant a big dinner in the Hart family, followed by board games and watching *A Christmas Story*. She was looking forward to it, even more so because Ben had accepted her invitation to join them for the evening. She'd asked him yesterday after she helped him decorate the Christmas tree he'd picked out at the tree farm.

For the first time in four years, she was enjoying the holidays, and tomorrow, on Christmas Day, she would surprise Ben with the news that Summerwood would be her home from now on. She couldn't wait to see his expression when he found out. If the last week was any indication, he would be thrilled. And now that she'd made the decision, she couldn't wait to put Los Angeles behind her. She wasn't sure what the future held, but she knew Ben and the community theater would be a part of it.

"I'm so glad I decided to close early," Mallory said as she entered the kitchen. She plopped down on a stool across from Maddie, folded her arms on the counter, and buried her head in her crossed arms. "I'm exhausted."

"I imagine you would be since you stayed up all night baking pies."

Mallory lifted her head, the dark circles under her eyes the result of her late-night baking spree. "I was so busy I forgot to bake the pies for tonight. Dad would be heartbroken if he didn't have his favorite pies." With a groan, she sat up and scanned the kitchen. "Thank you for helping me this week and cleaning the kitchen."

"You're welcome. I enjoyed it." Maddie tossed the dishtowel she'd been using into the hamper under the counter.

Mallory tucked her hair behind her ear. "Tell me the truth. After four years, why did you choose to come home this year?"

A few weeks ago, she wouldn't have welcomed Mallory's question. But now that she'd opened up to her parents, it was easier to be completely honest with her sister. "I think subconsciously I knew Los Angeles wasn't right for me. And it wasn't until recently that I admitted I left for all the wrong reasons."

"What reasons?"

"One of them was proving to Mom and Dad I could be successful." She pulled one of the stools from under the counter and slid onto it. "You and Lauren set a high bar."

Confusion shadowed Mallory's expression. "Me? I think you mean Lauren. Honestly, I worry I'm going to go out of business every month."

"But you've been so busy."

"Yes, because of the holidays. Why do you think I bust my ass making all those pies and cookies?" A tired sigh escaped her lips. "Dreaming of owning my own shop has turned out to be different from actually doing it. There are days when I wish my only responsibility was baking. I'd be in heaven."

"I had no idea you felt that way," Maddie said, surprised she and her sister had more in common than she thought.

"I guess you're not the only person in our family with acting talent." She paused, her lips flattening. "Please don't mention anything about this to Mom and Dad. I don't want them to worry. I'm just really, really tired. I do love the shop."

"I won't say anything, but promise me if you feel overwhelmed, you'll talk to me about it."

"I will." Mallory nodded. "So if you left Summerwood for all the wrong reasons, does that mean you're coming home for good? Or do you still need to prove yourself to Mom and Dad?"

"No. I finally came clean and told them how I felt. I don't think I need to prove anything to them or anyone else."

Mallory's eyes lit up. "Does that mean what I think it means?"

"Yes." She grinned, happy to share the big decision with her sister. "I'm in Summerwood to stay. It's my home."

"Have you told Ben yet?"

She shook her head. "I'm going to tell him tomorrow. It'll be a Christmas surprise. I'll need to go back to LA and pack up my apartment, though. I want to be out by the end of the month."

"Don't you have to give thirty days' notice?"

"I spoke to my landlord yesterday, and he waived

the stipulation. He's got a waiting list a mile long, and the next person on the list can move in on the first."

"Do you need help? Now that the Christmas rush is over, I can take a couple of days off and go with you."

"I'd love that," she said, not only grateful for Mallory's help but to be able to spend some one-on-one time with her.

Mallory's phone chimed. She pulled it out of the pocket of her apron and gasped. "It's a text from Tanner."

A tight knot formed in Maddie's stomach. "What does it say?"

"Merry Christmas."

That didn't sound ominous. Either Tanner wasn't a stalker, or he was playing some kind of game. "That's it?"

"Yes." Mallory looked up, worry carved on her face. "Should I respond?"

"Do you want to?"

"No," she said adamantly.

"Then don't. It's probably for the best. It might encourage him."

"You're right, but I can't help but feel like I'm rude."

"He may be counting on that. And you're not rude. You dated him for a short time and then broke up with him. So it's not like you were good friends."

Mallory bit her lower lip and nodded. "I don't look forward to him coming back to Summerwood."

Maddie didn't either. Something about Tanner didn't feel right. She glanced at her watch. "Take a screenshot and send it to me. After I leave here, I'm dropping by the police department to see Ben. I'll show it to him. And call me if you get another one."

"Okay." Mallory's eyes were shadowed with concern. "Let me know what he says."

Maddie entered the police department building through the front door. She nodded to a woman sitting on one of the visitor chairs and crossed the lobby under the watchful gaze of Cora Jean Beck.

"Hi, Cora Jean. Merry Christmas." She pulled off her gloves and stuffed them into her coat pocket. "I'm here to see Ben."

Cora Jean peered up at her, smiling warmly. "I was hoping you'd stop by." Behind her wire-rimmed glasses, a friendly sparkle lit up her brown eyes. "I wanted to personally thank you for filling in for me while I was in Seattle."

"I was happy to do it. How is your daughter?"

Cora Jean's expression immediately darkened. "She's fine now that she's divorcing that no-account, lying, cheating scumbag she called a husband."

Maddie doubted Cora Jean's daughter was fine, considering she'd been cheated on, but maybe she'd get there in time. "I was sorry to hear about her situation, and I'm sure you helped her tremendously by being there for her."

"I did what I could." Cora Jean ran her fingers through her short salt-and-pepper hair to tame a few wayward strands. "I told her she and my grandkids could come live with me if need be, but I doubt she'll take me up on the offer. She doesn't want to uproot the kids."

"That's understandable." Maddie discreetly scanned the desk; it appeared Cora Jean had added another knickknack to her collection. The miniature porcelain replica of Seattle's Space Needle hadn't been there before. "So is Ben—"

"I hear you're dating a famous actor," Cora Jean interrupted, leaning forward with an excited sparkle in her eyes.

Momentarily taken aback, Maddie frowned, then suppressed a delighted grin. Her plan to see if the fake piece of information she'd shared with Kay Yoffee would turn into the latest town gossip had worked. She couldn't wait to tell Ben.

She assumed a dejected expression and pressed her lips into a thin, grim line. Then she sighed and shook her head. "He broke up with me," she said softly. "In a text message."

Cora Jean's mouth gaped. "A text message!" Her eyes blazed with anger. "He's a coward, that's what he is, and I don't care how famous he is; you're well rid of him. You deserve better."

"Thank you," Maddie said, letting her lower lip tremble slightly. Should she cry? Or was that laying it on a bit too thick?

The phone on Cora Jean's desk rang, but she ignored it. "Who is this uncouth degenerate? I want to avoid his movies at all costs. He won't make a dime off me."

Maddie put a hand to her chest and met Cora Jean's gaze with a sad one of her own. "I'd rather not say; it's…it's too painful. But if you'll avoid those superhero movies in the future, you'd be doing me a big favor."

"Cora Jean, are you gonna answer that phone?" Maddie heard Ben's irritated voice before he strode into the room from the back. He paused at the doorway, the annoyance in his eyes softening when he set eyes on her. "Hey," he said, and a smile slowly tipped up the corner of his mouth. Unfortunately, the sexy smile didn't last long. The phone continued to ring and ring. "Cora Jean. The phone."

Cora Jean fumbled for the handset. "Summerwood Police Department. How may I assist you?"

As Cora Jean took the call, Ben motioned Maddie to follow him.

"Like she ever assists anyone," he muttered as they entered his office. "I didn't think I'd see you until tonight at your folks' house." He closed the door, and before she could sit in his visitor chair, he slid his arm around her waist, pulled her to his side, and quickly kissed her cheek. "Your father is down the hall, so unfortunately, that's it until we're alone."

"Darn. I was hoping you would close the blinds, lock the door, and take me on your desk." Maddie playfully cupped his butt cheek. "I guess that's one fantasy that won't be fulfilled."

He flashed her a wicked grin. "I have a desk at home."

"Color me ecstatic," she said as he released his hold on her.

"So other than tempting me, what brings you by?"

"I wanted to see you, but now I'm also here because Mallory got a text from Tanner." She pulled her phone from her purse, brought up the text picture, and handed the phone to him. "On the surface, it's not threatening."

Ben rounded his desk, sat down, and stared at the photo. "He could be trying to open the lines of communication. But if he was deliberately trying to frighten Mallory that night outside the bakery, he could be playing mind games with her." He glanced up at her as she sat in his visitor chair. "Did she respond to the text?"

"No."

"That's probably for the best. The less engagement, the better."

A sharp rap on the door startled her. She turned as the door opened, and Carolyn stuck her head inside.

"Hi, Maddie. Cora Jean mentioned you were here. I hate to interrupt, but do you have a few minutes to come to my office? I accidentally deleted some formulas on that FMLA and Workers Comp spreadsheet you created for me."

Maddie got to her feet. "Of course. I'm sure I can fix it." She smiled at Carolyn, then glanced at Ben. "It shouldn't take long," she said and followed Carolyn out of the office.

****

After Maddie left his office, Ben stared at the picture of Tanner's text. It wouldn't be the first time a text was sent from a man to his ex-girlfriend. Many couples parted amicably. The innocuous text could be perfectly innocent or the beginning of an ongoing harassment campaign.

He set Maddie's phone down on his desk and sat back in his chair. The new ergonomic chair didn't make that horrible squeaking sound. When Carolyn wheeled it into his office this morning with a big red bow on it, he'd wanted to hug her.

As he responded to an email from his boss, Maddie's phone rang. He swung around, saw the initial M on the screen, and reached for the phone. Maddie said Mallory would call if she got another text. That had to be her calling.

"Hey, Mallory."

"Oh, I'm sorry, I must have the wrong number," a

woman said.

"Are you trying to reach Maddie?"

"Yes." The woman sounded relieved. "I had a problem with my phone this morning and had to manually replace most of my contact list. I'm so glad this is the correct number."

"She isn't here now, but I can have her call you back."

"Please do, and tell her it's important. I'm her agent, Margo Loughlin, and I have wonderful news. She got the part in the pilot." Margo groaned. "Oh, hell. I probably shouldn't have given you that much information, but I'm so happy for her it slipped out. She's been waiting a long time for a break like this. But since you have access to her phone, you're probably a friend and know that already."

"Yeah, she's been waiting a while," he said, unable to stop a sickening knot from tightening in his gut.

"Please have her call me as soon as possible. The casting director is on a tight timeline and needs a decision right away. I don't want her to miss this opportunity."

"I'll do that." He forced the words out between gritted teeth.

After Margo ended the call, he stared at the phone with the scenarios of what relaying her message to Maddie would bring racing through his brain. His conclusion was there were two ways this could play out. Either she'd decline the role and stay in Summerwood or accept it and return to Hollywood.

She'd told him about the pilot. And she'd also said to him that most pilots rarely got picked up by the television networks. The entire endeavor could be a bust, and she'd be right back where she started. In Hollywood, a place she'd grown to loathe, going from audition to audition and living a lonely life. She'd admitted as much to him.

If she based her decision on that, she would most likely decline the offer. But what if she didn't? What if she left again, seeking that elusive validation she'd always craved, not realizing she was making a huge mistake? She would be miserable and regret it, just like she regretted leaving the first time. Dropping the phone on the desk, he pressed two fingers to his temple and rubbed. But it didn't lessen the throbbing in his head.

He had to give Maddie the message. But he didn't want to.

Don't even think about it, man. It's not your decision to make.

"Ben, look what Carolyn gave me."

He jerked his head up. Maddie stood in the doorway holding a small gift box with a red bow. For a moment, he just stared at her. Her wide smile and sparkling blue eyes almost took his breath away. She was truly happy, and that's how he wanted her to stay.

Somehow he pulled off a fake smile. "It's probably socks. She gives everyone socks."

"You can never have too many socks." She laughed and moved to sit in the chair across from him. "Did Mallory call?"

He gave her phone a cursory glance and shook his head. "No. No one called."

****

Once she'd finished helping her mother clean the kitchen after a fantastic dinner, Maddie walked into the family room and plopped on the sofa next to Ben, who was watching a game show on the large flat-screen mounted on the wall. "Where's Dad and Mallory?" she asked, snuggling closer to his warm body.

"In the garage," he said, not taking his eyes off the screen. "He's checking Mallory's car. She said it was making a strange sound."

"I hope he doesn't try to fix it. The last time he repaired a car, it didn't turn out so well."

He turned to look at her, a brow raised in question. "What happened?"

"In a word. Carbeque."

"Is that really a word?"

"It is now." She chuckled. "We laugh about it these days because no one got hurt, but it was scary at the time."

"I bet," he said, turning his attention to the game show.

"I forgot to tell you that the fake rumor I started about myself dating a famous actor made it to Cora Jean." She smiled, pleased her experiment worked. "She asked me about it yesterday, and I told her he broke up with me in a text message. How long do you think it will take for that piece of information to circulate around town?"

He didn't respond or even acknowledge she'd spoken. With a slight frown, she studied his profile. Ever since he arrived at the house, he'd been uncharacteristically subdued, saying very little. She doubted anyone else noticed, but she had. Had something happened at work?

"You've been quiet all night." She put her hand on his forearm. The fabric of his long-sleeved blue shirt was soft under her fingertips. "Is everything all right?"

"Yeah." He turned to meet her gaze and gave her an apologetic smile. "My mind is on work. I'm sorry."

"It's okay." She squeezed his arm. "I know you're having Christmas dinner at your dad's house tomorrow after you get off work. What time do you think you'll be home?"

"Not too late."

"Do you mind if I come over? I think you'll be *very* satisfied with your Christmas gift."

That coaxed a smile out of him. "Is that gift you, in sexy lingerie?"

"It could be. Or it could be me in the only underwear I packed for this trip."

"Either one works for me." His gaze lowered to her lips. "I'll be home by eight."

She grinned. "I'll be there at eight-o-one."

He reached for her hand with an amused smile, covered it with his, and they watched the game show in companionable silence until the commercial break. "Where's your mom?" he asked.

"On the phone with my grandparents. They went to Tennessee this year; that's why they weren't here for dinner."

His brows knit together. "Tennessee?"

"Specifically Dollywood. They're huge fans of Dolly Parton. As they should be, she's—" Maddie broke off as her phone rang. She reached for it on the coffee table and winced as Ben tightened grip on her hand. "Owww. That's some grip you got there," she said, and he immediately let go of her hand.

"Sorry about that."

Flexing her fingers, she checked her phone and dismissed the call. "Unknown number. I never answer those," she said, reclining to snuggle against him.

"If you were in LA right now, what would you be doing?"

"Hmmm." She squinted as she thought about it. "I'd probably be holed up in my apartment doing my nails or giving myself a facial. The holidays weren't the same for me when I was there."

"Why not?"

"I missed my family and you." His eyes flickered with an emotion she couldn't interpret, and for a second, she thought about telling him right now she was staying in Summerwood. But she fought the urge. She wanted to give him the good news on Christmas Day when they were alone together. Not when a member of her family could walk in on them at any moment.

His unreadable gaze roamed over her face. "I missed you too. That's why I—"

"Are we ready for the movie?" Her mother breezed into the room and put her hands on her hips. "Where are your father and Mallory?"

"In the garage. Dad's taking a look at Mallory's car."

Her mom rolled her eyes. "I'll go get them." She headed for the door. "The last thing we need is another carbeque."

Maddie burst out laughing and nudged Ben's side with her elbow. "Told you it's a word." She met his amused gaze. "What were you going to say before Mom came in?"

His smile faded, and a frown creased his forehead. "I don't remember. I guess it wasn't important."

She leaned her head on his shoulder. Something she thought she'd never do again. This was, hands down, the best Christmas ever. A second chance with Ben was the best gift she could have ever received.

And just like it was when she was a kid, tomorrow couldn't come fast enough.

Chapter Seventeen

"I wonder what it could be." Holding the Christmas gift from her parents, Maddie shook it. "It's not clothes. Something shifted inside. Something heavier."

"Open it already," Mallory said with a groan of impatience.

She shifted on the sofa and met her sister's exasperated gaze. "I'm savoring the moment."

"There's something wrong with you. You know that, right?" Mallory looked at their parents, sitting together on the love seat adjacent to the sofa. "I could bake and frost a cake in the time it takes her to open a present."

"Fine." Maddie chuckled and plucked at the wrapping paper, tearing through the tiny snowmen embossed on foil to get to the box underneath. "You win," she said, and after divesting the box of the paper, she lifted the lid and let out a delighted gasp. "It's the purse I almost bought last week."

"I noticed you were looking at it while we were shopping and went back to get it the next day," her mother said.

"It's beautiful." She pulled the deep-blue pebbled leather crossbody bag out of the box and admired it. Her mother had a knack for selecting thoughtful gifts. Probably because she was so observant. "Thank you."

"You're welcome, honey." Her mom's smile was

full of warmth. "And thank *you* for setting up the video chat with Lauren. She seemed in better spirits than when I last spoke to her."

"I agree." Maddie carefully replaced the purse in the box and set it on the floor next to her feet. Feet sporting new faux fur slippers courtesy of Mallory. "She looked like she got some much-needed sleep."

Mallory shifted on the sofa, curling her legs to the side. She'd arrived wearing sweats and a hoodie but had changed into the heather-gray leggings and soft, oversized pink sweater Maddie had gotten her for Christmas. "It's amazing what a good night's sleep can do. I slept like the dead last night. If I hadn't set the alarm on my phone, I'd probably still be sleeping."

Her father leaned forward and rubbed his hands together with undisguised glee. "Okay, now that we've talked to Lauren and opened our presents, who's ready for breakfast?"

"I am." Maddie raised her hand like an excited kid in class. The Hart family breakfast tradition was one of her favorite parts of Christmas.

"I'm starving," Mallory chimed in.

"I'll help you," her mother said as their parents both stood. She winked at Maddie and Mallory before following her dad to the kitchen.

"I hope Dad doesn't overcook the pancakes." Mallory stifled a yawn and stretched her arm along the back of the sofa. "Last year, they were as hard as hockey pucks."

Maddie leaned against the cushion and smiled. "With Mom supervising, that won't happen." Her gaze fell upon the Christmas tree placed in the corner of the room. It was a beautiful tree, decorated with a mismatch of vintage ornaments from Christmases past, wrapped with tiny multicolored lights, and still emanating a fresh pine scent. Last night, after Ben had left and her parents had gone up to bed, she'd turned off the lights, sat on the sofa, and gazed at it for a long while before turning in for the night.

"I'm so glad I came home," she said more to herself than to Mallory.

Mallory stretched out one leg and gently poked Maddie's thigh with her toes. "Me too. Love you, Mads."

Mallory's heartfelt words infused her with warmth. She'd missed moments like this with her sister. "Love you, Mal."

That evening Maddie stood at the foot of her bed, trying to decide which outfit to wear to Ben's house. She had stayed in Summerwood much longer than she originally planned, leaving her with limited options. Tonight, she had narrowed her choices to a pair of black jeans and her cream chenille sweater or the black sweater dress she'd worn when she and Ben had dinner at La Rambla.

Ben wouldn't care what she wore, so in the end, it came down to comfort. She scooped up the dress from the bed and hung it in the closet. Pants and sweater for the win.

She couldn't wait to see Ben and tell him about her decision. Keeping it under wraps had taken all of her willpower.

As she tugged the sweater over her head, her phone rang. Moving to the nightstand, she pulled the hem down to cover the waistband of her pants and picked up the phone. Seeing the M on the screen, she frowned. Why was Margo calling her?

She pressed the accept call button. "Hi, Margo. Merry—"

"Why haven't you called me back?" Margo demanded. "I know it's a holiday, but as I said in my message, time is of the essence."

"Call you back? I don't know what you're talking about," Maddie said. "I didn't get a message from you." She knew that for sure; she checked her phone several times a day.

Margo let out an exasperated sigh. "I didn't leave a voice mail. I spoke to your friend."

"Which friend?"

"I don't know. I didn't get his name. But he answered your phone."

Now she really was confused. If Margo had called the wrong number by mistake, why would a stranger take a message? "When?"

"Yesterday. Around one thirty or so. He assured me he would give you my message."

Maddie drew in a stunned breath. *Ben.* She'd left her phone in his office yesterday. Her fingers tightened on the phone. "I'm sorry, Margo. I didn't get the message. What's going on?"

"The casting director for the pilot changed her mind. She called me yesterday morning and said the role is yours if you're still interested. But she needs to know by tomorrow afternoon."

Dumbfounded, Maddie sank to the bed. This was what she had been waiting four years for. Her big break. If she wanted it. The big break she might have missed out on because Ben hadn't given her Margo's message. Her heart pounded, and a heated flush spread throughout her body. She would never have believed Ben capable of something like this in a million years. She took a breath and fought the urge to hurl her phone at the wall.

"Maddie, are you still there?"

"Yes." She put her hand to her chest to calm her racing heart. "Sorry."

"I thought you'd be more excited."

"I'm…I'm surprised. After the first rejection, I wasn't expecting this."

"That's understandable. So shall I call her tomorrow and tell her you'll accept the role?" Margo asked, her tone upbeat.

Lifting her hand from her chest, Maddie squeezed her eyes shut and rubbed her temple. Her mind was spinning in a million different directions, and suddenly, nothing made sense. "Umm. You said I had until tomorrow afternoon to make a decision, right?"

"That's correct," Margo replied after a brief silence. "I'll need an answer by noon."

"Right. Okay. Got it." She bit her lower lip, nodding her head. "Noon tomorrow."

"Maddie?" The tight note in Margo's voice signaled concern. "Are you all right?"

No. Not really.

"Yes," she said, still rubbing her temple. "I'm a bit overwhelmed right now."

"I'm here for you," Margo said in a comforting tone. "Please call me if you need to talk this out before noon."

"I will. Thanks, Margo."

"You're welcome. Merry Christmas, Maddie," she said, and the following beep indicated she'd ended the call.

Maddie placed her phone on the nightstand and stared blankly at the wall.

Why?

Why had Ben, honorable, decent, law-abiding Ben, deliberately withheld Margo's message? And it *had* been deliberate. She had been in Carolyn's office no longer than five minutes. Ben wouldn't forget speaking to Margo in that short amount of time. And when she asked if Mallory had called, he'd said no one had called at all.

Closing her eyes, she drew in a deep breath and slowly exhaled. It didn't do anything to assuage her anger. She didn't know what Ben's motives were, but there was one thing she *did* know. She had to talk to him. Straightening her shoulders, she rose from the bed, collected her coat and purse, and left the bedroom.

Instead of calming her down, the fifteen-minute drive to Ben's house ratcheted up the resentment simmering inside her. She pulled into his driveway, parked her car, and turned off the engine. Staring at his house, she took a fortifying breath. Confrontation wasn't something she was good at. Her reluctance to confront her fears was one of the reasons why she'd skipped out of Summerwood in the first place. But that was then. Now she needed answers, and she was damn well going to get them.

After unbuckling her seat belt, she got out of the car, slammed the door, and marched up the flagstone path to his porch. When they decorated his tree, he'd hung a wreath made of evergreen branches and pinecones on his door. She resisted the temptation to tear it down and toss it into the yard. It wasn't the wreath's fault Ben was a liar.

Closing her hand into a fist, she pounded on the door three times. Seconds later, he opened the door, the warm smile on his face slowly fading as her eyes bored into his with all the force of her pent-up anger.

"You know, don't you?" he said, then averting his gaze, he pulled the door open and stayed silent as she stalked past him into the living room.

Tossing her purse on the sofa, she spun around to face him. "Why didn't you tell me Margo called?" she demanded. "You're not stupid, Ben. You had to know I'd find out. And if you're going to say you forgot, don't bother. I wondered why you were so quiet last night. But now I know why. You were keeping this from me."

He closed the door and met her gaze with no trace of remorse in his blue eyes. "I honestly believed I was acting in your best interest."

"Really?" She stared at him in disbelief. "How is lying to me in my best interest?"

"I didn't lie." Scowling, he crossed his arms over his chest. "I just didn't give you the message."

Was he seriously using that pathetic excuse? She rejected it with a decisive sweep of her hand. "Don't mince words. It was a lie of omission."

"You hate Los Angeles, and you said you were ninety-nine percent sure you were staying in Summerwood. If that's the case, then you wouldn't be accepting the role anyway." He cocked his head, his eyes suddenly filled with suspicion. "Unless the only reason you were going to stay is because you weren't getting any roles."

His baseless assumption kicked Maddie's pulse into overdrive. She refused to let him shift the blame from where it belonged. "Stop deflecting. This isn't about me; this is about you. You wanted me to stay in Summerwood, and you didn't give me Margo's message to ensure that's exactly what I would do."

His eyes flickered with irritation. "Yes, I want you to stay. But it's more than that. You've admitted you weren't happy in Los Angeles, and you were more fulfilled doing community theater. You're the one who told me you missed this town, this community, and me. I was afraid you would take the job because you still have a deep-seated need to prove something to your parents."

"So you're saying you don't trust me or my judgment?" She stared at him, unable to process what he'd done and why. "You believe I haven't learned anything in the past four years?"

A frown tugged at his brows. "I didn't say that."

"Maybe not in so many words, but your actions prove otherwise."

"For good reason. You tried Hollywood once, and you were miserable. I was trying to save you from making another mistake."

"Save me?" she snapped angrily. "You don't need to save me. You're not some hero on a white horse. And as for mistakes, maybe the biggest one I could make is to be with a man who doesn't trust me enough to tell me the truth."

Uncrossing his arms, he scrubbed a hand over his jaw and sighed. "You're overreacting."

"Overreacting? Because I'm angry you withheld information from me?" Her sharp laugh sounded as hollow as her heart. "That's rich, Ben. And so typical. If a woman gets angry, she's overreacting. Or she's a bitch."

"I didn't mean it that way," he said defensively. "You're blowing this way out of proportion."

"Are you kidding me?" She turned and picked up her purse. Her gaze landed on a box of chocolates from

Chocolate Madness, a gourmet chocolate shop on Main Street, sitting on the coffee table. They were her favorite, but she was too angry to be touched by his thoughtfulness. "If that's what you believe, then I think it's time for me to go," she said as she pivoted to face him.

"Go where?" His eyes widened. "Back to Hollywood?"

"What I do is no longer your concern. I don't want to be with someone who would resort to lying and manipulation to get his way." She brushed past him to the door, and after pulling it open, she looked at him over her shoulder. "That's one mistake I will *not* be making," she said and closed the door with such force the wreath fell to the porch.

She stared at it and considered picking it up and hanging it back on the door for a hot second. But instead, she kicked it and watched it skid across the porch before she hurried to her car and drove away from Ben for the second time in four years.

****

Early the following day, Ben stared at his reflection in the bathroom mirror and didn't like what he saw. And what was worse, he couldn't stop replaying Maddie's angry words in his head in a never-ending loop.

What I do is no longer your concern.

Swearing under his breath, he bent over, splashed water on his face, and reached for a towel. Cold water and a shave hadn't helped. The dark circles under his eyes and his sallow skin told the story. After Maddie stalked out of the house, he'd broken open a new bottle of whiskey and downed almost all of it.

He didn't drink the hard stuff often. But last night,

he'd needed to forget what he'd done. And why. The whiskey had done its job. At least for a while.

After dressing in his uniform, he retrieved his gun and holster from the safe in his closet and left the house. His shift didn't start for an hour, but he needed coffee, and he hoped to catch Sam at Callie's.

Driving down Main Street, he passed the plaza without looking at the Christmas tree, just like he'd left his house without looking at the tree he and Maddie had decorated together. He didn't need to be reminded that he'd fucked up Christmas. Royally.

He breathed a sigh of relief at the sight of Sam's truck parked outside of Callie's. He parked next to it and headed for the diner. Once inside, he spotted Sam at the counter, nursing a coffee and his usual glazed doughnut.

Sam glanced up as Ben draped his jacket on the stool and sat next to him. "You're here early," he commented, then frowned. "You look like shit."

"I feel like shit." Ben turned over the coffee cup sitting in a saucer in front of him and nodded as the server came over holding a pot of coffee. "Thanks," he said after she'd filled his cup. He took a sip, eager to get the caffeine into his system.

The door opened, and a young couple entered and sat down on the two stools next to him. He glanced at Sam. "I need to talk. Do you mind if we grab a table?"

Sam's brows rose, but he nodded and shoved the last of his donut into his mouth as he slid off his stool. "There's an open table near the back," Ben said and picked up his coffee cup and the jacket he'd covered his stool with.

He followed his brother, and after they sat down, Sam peered at him over the rim of his coffee cup.

"Did you get shitfaced last night?"

"Unfortunately, yes," he said, wishing he could forget why he'd gotten drunk. What he'd done to Maddie was out of line, and he deserved every bit of her anger.

"That's not like you." Sam lowered his cup, studying him with sharp eyes. "Especially when you have to work the next day."

"A lot of things aren't like me." He caught a strong whiff of bacon and fought back the bile inching up his throat. This was why he rarely got drunk. His stomach couldn't handle it.

"Care to explain?"

As much as he hated admitting what he'd done, talking things out with Sam had always helped him put things into perspective. "I kept something from Maddie, and she found out."

"What did you keep from her?" Sam asked, his expression wary.

"I answered Maddie's phone, thinking it was Mallory, but it was her agent. She let it slip that Maddie is being offered a role in a pilot for a television series. She asked me to have Maddie call her, and she made a point to tell me time was of the essence."

"And let me guess." Sam gave him a pointed look. "You didn't pass along the message?"

"No. I didn't."

His brother shook his head and groaned. "Why would you make a boneheaded move like that?"

"Because I wasn't thinking straight. I convinced myself it was in Maddie's best interest, and that's what I told her last night."

"I'm sure she didn't like that."

"She was angrier than I've ever seen her. She

accused me of manipulating her for my own ends."

Sam's brows ticked up in question. "Weren't you?"

"Damn it, Sam," he said, annoyed at the knowing gleam in his brother's eyes. "Don't look at me like that. She hates Hollywood, and she was so close to finalizing her decision to stay here in Summerwood. I was only trying to—"

"Trying to what? Run her life? Make decisions for her?" Sam pointed a finger at him. "I seem to remember how angry you were at Dad when he tried everything he could to talk you out of joining the police department."

Ben's stomach tightened. "That's different."

"The situation may be different, but not the intent. You complained to me every damn day about how Dad was trying to run your life. You said it was your life, you were an adult, and you had the right to make your own decisions." He leaned back in his chair and inclined his head. "Doesn't Maddie deserve the same courtesy?"

He stared at Sam for several seconds, unable to continue to defend his actions. "Damn it. I hate it when you're right."

"You already knew it was wrong," Sam said, surprising him by not gloating. "Or else you wouldn't have gotten drunk or sought me out this morning."

There were times when Sam knew him better than he knew himself, and this was one of them. "I didn't want her to leave, and I was afraid she'd pack her bags and go back to Los Angeles if she got the message."

"Or maybe she would have turned down the job and stayed."

"I didn't want to take the chance." Even as he said the words, he knew they were ridiculous. Of course, Margo would have called Maddie back when she didn't hear from her. And he could have come clean on Christmas Eve, but he'd kept his mouth shut even while knowing it was only a matter of time until she discovered what he'd done.

"Nothing good ever happens when you lie. Didn't you learn anything from what Mom did to us?"

Ben's gut churned sickeningly at the thought of even being remotely like his mother. But maybe the proverbial apple hadn't fallen far from the tree. "You'd think so. Maybe I'm more like her than I thought. Maddie was right; I was trying to manipulate her."

"First, you're nothing like Mom," Sam assured him. "And second, you're human. You made a mistake."

"A mistake that cost me a future with Maddie."

"You don't know that."

"You didn't see her face when she left my house. She hates me."

"I doubt that. Why don't you talk to Maddie? It can't hurt."

He picked up his cup and sipped his coffee. Sam was right; he needed to talk to her. But would she speak to him? And would anything he said make a difference? At this point, he wasn't sure.

Twenty minutes later, Ben gave Sam a wave as his brother took off in his truck to go to work. As he knew it would, talking to Sam had put things into perspective. He needed to talk to Maddie as soon as he could so he could apologize and, hopefully, make things right between them. He pulled his phone out of his jacket pocket and called her, only to end the call when it went straight to voice mail. A message was too impersonal; he had to talk to her one-on-one.

As he was heading to his car, his phone chimed. He

glanced at the screen, hoping the text was from Maddie. Instead, with a dejected sigh, he read Carolyn's message reminding him of a mandatory sergeants' staff meeting at 0800 sharp. Shoving the phone back into his pocket, he looked up, and a jolt of adrenaline shot through his body. Walking at a leisurely pace toward him and dressed in jeans and a gray sweatshirt with the hood pulled up over his dark blond hair was Tanner Gates.

As Tanner approached, Ben stepped directly into his path. He scowled and changed direction, but Ben sidestepped to block his way. "Tanner Gates, right?"

"Yeah." Frowning, Tanner cocked his head. "Am I in some sort of trouble?"

"Not at the moment," he said in a cordial tone. "In case you were unaware, there's a city ordinance against loitering."

Tanner blew out an indignant huff. "I'm not loitering. I'm going to Callie's for coffee."

"I'm not talking about right now. On the night of the tree lighting ceremony, we received a complaint you were loitering outside of Sweet Temptations bakery."

Annoyance flared briefly in Tanner's eyes, but his expression stayed neutral. "I don't know what you're talking about. I was at the tree lighting ceremony, and afterward, I walked along Main Street looking at the store windows. Like a lot of other people."

"If that's the case, we don't have a problem. But so there's no misunderstanding, the police department takes city ordinance violations seriously. Understood?"

A muscle spasmed in Tanner's jaw as the silence stretched between them. "Yes," he finally said, his tone terse. "Can I go now?"

"Of course." Ben made a sweeping motion toward

Callie's front door with his hand. "Have a nice day." Bracing his hands on his utility belt, he watched Tanner walk away, wishing he'd gotten a better read on the guy. Tanner's reaction could have fit a guilty or an innocent man. Until he knew for sure, he'd continue to keep an eye on Tanner Gates.

As Ben expected, the sergeants' meeting took up most of the morning. After leaving the conference room, he returned to his office to drop off the materials he'd used in the meeting and grabbed the keys to his patrol vehicle. He couldn't wait any longer to talk to Maddie.

Ben spent the drive out to Maddie's parents' house thinking about what he wanted to say to her. After how he'd behaved last night, she might slam the door in his face. And who would blame her if she did? No one. He'd acted like a selfish prick.

As he pulled into the driveway, he noted that Maddie's car wasn't there. Just Rena's mid-sized SUV. But that didn't stop him from parking and getting out of the car. Maddie's vehicle could be in the garage, or maybe Rena had borrowed it. He trudged up the walkway to the house, climbed the stairs to the porch, and rang the doorbell. The door opened a few seconds later, and Rena smiled at him.

"Well, hello. I didn't expect to see you again so soon." Her gaze roamed over him, and her smile faded, and fear flickered in her eyes. "Did something happen to Eli? Is that why you're here?"

"No. The chief is fine," Ben reassured her.

"Oh, that's a relief." She put a hand to her chest and let out a deep breath. "I don't worry as much now that he's working in administration, but you never know." Her smile resurfaced. "So why did you stop by?"

"To see Maddie." He glanced over his shoulder. "Her car isn't here. Did she drive into town?"

Rena frowned. "I thought you knew. Maddie went back to Los Angeles. She left early this morning."

Ben's breath jammed in his throat. "I guess I got the days mixed up," he said, taking a step back. He tried to smile, but the tight knot in his stomach wouldn't allow it. "I'll give her a call when I get off work to wish her well."

"She's—"

"Thanks, Rena. I've gotta get back to work." He turned and hurried down the steps, striding as fast as he could to the car.

He drove back to the station on automatic pilot, replaying the argument with Maddie in his head. Each time the knife in his gut twisted a little more. He'd driven Maddie away. Of that he had no doubt. If only he'd given her that damn message. Then maybe, just maybe, he wouldn't have lost the only woman he ever loved.

Again.

Chapter Eighteen

Maddie propped her hands on her hips and surveyed her small living room. Although she'd lived in the apartment for four years, she hadn't accumulated a lot of possessions. Against one wall, she and Mallory had stacked two boxes filled with some kitchen items. Two more boxes had been stuffed with her meager assortment of towels and sheets, and three additional boxes contained clothing and shoes she hadn't been able to fit into her suitcase. Maybe it was a good thing she never had any extra money to shop.

The small apartment was in an older complex and rather drab. The landlord had refused her requests to paint, and she had vowed that wherever she landed next, she would paint every room in whatever color suited her. Life was too short to live in a home she didn't love.

The front door opened, and Mallory stepped inside. Closing the door behind her, she wiped the back of her hand across her forehead. "How do you live in this city?" she asked and, with her fingertips, plucked at the fabric of her *P!NK* T-shirt, lifting it from her skin to cool herself off. "It's almost January and nearly eighty degrees out there."

"You get used to it," she said. "Did you get the suitcases into the car?"

Mallory nodded. "I pulled down the second-row seats. There's plenty of room for the boxes." She pointed toward the flat-screen propped up against the wall near the bedroom. "And I think we should wrap the TV in one of your blankets and pack it last. Then we can slide it on top of the boxes."

"Good idea."

"I need some water." Mallory moved into the tiny galley kitchen off of the living room and opened the small fridge. "When is the charity coming for your furniture?"

"In about a half hour." Maddie checked her watch. It was almost noon. "We need to get on the road as soon as we can. Traffic is bad all the time, but it's worse during rush hour."

Mallory returned to the living room and plopped down on the sofa Maddie had purchased at a nearby thrift store. It was in decent shape, but she had no emotional attachment to it. So she was donating it, along with her other furniture, to a charitable organization supporting women in need. "Have you heard from Ben?" Mallory asked as she twisted the cap off the bottle.

"No." A heavy weight settled in her chest. A future without Ben wasn't what she'd been hoping for, but how could she be with him after what he'd done? He wasn't the man she'd thought he was, and it was disappointing on so many levels.

"So you're still mad at him."

"He lied to me, and he wasn't sorry about it."

"I'll take that as a yes." Mallory took a long drink of her water. "By the way, he left me a voice mail yesterday."

Maddie's stomach fluttered, but she hid her reaction with what she hoped was a nonchalant expression. "He did? Did he ask about me?"

"No. He called to let me know that Tanner's back in Summerwood and he had a little chat with him." She lifted her free hand and crossed her fingers. "Hopefully, that's the end of the Tanner drama."

Oddly disappointed that Ben hadn't even mentioned her, she nodded, silently chastising herself for caring. "I hope so."

Mallory tilted her head, studying her with shrewd eyes. "Did you want him to ask about you?"

"I don't know." Sadness closed like a fist around her heart. "But it doesn't matter what I feel," she said, sitting next to her sister. "Whatever Ben and I might have had is over."

Mallory's eyes softened. "I'm sorry, Mads," she said, reaching out and hugging her.

"Thanks." She picked at a stray thread on the cuff of her shorts. Only in LA would she be wearing shorts three days after Christmas. She shifted on the sofa and met Mallory's sympathetic gaze. "And thanks for coming down here to help me. Having you here has made everything so much easier, and I don't mean because you helped me pack."

"Anything for my little sister." The doorbell rang, and Mallory flinched. "Holy shit, that's loud."

Maddie chuckled. "It awful, isn't it?" She rose from the sofa. "It's probably the charity."

To avoid a repeat performance of the doorbell from hell, she hurried to the door and opened it. Her heart started to race, but the rest of her was frozen in place, and she couldn't seem to move.

"Ben?" she whispered. *What is he doing here?* And why did he have to look so damn gorgeous? Faded blue jeans and a casual white shirt with the sleeves rolled up exposing tanned forearms were one of the sexiest things a man could wear.

"Your mom gave me your address." He shoved his hands into his front pockets as his gaze roamed over her face. "I could have called, but I wanted to see you in person." A halfhearted smile lifted the corners of his mouth. "So here I am, hoping you'll give me the chance to talk to you."

"Did you drive from Summerwood?"

He shook his head. "I took a flight out of Portland and rented a car here at the airport. I needed to get here as soon as humanly possible."

"Why?"

"May I come in?" he asked, glancing over her shoulder. "Hey, Mallory."

Maddie pulled the door open as Mallory jumped up from the sofa. "Hi, Ben." She beamed at him with a huge smile. "I think this is my cue to walk over to that cute little café down the block and check it out."

Ben stepped inside to allow Mallory to leave the apartment. As Maddie closed the door, Mallory spun around and gave her the thumbs-up sign along with a goofy grin. Maddie rolled her eyes and shut the door.

When she turned to face Ben, she found him staring at the boxes stacked against the wall. "Are you moving?" he asked, turning back to look at her with a curious glint in his eyes.

"Yes. Mallory came down to help me."

A slight frown knitted his brows. "Did you find another apartment?"

"No." She tucked her hair behind her ear and straightened her shoulders. "Why are you here, Ben?"

"To apologize." He lifted a hand and ran his fingers

through his tousled hair. "I'm sorry I didn't give you Margo's message. And I'm sorry when you confronted me about it, I acted like a complete jerk."

Her pulse accelerated. She hadn't expected an apology, but she needed more than just an *I'm sorry*. She needed answers. "Why didn't you give me her message?"

His gaze roamed over her face before meeting her eyes. "I was afraid you would leave town and never come back once you heard you'd gotten that part on the TV pilot."

"Even though I told you I was almost certain I was staying in Summerwood?" She crossed her arms across her chest and held his gaze.

"Almost being the operative word." Blowing out a long breath, he ran a hand through his hair. "It wasn't an absolute certainty, and I wanted it to be. I wanted you to stay in Summerwood so badly I was willing to go against everything I stand for."

"But I'm sure you knew Margo would call me back when she didn't hear from me."

"Yes. But I wasn't thinking about that when I didn't give you the message. And when you came to my house and confronted me, instead of telling you why I didn't give you the message, I got defensive and spouted all that nonsense about looking out for your best interests." He paused, his expression filled with genuine remorse. "The truth is, the only interests I was looking out for were my own."

She held his regretful gaze, her thoughts jumbled. Why had he flown to Los Angeles to apologize? They both had phones. "You could have called."

"It was important to me that I apologize to you in

person. And with you living in LA, I wasn't sure when I'd see you again."

"I won't be living here much longer." She lowered her arms and shot a glance at the moving boxes. "Mallory and I are driving back to Summerwood as soon as we get the car loaded and my furniture is picked up."

His brows rose. "You're not doing the TV pilot?"

"After I left your house, I considered it, but it was only because I was hurt and so angry at you. When I went home for Thanksgiving, I had every intention of coming back here and auditioning until I finally got that big break. The role that would prove to everyone I'm a success. But while I was home, I discovered that, in my own way, I'm already a success; I just didn't know it. And once I realized I didn't have to prove myself to anyone, I knew I could leave LA and not look back."

He stared at her, wide-eyed for a couple of seconds. "You're coming home?"

She nodded. "I made up my mind on Christmas Eve. I was going to surprise you with the news on Christmas Day."

A pained wince twisted his mouth. "If I'd trusted you to make your own decision, none of this would have happened. I'm sorry, Maddie. If you believe anything, please believe that."

The absolute sincerity in his eyes almost brought tears to hers, and her heart constricted. She had no doubt he was sorry for what he'd done. "I believe you."

"Can you forgive me?"

Fully aware she'd made mistakes too, her heart had only one answer for him. "You set the bar for forgiveness when you forgave me for hurting you. I didn't mean to hurt you four years ago, and I don't believe you intended to hurt me now, so yes, I can forgive you."

His shoulders relaxed, but an air of anxiousness still surrounded him. "There's something else I need to tell you."

"Something bad, or something good?" she asked.

"Good. Or at least I hope you'll think so." He stepped forward and lifted his hand to caress her cheek gently.

The woodsy scent of his cologne surrounded her as she leaned into his tender touch.

"I love you, Maddie," he said, his voice low and husky. "I thought I was long over you, but I was kidding myself. I never stopped loving you."

Her heart skipped a few beats, joy suddenly replacing the misery of the past few days. "That's a coincidence." She gazed into his blue eyes and finally admitted what she'd kept locked inside her heart for four years. "I never stopped loving you either."

Ben's beautiful blue eyes darkened, and a slow sexy smile played upon his lips. "I do love a good coincidence," he said and leaned forward to capture her mouth with his.

His hungry kiss ignited a scorching fire that spread through her body, and all coherent thought evaporated in her brain. All that registered was Ben and the warmth of his body and the arousing scent of his cologne as he wrapped his arms around her and pulled her against him. She melted against him, clutching at his shirt and returning his searing kiss with a fierceness that surprised her.

The awful sound of her doorbell startled her, and she pulled back, breathless from their kiss *and* being so rudely interrupted. "It's probably the guys from the charity," she said, trying to catch her breath.

"That's the most obnoxious doorbell I've ever heard," he said as Maddie backed out of his arms and tugged the hem of her blouse down to her hips.

"I won't miss it," she said as she hurried to the door. She turned to him before she opened it, happiness filling her heart. "And I won't miss Los Angeles. It's the past. Summerwood, and you, are my future."

****

Ben pulled Maddie's car to a stop alongside the passenger drop-off curb at the Hollywood Burbank Airport and shifted into park while Mallory and Maddie climbed out of the passenger seat they'd been sharing. He opened his door, hopped out, and walked to the back cargo hold to retrieve Mallory's suitcase. He set it next to Mallory, who gave him a quick hug.

"Thanks for driving back to Summerwood. And for buying my airline ticket."

"No thanks are necessary, but I wouldn't mind one of your—"

"Lemon meringue pies," she said with a laugh and turned to give Maddie a bear hug. "I'll see you when you get back."

While Maddie and her sister said their goodbyes, Ben jogged to the driver's side and climbed into the car. Other cars were lining up to drop off friends or family; lingering too long at the curb was frowned upon. At any airport.

Closing his door, he shifted into drive as Maddie got back in the van.

"Bye, Mal," she called out to Mallory's retreating back.

Mallory turned and waved before heading for the

airport doors.

"This was a brilliant idea." Settling into her seat, she buckled her seat belt.

Ben thought so too. He'd taken vacation time to fly down to LA to talk to Maddie, and he had five days left. He hoped to talk Maddie into taking their time going home. He wanted to spend as much time alone with her as he could.

"Between here and Summerwood, where is one place you've never been that you'd like to visit?" he asked, tapping his fingers on the steering wheel.

"Hmm. I've always wanted to go to Big Sur."

"We can do that. And maybe stop in Carmel and Monterey."

"I love that idea." Her eyes sparkled with happiness, and he was the luckiest man on the planet.

Stepping on the gas, he navigated out of the drop-off area and followed the arrows directing him toward the freeway. "What did Margo say when you told her you turned down the pilot?"

"She was surprised, but she understood."

"Have you thought about what you want to do when you get home?" he asked as he merged into traffic.

"Aside from seeing a lot of you?"

"That's a given." He grinned. "If we get approved for a new position at the department, will you apply?"

"I'm not sure." She reached for her sunglasses on the dashboard and slipped them on. "I enjoyed working at the police department, but there may be an opportunity with the community theater. Stevie needs an assistant, and she said she'd love to hire me if I was staying in town." She smiled at him. "I have options."

Ben reached for her hand once they were on the

freeway heading north. "How would you feel about spending New Year's Eve with me?"

"Celebrating a brand new year and a new beginning for us?" She leaned over and kissed his cheek, her soft perfume teasing him with the promise of what was to come. "I can't think of anywhere else I'd rather be."

As he left Los Angeles in the rearview mirror, Ben was damn glad he'd kept the diamond ring he bought for Maddie four years ago. Just like her, it was exquisite, and he couldn't wait for the day, in the not-too-distant future, when he could slip it on her finger and call her his fiancée. This time, though, he would ensure they were both ready, and he wouldn't ask her to marry him on his porch. He wasn't superstitious, but he wasn't taking any chances.

Not this time.

A word about the author...

Alison's love of the romance genre goes all the way back to her high school years when she gobbled up every Harlequin novel she could get her hands on. Back then, she never dreamed of writing her own stories, but years later, her inner writer emerged and she's now a multi-published author of contemporary romance.

When she's not plotting her next book, she hangs out with her adorable rescue dog, Bailey, consumes more chocolate than she should, and spends time with her friends and family.

Visit her website at www.alisonpackard.com to subscribe to her newsletter, get information about her previous books, and updates about upcoming releases.

~*~

Find Alison online at:
alisonpackard.com

www.ingramcontent.com/pod-product-compliance
Lightning Source LLC
Chambersburg PA
CBHW060538260626
47161CB00003B/953